Eight Years of Lies

ALSO BY LISA HALL

The Day She Disappeared
Eight Years Of Lies

EIGHT YEARS OF LIES

LISA HALL

Joffe Books, London
www.joffebooks.com

First published in Great Britain in 2025

© Lisa Hall

This book is a work of fiction. Names, characters, businesses, organizations, places and events are either the product of the author's imagination or are used fictitiously. Any resemblance to actual persons, living or dead, events or locales is entirely coincidental. The spelling used is British English except where fidelity to the author's rendering of accent or dialect supersedes this. The right of Lisa Hall to be identified as author of this work has been asserted in accordance with the Copyright, Designs and Patents Act 1988.

No part of this book may be used or reproduced in any manner for the purpose of training artificial intelligence technologies or systems. In accordance with Article 4(3) of the Digital Single Market Directive 2019/790, Joffe Books expressly reserves this work from the text and data mining exception.

Cover art by Nick Castle

ISBN: 978-1-83526-953-4

PROLOGUE

It was just a normal day. Another boring, mundane day in our boring, mundane lives. But it's shocking how quickly things can go from mundane and boring to earth-shattering and soul-destroying.

One minute, you're living your life as you've always done — running the kids to school, going to work, hoping you'll be back early enough to make a decent home-cooked meal before eventually climbing into bed, giving the ritual peck on the cheek before you roll away from each other, and sink into another night of oblivion.

The next minute, everything has changed, and everything you ever believed to be the truth is unveiled as a lie. The life you've made for yourself is built on sand, shifting with any tiny movement, and your feet can't hold you steady for much longer. You no longer know what's real and what's a twisted distortion of the truth. You no longer know the person who lies in bed next to you every night. And you never did.

CHAPTER 1

Sunlight streams in through the thin curtains, dancing across my closed eyelids and pulling me into consciousness. Squinting, I peer at the clock on the bedside table, brushing aside the clutter that surrounds it. *6.58 a.m.* Two short minutes until the alarm squawks into life and another day starts in the Bennett household. I roll over and brush my fingers lightly over Tom's bare shoulder, tracing the pattern left by the sprinkle of tiny freckles that litter his pale skin, hoping he won't push me away. Mumbling, he turns over, throwing an arm over me and pulling me into his chest.

'What time is it?' His breath is hot as he murmurs into my hair.

'Just before seven. The alarm is about to—' Screeching fills the air and I lean over to slam my hand down on the clock before it wakes Isla in the next room.

'Bagsy first shower.' Tom jumps out of bed, as I groan and tug the duvet further up over my shoulders. I envy his ability to leap out of bed the moment his eyes open, but I'm more of a night owl, groggy and dull in the mornings until I get my first hit of caffeine. 'Sorry, Claire, I've got a hectic day ahead . . . but you're about to get an extra ten minutes in bed, so don't complain.' I snuggle into the pillows with a smile, watching appreciatively as he walks around the bed naked, kicking our discarded clothes from the previous evening out of the way.

Last night, after a steak and red wine dinner, we managed to make the most of some alone time together — for the first time in ages, something I'm trying to put down to our busy schedules rather than the way Tom seems to be more distracted than usual lately. We've always tried to keep regular date nights ever since our daughter, Isla, was born — until recently, when Tom has seemed oddly distant. I was starting to think I'd done something to upset him, but when I tried to talk to him about it, he'd brush me away with vague reassurances that everything was fine, his mind apparently on other things. But last night, he was more like his old self, whispering to me once Isla was asleep that perhaps we should take the rest of the bottle of red up to bed. Now, he walks around to my side of the bed, leaning over to kiss me, his hand sliding under the duvet and brushing over my nipple in a way that makes me gasp.

'Mmm. Come here.' I tug him closer, wanting to make the most of his good mood, but giving a little shake of his head he backs away, a smile on his lips.

'Let's put this on ice,' he winks. 'I'm going for a shower. Make yourself useful — go downstairs and get the coffee on.'

He disappears into the en-suite bathroom, and I sigh, lying back on the plump pillows behind me. Eight years together and I still look at him the way I did when we first met. We still have that spark between us, the chemistry that meant it felt inevitable that we would end up together, even if things have been a little strained between us lately. Don't all marriages have those moments though, where things don't seem to fit quite as well as they usually do? I hope his cheerful demeanour this morning means he's over whatever has been playing on his mind. I try not to think about the way he sneakily checked his phone last night after he thought I was asleep, the blue glow from the screen lighting his side of the darkened bedroom. From the en-suite bathroom comes the thunder of water, steam beginning to billow under the door, and I lie back on the pillows, my mind wandering back to Tom and his strange behaviour over the past few weeks. Maybe I was imagining it, reading into something that wasn't really there. I know I have a tendency to overthink things, and his behaviour at dinner last night was that of the old Tom, the Tom I know and love, and I'd be lying if I said I wasn't relieved after weeks of walking on eggshells. I drift back to sleep, until the scent of frying bacon and the chatter of conversation downstairs brings me back to consciousness, and I hear Isla shriek, followed by Tom's voice, warm and full of laughter. I swing my legs out of bed, pull on sleep shorts and a vest and head downstairs, to start the day with my perfect little family.

* * *

When I reach the kitchen, Isla sits at the table in her nightdress, her mouth full of pancake, maple syrup on her chin. Tom is at the stove, pancake batter in the pan, wearing the light-blue polo shirt that I love because it brings out the colour of his eyes. The warm, toasted aroma of ground coffee beans fills the air. I had worried about Tom being the stay-at-home parent when Isla was born, and we'd made the decision that I would be the one to return to work full-time after my maternity leave ended. It was easier for Tom to go part-time as an estate agent, and my salary as a conveyancing solicitor was more than enough to keep us, but I'd been concerned that Tom would feel emasculated if I was the breadwinner, that he'd hate spending half his time at home. As it turned out, I worried over nothing, and Tom leaned into being the main caregiver with gusto, enjoying every minute of his time at home with Isla far more than I ever could.

Now, I take a minute before they notice me in the doorway, to just soak it all up — my family, a perfect picture of everything I could have ever wanted. Granted, both of us thought that there would be more than one child — I was hoping for at least one more, and I know Tom was too — but Isla is perfect, and now, the more time that passes, the less I try to think about it. Tom turns to me and grins before flipping the pancake in the pan, and I reach out and top up his coffee cup, pouring one for myself while I'm at it.

'Mmm, my hero. Isla, run up and get dressed for school.' Tom slides the cooked batter and bacon onto a plate and passes it to me, before he grabs his coffee and appreciatively draws in a deep breath over his mug. 'What are your plans for the day?' he asks, as I peer into the refrigerator in search of the orange juice, looking past the container of homemade chicken nuggets Tom has made for Isla's dinner tonight, and those awful protein bars he insists on buying for snacks because they're healthier than chocolate. 'And aren't you late? You're normally gone before Isla and I are even dressed.'

I find the orange juice and sit at the table, ready to tuck in. 'I thought we could have breakfast together, after we had such a lovely evening last night.' My fork poised in front of my mouth, I can feel my cheeks heating as Tom turns away, a smile tugging at the corners of his mouth. 'I've got a late meeting this morning, and then I've got a tonne of paperwork to sort out on the Manley house. The buyer is chasing me night and day and the seller's solicitor is horrendously slow with the enquiries. I'd rather stay home with you, to be honest.' I wink at him, and he laughs. 'And I might meet Gwen for a glass of wine tonight.' I haven't seen Gwen, my younger sister, for over a week and I'm desperate to catch up with her.

Tom nods approvingly. 'Good idea. Invite her over for dinner next week, while you're at it. Is she still dating that guy? The vegan?'

I shake my head. 'Hell no. You know Gwen, three dates and she's bored.' Gwen has been single ever since she skipped out on her own wedding five years ago. Now, she lives alone in a cottage with a garden that Isla is sure houses fairies, selling her own pottery and dating guys she knows she doesn't have a future with.

Tom drains the last of his coffee, shouting up the stairs to Isla to get a move on, before positioning himself in front of me as I stand to take my breakfast things to the sink.

'Busy day ahead, Mrs. Bennett.' He lays his palm flat against the nape of my neck, pulling me towards him, his mouth toying with a smile. I resist the urge to reach up and kiss his plump lower lip, still a little unsure of the reception I'll get, even after last night. A lightness fills my chest when he takes the initiative, leaning down to kiss me gently.

'Indeed, Mr. Bennett. I'm guessing you're in the same boat.'

'Well, those houses won't view themselves. I've got a viewing at ten thirty, then two more this afternoon. It's the third time this guy has wanted to view the property, so God help me.'

I reach up and pat his cheek. 'You could sell snow to the Inuits, what's one more viewing?'

Tom laughs, rich and warm. 'I'll be done by three o'clock, just manifest me that sale.' He holds up crossed fingers. 'Listen, meet Gwen tonight. Get dinner together. I'll just grab something quick for Isla and me — those nuggets in the fridge. Shit.' Tom looks at his watch. 'We're late.' He pulls away from me, reaching towards the worktop for his wallet and car keys. 'Isla? Are you ready? Have a good day, Claire, OK? I love you.'

At the bottom of the stairs, he reaches for me again, kissing me long and hard the way he used to, and I feel it again, that little thrill of relief that whatever has been bothering him has passed, and he's back to being my Tom again. Isla thunders down the stairs, school bag flying.

'Yuck. You two are gross.' She wrinkles her nose at me as she tries to tie her shoelaces before sticking her foot out. 'Please, Mummy?'

I bend to tie them for her, catching Tom's eye and grinning. 'There you go. Go on, get out of here.' I ruffle her hair as she ducks away from me and out the front door.

'Claire, I do love you, you know.' Tom kisses me one last time, the light catching the tiny diamond in my engagement ring as I put my hand to his shoulder, steadying myself.

'I know. What is this? Is everything OK?' My eyes search his face, hoping I'm not being too hasty in my relief that things seem to be back on track.

'Everything's fine.' He gives me that old familiar Tom grin, and I return it tentatively. 'Promise. I just wanted to tell you, that's all.' Tucking his wallet into his back pocket, he heads out to the car, and I watch from the front door as they pull away from the house, Isla waving like a mad thing. Tom raises his hand in a single wave as he drives off, and I close the door on them, still not quite able to shake the feeling that there was something more Tom wanted to say.

* * *

Once they've left, the house is eerily quiet, although the stain of their presence is everywhere. Isla's trainers lay in a jumbled heap by the back door into the garden, Tom's jacket hangs on the newel post, and when I go upstairs to shower the smell of his aftershave scents the still-steamy air, a damp towel left on the end of the bed.

Showered and dressed, I check my watch, deciding there is time for more coffee while I check emails before heading to the office. Firing up the laptop, I refill the coffee machine while it boots up, then open my Facebook page for a quick scroll. Social media is something Tom can't seem to get his head around — he doesn't understand why people find it so important to keep in contact via the internet.

'What's wrong with the telephone?' he always asks, as I aimlessly scroll through the statuses of the two hundred or so 'friends' that fill my timeline. 'Why can't you just call them if you want to keep in touch? Do you even still know half these people?'

While I've tried to explain to him that I don't necessarily want to spend an hour on the phone to a friend after a long, exhausting day at work, that it's easier just to whizz through a screen filled with short snippets into people's lives, he doesn't understand it and can't be persuaded to set up his own profile. Maybe it's because Tom doesn't have a lot of friends — he has one or two guys that he'll go for a drink with, and that's it. He's never felt the need to surround himself with people just for the sake of it, preferring instead to keep his circle small.

Coffee poured, my finger runs lazily over the mousepad. Gwen has posted some arty shots of her latest pottery project, rustic-style plates that will sell out in a flash. Two hundred and fifty-six people have 'liked' it, including my mum, which means she will be boasting to all her friends about her talented artist daughter, making Gwen cringe. Kerry, from school, has posted a memory from five years ago — a picture of a group of us girls, taken at our school reunion. Smiling, I 'like' the picture, the memory fresh in my mind — too many Jaeger bombs and Tom carrying me from the Uber up to bed like the Prince Charming he is. I scroll further, sipping at the steaming hot coffee, as the sun travels across the dining table through the conservatory windows. I'm pretty content, enjoying the sunshine, when something appears on my screen that stops me in my tracks. It's a photograph, the caption beneath it reading, 'PLEASE CAN ANYONE HELP ME? HAVE YOU SEEN THIS MAN?' I click on the box to expand the text.

> PLEASE CAN ANYONE HELP ME? HAVE YOU SEEN THIS MAN? *This is my husband and child — they have been missing for several months and I am desperate to find them. There have been sightings of them in and around the Southampton area, and I believe that there may be some family connections in London. I would be grateful for any information that anyone may have — please help, I'm desperate to find them.*

Placing the coffee mug gently back down on the table, I squint at the screen, the coffee swirling in my stomach and rising up to give me heartburn. *This can't be right.* I close the screen. Wait for a moment. Pull the screen up again and log back in before scrolling down, hoping that whatever I saw was a trick of the light, not really there at all, but no. There it is. A photograph of a man and a little girl, seated at a table somewhere warm, bright sunshine and the golden sands of a beach in the background behind them. The little girl sits on her father's lap, the father's arms tight around her. Both have a light tan and are grinning wildly at the camera. A woman named Lydia French has posted the advert, a sponsored post designed to reach thousands, if not millions of people. Feeling off-balance, I run my eyes over the post again, taking in the urgency, the desperate plea for help, my mind a blur of questions and confusion as the words sink in. Without taking my eyes from the screen, I raise my cup to my lips, the slight tremor in my hands causing lukewarm coffee to slop over the side of the mug and into my lap. *What the hell is this?* This picture — the smiling faces, even the location — is familiar to me. I *have* seen this woman's family. *I took this photo.* Only, as far as I'm aware they're not Lydia French's husband and child. They're mine.

CHAPTER 2

There has to be a reasonable explanation, Claire, I tell myself as I pull my coffee-stained trousers away from my skin, shoving the cup to one side. The tiny hairs on the back of my neck lift at the sight of my family on a complete stranger's Facebook page as I read the post again. *Lydia French.* I toss the name around in my mind, almost tasting it, but it's unfamiliar. Is this a joke? I've heard of catfishing before — where people use someone else's profile to create a fake online persona, but would someone really do that with my photo? Things like that happen to other people, not me. My heart gives an anxious bump in my chest, my fingers slipping on the mousepad as I hover the pointer over the little blue name that takes me straight through to her profile page. When I finally click, I see the cover photo is missing, a blank white space in its place, and the profile picture is the one that dominates her most recent post. The photo of Tom and Isla, taken on my digital camera in the summer last year. I swallow down the little murmur at the back of my mind that reminds me how oddly Tom has been behaving over the past few weeks, as if there is something bigger than me and Isla pulling him away from us. Lydia French's profile page is literally that — the status about

Tom is the only thing that shows up. It's the kind of page that celebrities and local businesses set up to promote their wares. She has no likes, and by the looks of it, only joined the social media site recently. *Purely so she could post this picture?*

I sit back in my chair, running my hands over my sleek bobbed hair, not sure what to do next. Everything is the same, and yet not. Looking around my perfectly normal kitchen — gleaming surfaces, Tom's coffee cup by the side of the sink, the domestic setting with everything as it should be — I take a deep breath. I don't want to overreact, especially if it is just some kind of internet troll who gets off on riling people up over the web. I tap my manicured nails impatiently on the table as a jumble of chaotic thoughts cascade through my mind, my skin prickling beneath the soft collar of my shirt. Maybe Tom knows something about it? Tom talks about his past so rarely that when he does, I tend to file things away to turn over in my head later on. If he had mentioned Lydia French I would have remembered, I'm sure of it. Pushing my chair back, I go to the sink and pour a glass of water, purely for something to do as I think. Part of me tells myself, *It's probably nothing, just a mistake*, but another part of me, the part that still thinks Tom is out of my league even after all this time together, feels that this is too weird to leave alone. I don't want to jump to any conclusions, especially if it's just a mix-up — a miscommunication somewhere meaning that my photo has been used instead of somebody else's? — but I'm not happy about Isla's picture being plastered all over the internet for just anyone to look at. I'm pretty sure I've never posted this photo online before, so where did this woman get it from? I puff out a frustrated breath, wavering between action and passivity. The unsettling caption aside, the idea of people having access to a photo of my daughter without my permission — even if it is a mistake — finally spurs me into action and I decide to send the woman a private message. Satisfied I've made the right decision, I click on the message button on her profile.

Dear Lydia,
I've seen your recent post. Why do you have a photograph of my husband and daughter on your page? Please take it down before I report it.
Claire

I'm not holding my breath at getting a response, but I have no idea why she has that photo. *My photo.* A nasty, niggling thought strikes me, one that makes my mouth go dry. *What if the post isn't aimed at someone looking for Tom? What if they're really after Isla?* The thought of it makes my blood go cold. Surely not? I mean, things like that just don't happen to normal people — it's not like we're celebrities or anything. Without thinking, I click on the 'like' button to enable me to follow her page, to see if any further posts appear, then, bringing the photo back up to full size on the screen I study it carefully, until I realise I'm going to be late to the office.

* * *

I jump in the car, cursing under my breath, knowing now that I'm probably going to be late to meet my client, and as a partner at the firm, it isn't going to go down well. I reverse out of the drive without looking, almost knocking over old Mrs. Jackson from three doors down in my haste to get moving. This whole morning has a strange air to it now, a distortion that I'm finding hard to shake off, as if looking in a funhouse mirror. I hit the main road, itching to floor the accelerator to make up for lost time, only to find myself stuck in a traffic jam, thanks to the roadworks at the bottom of the hill. The image of Tom and Isla sitting at the table in the sun rolls around in the back of my mind. Picking up my phone while the lights are still red, I scroll down to Tom's number. He might be able to clear this up — there has to be some sort of reasonable explanation as to why the picture has appeared on my social media account. The handsfree activates and his phone rings five or six times before voicemail cuts in, his familiar tones telling me that he can't take my call right now. Frustrated, I swallow down the emotion that wraps a fist around my throat and ask him to call me back, before hanging up. The lights change and I lean on the horn, letting out a long sigh of frustration as the woman in front of me is so busy checking her make-up in the rear-view mirror that she is slow to pull away, meaning I miss the green light and end up stuck at the red again. Minutes pass and Tom doesn't call me back, so I redial, the ringtone screeching in my ear until voicemail cuts in again. Not that much of a surprise really, Tom is useless at remembering where he's left his phone, and he always keeps it on silent, not wanting his house viewings to be interrupted. Although just lately . . . something dark and vicious squeezes my chest in a vice-like grip. Lately, his phone doesn't seem to have left his side, the faint blue glow lighting his features as he sneaks glances at it in bed, when watching TV, even when running a bath last week. I commented on it then, remarking that he must be waiting for a very important call if he even needed to take his phone to the bathroom with him. He snapped back at me, saying I was always nagging at him for leaving it everywhere, and that he was trying to be more organised. I kept my mouth shut, not wanting to argue in front of Isla. Now, I don't know what to think.

 I tap the steering wheel impatiently as I wait for the lights to change again, contemplating calling Tom for a third time, but then I remember — he said something about a viewing this morning. Checking my watch, I realise he's probably touring a property, turning on the charm for some prospective buyer, so that would explain why he's not answering.

 Finally, the lights turn green and I pull away, anxious to put my foot down and make up some lost time, hating the thought of my client waiting for me in reception as I arrive flustered and flushed. I throw my phone down onto the passenger seat, the ringtone still stubbornly silent, my mind now wandering to my client and the contracts that need to be signed this morning. I'll speak to Tom tonight — maybe he knows who this Lydia French is and we can clear this up. I'm sure it's all just a mistake.

* * *

It takes me almost an hour to get to the office, hitting every red light possible on the way, and as I hurry into reception I'm aware that I'm sweating, perspiration beading my forehead and prickling under my arms.

'Claire, your eleven o'clock is here.' Nancy, the receptionist, gives me a slight frown, masked with a smile, as I hurry past her towards my office.

'Five minutes.' I hold up five fingers and smile, letting out a breath, closing my office door behind me. I lean against it, the wood cool through my cotton blouse, and gulp in the frigid dry air that the air conditioning pumps through the building. Moving to the desk, I pull out a lipstick and swipe it quickly over my lips, before spritzing myself with a puff of perfume and yanking the door open with a bright smile.

'Mr. Jeffrey? Come in, please.'

The meeting runs on for far longer than I hoped. I shuffle through paper after paper, gesturing for the buyer to sign on various dotted lines. I try to answer as many queries as I can as Mr. Jeffrey ploughs through the fixtures and fittings list, and questions every boundary line on the plan, but my head is full of that post from Lydia French. Every time I think I've convinced myself it's nothing to worry about, the image of Tom and Isla at the restaurant table in Alicante swims into the forefront of my mind. By one o'clock we are finally finished, and I seize the opportunity to get away for ten minutes to pick up a sandwich and get some fresh air.

I try Tom's phone again, but it rings out. I don't bother to leave another message. As I wait in line for a feta and sundried tomato bagel, the horrible thought I had earlier creeps back into my mind — what if this isn't about Tom? What if it's something to do with Isla? You hear all sorts of horror stories on the news, of paedophile rings and child trafficking. My stomach rolls as I remember the words in the post. Lydia French, claiming Isla as *her* child, when she's mine. I'm Isla's mother, not Lydia French, and it's my job to keep her safe. Kicking myself for brushing the thought away earlier, I know I won't be able to concentrate at work until I check that Isla is where she's meant to be. I grab the paper bag containing my bagel and hurry out onto the sweltering street, dialling the number for Isla's school. My stomach churning, I will myself to calm down, sucking in a deep breath as I wait for the call to connect.

'St. Mary's Primary — can I help you?' The familiar voice of Mrs. Cross, the school receptionist, tinkles down the line.

'Hello, Mrs. Cross, it's Claire Bennett, Isla's mum.'

'Mrs. Bennett! What can we do for you? Is everything OK?'

I pause for a moment. Racking my brains, I dredge up an excuse for calling. 'I just wanted to check Isla was all right — she wasn't feeling very well when she woke up. Tom said he might take her to the doctors this morning.' I cross my fingers behind my back at this little white lie and hope Mrs. Cross believes I'm nothing more than a concerned mum, checking up on her daughter's welfare.

'Oh, poor Isla. There are lots of bugs going around at the moment — I hope it's nothing too serious. I can check the register for you?'

'Yes, please. No, it's nothing serious. She's just been a little under the weather. I'm on my lunch break and wanted to make sure that she felt OK, that's all.' Strictly speaking, I am telling the truth.

'End-of-term blues, no doubt — they all get a bit exhausted once we reach this point in the school year. Teachers included.' Mrs. Cross gives a delicate laugh, and I hear her flipping the pages of the register. 'Right, I've checked the register. Isla was dropped off on time this morning — your husband must have felt she was well enough after all.'

'Right. Lovely. That's . . . well, that's brilliant. I'm so pleased she was feeling better. I'm sorry to have troubled you.' My knees feel oddly shaky as I hang up, breathing out a sigh of relief, and mentally chastising myself for being such a drama queen. I can just imagine Tom's response when he hears about this.

For the next few hours, I work on the enquiries I've been sent from another solicitor and pick at the bagel, finding I've lost my appetite before finally giving up and throwing it into the bin. Jasmine, my junior conveyancer, gives me a glance of disgust as she brings in a stack of papers for me to sign.

'Feta is bad enough inside the bagel, let alone scattered all over your desk,' she says, pausing as she catches sight of my face. 'Is everything OK?'

I sweep my hand over the desk, catching the tiny crumbs of cheese and bread and tipping them into the bin. 'Of course.' I try and smile, the muscles in my face aching.

'You have the enquiries on the Topper house all finished? I need to send them over,' Jasmine says, with another curious glance.

'Yes, I—' Before I can answer, the shrill ring of my phone stops me in my tracks, my heartrate tripling as I register that the number on the screen is Isla's school. *Shit.* A queasiness washes over me — *has something happened to Isla, while I've been sitting here picking at a bagel?* I almost drop the phone in my haste to answer, my fingers thick and clumsy as they stab at the screen to answer the call.

'Hello?' I speak breathlessly into the phone.

'Is that Mrs. Bennett?' The chirpy voice of Mrs. Cross tinkles down the phone line. 'This is St. Mary's. Do you know what time you'll be here to collect Isla? Only, it's almost four and the school day does finish at three o'clock. I tried to contact Mr. Bennett first, as per your school data sheet, but he doesn't seem to be answering his phone.'

Isla is still at school. Relief is sweet and the nauseous swirling in my stomach subsides as I thank God that Isla is OK, before my palms start to sweat as what Mrs. Cross is telling me registers. *Tom hasn't turned up to collect Isla, and he still isn't answering his phone.* The nausea returns, a thousand tiny butterflies swarming in my stomach as I take a deep breath and run my hand through my hair, trying not to bombard Mrs. Cross with questions. Instead, I apologise to the school receptionist, telling her there seems to have been some sort of mix-up.

'Of course, Mrs. Bennett,' the school receptionist says. 'If you could get here as soon as possible though?'

Hanging up, I ignore Jasmine's questioning look as I pluck my jacket from the back of my chair and reach for my car keys.

'You're leaving?' she says. 'What about the—'

'Can you do it?' I cut in, already halfway to the door. 'Please, Jasmine. I have a family emergency.'

Not waiting for a response, I push past her and hurry out to my car, unlocking it with one hand and tapping my phone with the other, impatiently waiting for the call to connect.

'Clairebear! What are you doing calling me in the middle of the afternoon? Playing hooky?' Tears sting my eyes at the sound of Gwen's voice and I picture my sister cradling the phone between her ear and her chin, her hands mucky with clay.

'Have you spoken to Tom today?'

'Huh? No, I've been in my studio all day. In fact . . .' She trails off. 'Claire? What is it?'

'It's Tom,' I manage, a strange lump forming in my throat as I speak. 'He's not turned up to collect Isla from school. I can't get hold of him.' It crosses my mind to tell her about the post from Lydia French, but I'd rather talk to her face to face about it.

'What? Where is he?'

'That's just it — I don't know. Stuck at work, maybe? I wondered if he might have called you.' I know that Tom and Gwen are close — he calls her his 'sister from another mister', given that he has no siblings of his own — and sometimes he'll call in on her at the studio if he's passing.

'I haven't spoken to him,' she says, 'but I'm sure he'll turn up. He's probably got stuck with a buyer or something. You know what he's like, he never wants to rush them along.'

Hoping Gwen is right, I hang up and turn onto the main road towards the school.

As I drive, Mrs. Cross's words tumble over and over in my mind, the biliousness in my guts intensifying each time I hear the words *he doesn't seem to be answering his phone*. I press the accelerator to the floor, jerking the car into a higher gear as I weave through traffic, all the while trying to figure out exactly why my husband hasn't collected our daughter from school.

CHAPTER 3

It's dark. Properly dark, not like when you go up to bed and the streetlights are shining in the window, or the moon is casting a white glow over the garden. It's completely pitch black, no essence of any light at all. I open my eyes and I still can't see anything. My head aches and my eyes are gritty and sore, the way they are after an all-nighter. I'm uncomfortable, I know that. The floor is cold, hard. Concrete, or compacted dirt maybe. Goosebumps run up and down my arms, shivering their way down my legs, the cold from the floor seeping into my bones. Blinking, I try to make out something — anything — in the pitch black, but it's useless. My eyelashes rub against something, something tight against my face, and I realise I'm blindfolded. Moving my hand in front of my face to pull it away, I realise I can't. There's a stabbing pain in my shoulder as I try to pull the fabric from my eyes, and the sharp tug against my wrists tells me something is very wrong. I twist my fingers around to grasp a metal pipe that runs vertically away from me. I tug again, a metallic clanging filling the room. Bile burns the back of my throat as I realise I'm blindfolded and handcuffed. Trapped.

CHAPTER 4

Twenty minutes later, Isla slides into the passenger seat of my car, wearing a stubborn pout at being the last child left at school. I climb in next to her and turn the car on, positioning the air conditioning vents so that they puff cool air over her cross little face.

'I'm sorry, darling. I got stuck in traffic. I got there as quickly as I could.' I check my mirrors and pull smoothly out of the car park onto the main road heading towards our house, trying my best not to let the tickle of concern over Tom's absence show on my face. I try to pay attention to her chattering, my mind wandering, questioning where the hell Tom could be. *Maybe he got held up on his afternoon viewings? Gwen was right when she said he hates to hurry prospective buyers along. But then, surely, he would have made his excuses to call and ask me to fetch Isla?*

'Hmmm? Sorry darling, say that again?' I realise Isla is waiting impatiently for me to reply to a question that I never heard her ask.

'*I said* it's rubbish being the last one left at school, Mummy. All the other kids went home *ages* ago. Didn't Daddy tell you you were supposed to be picking me up?' Isla fiddles with the radio, something that usually drives me mad, but today I let her flick through the stations, trying not to find the jump from programme to programme irritating.

'Didn't Daddy tell me? He must have done, and I . . .' I trail off for a moment. 'Did Daddy tell you that? That Mummy would be picking you up?' Isla stops fussing with the radio and starts fiddling with other buttons on the dashboard, turning the air conditioning up and back down again.

'He said he had to go somewhere and he might not be back in time to come and get me. He said, "Mummy might have to pick you up tonight, so make sure you don't forget your lunch box."'

I force my concentration back to the road, a small ripple of unease snaking its way along my spine. *Tom said he might not be there to collect Isla?* I rack my brains trying to think if Tom said anything to me about it. He mentioned that he might have to go to a conference in Birmingham, but I thought that was next week. *Maybe Isla got the wrong end of the stick?* She is only seven after all, and she often gets things confused.

'Well, I hope you did remember your lunch box!' Trying not to let my uneasiness show, I lean over and tickle her knee but she still isn't happy, a frown creasing her brow. 'Come on, pickle — you normally like it when I pick you up.'

'Yes, well, that's when you come at the right time. Normally, if Daddy can't pick me up, he asks Hannah to come and get me and I get to go home and play with Brody and Matilda.'

Something registers in my brain at her words. *Hannah.* Of course, I don't know why I didn't think of it before. Hannah might know something about all of this, Tom might even have spoken to her about it — we're good friends with Hannah and her husband Robert, and Tom and Hannah spent a lot of time together with the kids.

'Mummy? Are you even listening? Daddy is supposed to be taking me to play at Brody and Matilda's *today*!' Isla's voice is impatient, and I give her a distracted smile.

'Daddy didn't tell me that.' *It seems like Daddy didn't tell Mummy lots of things today.* 'If you say it's all arranged, then we should probably still go, right?'

Mollified, Isla nods an enthusiastic *yes*, and I agree to go home and let Isla get changed out of her school uniform before we go to Hannah's. If we head over there now, by the time we get home Tom should be back from work, and once Isla goes to bed, we can sit and talk about what was so important that he missed the school run. Maybe he'll even tell me what it is that has been on his mind for the past few weeks.

Back at the house, I wait for Isla to get changed and gather her rucksack of very important things that she absolutely *must* take to Hannah's, quickly checking my emails to see if Jasmine has returned the enquiries I abandoned on my desk. As I reach for my jacket, slung over the newel post on top of Tom's, my phone pings with a Facebook notification. In my dash to fetch Isla and my worry over Tom not turning up to collect her from school, the social media post from this morning had briefly slipped my mind, but now, at the sight of the blue logo on my phone, it hits me again. *Was there really a photo of my husband, my daughter?* Today has been such an odd day, I almost feel as though I could have imagined it.

I tap on the notification as Isla dances around beside me, suddenly afraid that it's a response to the message I sent to Lydia French this morning. My breath leaves my body in a rush as I see it's just a friend request from someone I worked with years ago, and I pause for the briefest of moments before I type in Lydia's name and tap on her profile, forcing myself to look at the plea she posted again. There is a fresh pang of unease as I take in the advert, my eyes running over her words. Something tugs deep in my belly at the sight of Tom and Isla grinning at the camera, at the thought of people believing they belong to Lydia French, that she is the woman who takes care of them, loves them, lives every day with them. A pulse of anger quickening in my veins, I screenshot Lydia French's social media page and email it to myself, almost to prove to myself that it's real. Switching to Messenger, I see there has been no response to the message I sent asking Lydia French to explain herself, the message still sitting on delivered, and my stomach gives another sickening lurch. Snatching up my house keys, I follow Isla down the garden path to walk the short distance to Hannah and Robert's house, giving myself time to calm down before I speak to Hannah.

* * *

If she is surprised to see me rather than Tom on her doorstep at almost five in the afternoon, Hannah makes a good job of hiding it. Smiling, she gestures for me to come in, and I make my way through the bombsite that is her hallway to the kitchen. Shoes, bags and toys litter the floor and I have to take care not to tread on anything as I pick my way through. I can hear Brody and Matilda arguing somewhere upstairs as Isla charges up to join them, and Hannah brushes her messy, blonde hair out of her eyes as she flicks the kettle on.

'Kids, eh?' She raises her eyes to the heavens and busies herself fetching mugs and finding teabags. 'I wasn't expecting you, Claire. I thought Tom was dropping Isla off.'

I pause before I speak, aware that Hannah might know full well why Tom has been so distant from me lately and may be reluctant to talk about it, so I weigh up my words before I say anything, smoothing my clammy hands over my trousers.

'Yeah, I thought he was too.' I give a tiny huff of laughter that comes out more like a groan. 'It's been kind of a weird day, to be honest.' I take the steaming mug of tea that she holds out to me.

Hannah's smile falters as she takes in the expression on my face. 'We all have days like that, Claire. Is everything OK?'

'I'm not sure . . . Hannah, have you seen Tom today?' Clearing my throat in an attempt to disguise the slight wobble in my voice, I try to gauge her reaction, to see if she's hiding anything, but there's only puzzlement on her pale features.

'No, sorry. Well, I saw him briefly when he dropped Isla off at school this morning, but we didn't speak. He dropped Isla right at the gate and then headed off in the car straight away. I guessed he must have just had a busy morning ahead. Claire, what's going on?' Her brows knit together and she bites down on her lower lip as she studies me closely. My stomach sinks with disappointment — I was hoping Hannah would tell me she spoke to Tom this morning, that Tom had told her he might not make the school run. Part of me was still hoping Tom did tell me and I just hadn't listened.

'I'm sure everything's fine . . . he probably just got held up somewhere.' I pause with the cup halfway to my mouth as a thought strikes me. 'Does he normally drop Isla and run in the morning?' I realise I don't actually know a great deal about Tom's morning routine — I'm usually so busy rushing out of the door to get to the office early that I take little notice of it. It's his job to get Isla to school on time, and mine to make sure I bill enough hours every month.

'I . . . well, I suppose it's a little unusual. Most mornings he'll park at the bottom of the hill and walk up, so he can say goodbye to Isla properly at the gate. I didn't think anything of it this morning, I just thought he must have an early viewing at work.' This might not mean anything, but today's drop-off does seem to be a break in Tom's usual routine. He told me he had a viewing, but not until ten thirty — I would have expected him to walk Isla up the hill to the gate if that was the case.

'Claire—' Hannah lays a hand on my arm when I don't respond — 'why aren't you at work? Not that I'm not happy to see you, of course I am, but I'd arranged the play date with Tom. What's going on? Where is he?'

I look down at my manicured nails, resisting the urge to pick at the polish around the edges.

'I'm hoping he's still at work, but to be absolutely honest with you, Hannah, I have no idea.'

* * *

Hannah makes fresh tea and sits me down at the pockmarked, worn oak table in her warm but messy kitchen. The smell of fresh laundry scents the air, and her bread machine beeps before whirring into life. A perfect picture of domestic bliss. After checking the girls are happily playing together upstairs, I turn to Hannah and pull my phone from my pocket.

'Hannah, can I show you something?'

'Of course.' Her eyes are wide as she stares at me. 'Claire, you're being really . . . you're scaring me a bit.'

I don't reply as I fumble with the passcode on my phone and then, bringing up the screenshot of the post, hand the phone to Hannah.

'Claire?' I watch as her eyes scan over the post, taking in the words and the photograph that accompanies it. 'What is this?'

'I have no idea. It was on my timeline this morning. I was hoping you might know something . . . *anything*.'

'Me? I don't know anything about this!' Hannah is indignant as she re-reads the post, her eyes flicking over the words, returning time and again to the photograph of Tom and Isla, laughing in the sun. 'You don't know this . . . Lydia?'

I shake my head. 'I've never heard that name in my life. As far as I know, Tom doesn't know any Lydia either.' I squash down the memory of him checking his phone after he thought I was asleep, push away the thought that naturally follows.

'Is this a sponsored post?' Hannah peers closely at the picture on my phone, splaying her fingers to enlarge it so that it completely fills the screen.

'Yes, it looks as though she's paid for an ad to make sure she reaches a large number of people.' Pushing my hands through my hair in frustration, I watch as Hannah raises her eyes to mine, her cheeks pale. 'I'm hoping it's just some kind of weird catfish, internet troll thing . . .' I trail off, desperately hoping she'll be able to shed some light on the situation.

'Can you log in to your account, so I can get a better look at it?' She hands me the phone and I quickly log in, typing Lydia French into the search bar at the top of the page. Dozens of Lydia Frenchs appear, but not the one I'm looking for. I scroll down my timeline, hoping the photo of Tom and Isla will spring out at me, but there's nothing. The advert isn't there.

'It's gone,' I say, looking at Hannah in alarm as my pulse quickens. 'The advert has disappeared.'

'Let me see.' Hannah takes the phone from me, and I watch as she taps at the screen, peering intently into the phone.

'You're right, it's definitely not there now. The fact that it's a sponsored post could explain why it's disappeared.' Hannah hands the phone back to me. 'The ad will only show for as long as there is funding behind it — when the money runs out, the ad disappears. Look.' Hannah pulls out her own phone, bringing up a page for her Etsy shop. 'See? I can enter the search criteria that I want to use to target the people that might be interested.'

'So, this Lydia French could have set the advert to target me? To make sure I saw it?'

'Possibly?' Hannah gives an uneasy shrug. 'Or she's just spread the net as wide as possible in the hope that someone Tom knows sees it. Either way, it's definitely been removed — it's not showing at all when I search for her. If the ad had just run out of funding, then the page would still be there if we looked for it, but there's nothing.'

I'm not sure if this is a good thing or a bad thing, and judging by the solemn look on Hannah's face, neither is she. The creeping feeling that maybe the page has been removed because Lydia French doesn't need it anymore, because she's already found Tom, makes me finally voice internally the thought I've been trying to avoid all day.

'Do you think . . .' I swallow, the words catching like barbs in my throat. 'Do you think Tom could have had an affair with her? With this Lydia? Why mention Isla?'

Hannah gives a snort, pressing her hand to her mouth. 'Sorry, Claire, but are you joking? There's *no way* Tom would cheat on you. He adores you, adores Isla. He worships the ground you walk on — even when I moan about Robert, Tom never, ever joins in and says things about you. It's absurd to think he would do that.'

While I'm relieved at Hannah's vehemence — I don't think Tom could ever have an affair either, deep down — her words do give me pause, because if Tom isn't having an affair, then that means something might have happened to him, something that's stopped him from coming home.

'That still doesn't explain why this woman is using my photograph on social media, does it? Hannah, you spend heaps of time with Tom — has he seemed different in anyway lately? He didn't turn up to collect Isla from school, and he's not answering his phone, and to be honest I'm worried.' If just one thing had happened today to make this day so strange, if I had *either* seen the post from Lydia French *or* Tom hadn't collected Isla from school, then maybe I would have lasted a little longer before the anxiety really kicked in. As it is, that uneasy feeling still snakes along my spine, and I sense the beginnings of a tension headache as worry settles on my shoulders.

'What? I thought . . . I thought he arranged for *you* to collect Isla? But Tom was supposed to?' Hannah frowns as she processes what I've said.

'No, I was expecting Tom to collect Isla as usual, but then I got a call from the school to say that he hadn't arrived and Isla was still waiting. I tried calling Tom but there was no answer. I've tried him a few times today . . . nothing.' Shaking my head, I try to adopt a more normal tone, but when I speak my mouth is dry, the words feeling too big for my mouth. 'I'm sure he's just been held up at work or something. Nothing serious.' I pause for a second, not wanting to voice things out loud as my heart starts to beat a hard, insistent tattoo against my ribs. 'But with that weird post . . . I don't know if he's been keeping something from me. That's why I wondered if Tom has seemed OK to you over the past few weeks.' I clear my throat and swallow hard. While the four of us are all close friends, Tom spending time with both Hannah and Robert, I don't think Tom would appreciate me spouting off about how he's been cold-shouldering me, or the strange, thick atmosphere that seems to have invaded our home.

'No.' Hannah shakes her head slowly, before brushing her fringe back out of her eyes. 'I mean, he's been a bit quiet the last few days, but that's nothing unusual. You know Tom, he's not exactly outgoing, so I didn't think anything of it. You guys didn't have a fight or anything, did you?' I shake my head convincingly, and she carries on thinking aloud. 'He was just normal, I'm sure of it. Although . . .' She stops, as if something has just occurred to her.

'What? Hannah — what is it?' My feet start to tap restlessly under the table as I wait for her to continue speaking. She drags her eyes reluctantly away from the picture of Tom and Isla on my phone screen.

'There was a phone call. Last Thursday? We'd picked the children up from school and come back here for a coffee.'

I think back to last Thursday — I'd had to go up to London for a meeting and was late back. Tom had been asleep by the time I got home and I'd barely spoken to him, just climbed into bed and kissed his bare shoulder as he slept. Now, I wish I'd woken him, talked to him, asked him how his day was.

'And? What was the phone call?'

'That's just it — Tom's phone rang and he ignored it. It was weird, because he'd had his phone on the table all afternoon — you know what a nightmare he is with his phone, he's always got it on silent — and I thought he must have been waiting for the call. But he didn't answer, he just let it ring out — and then it rang again straight away. It happened a couple of times before he blocked whatever number was calling him. I asked him if everything was OK, but he said it was just some insurance company that was hassling him. He was a bit jumpy though, afterwards. He still left his phone on the table and kept checking it, like he was expecting someone to be trying to get hold of him.'

It sounds like strange behaviour to me, especially given the way Tom usually keeps his phone on silent. It's not giving me much to go on, and the thought that Tom might be having an affair tickles the back of my mind again. It would certainly explain why he kept his phone close . . . but then I shake the thought off. This is *Tom*.

'Maybe he was just tired? I know he'd had a long week at work and he wasn't looking forward to solo parenting that evening. Sorry.' Still speaking, Hannah keeps her eyes on the table, scratching at a drop of sauce that has dried thick and hard, and I feel a slick of shame wash over me at the realisation I didn't know Tom felt that way.

'Maybe it *was* an insurance company that was calling him. But it still doesn't explain the picture. How did Lydia French get hold of it? A picture that I took, on my camera, that no one else has had access to. I mean, even I had forgotten about it — it was just sat on my digital camera.' I bring up the photo again, drinking in the light as it bounces off Tom's dark hair, the gap in Isla's smile where her front tooth was missing.

'And there's no way anyone else could have gotten hold of the picture? You didn't take the SD card into any place for the photo to be printed off into a physical copy?' Hannah's voice breaks into my thoughts and I flick my eyes towards her, her face pale with worry.

'No — of course not.' I glance down at the picture again, when I remember. Sweat breaks out across my temples as I realise that I have done something very, very stupid. 'Oh shit, Hannah. There is a way that someone could have got their hands on this photo. And it's all my fault.'

CHAPTER 5

Hannah stares at me silently, waiting for me to carry on. Taking a deep breath, I swallow hard and give a brief glance towards the hall, where the sound of laughter drifts down the stairs, before leaning in and lowering my voice.

'Remember the cruise? The day this picture was taken?'

'Of course.' Hannah takes my phone and stares at the photo, running a finger over Isla's smiling face. 'That was probably the best day of the entire holiday.'

Last summer we took a cruise with Hannah and Robert. Not something either myself or Tom would have thought of for our holiday, but the subject of a cruise had come up over a boozy Sunday lunch at theirs one day, and I think both Tom and I got caught up in the excitement. We hadn't had anything booked for the summer holidays, and as the cruise — a fourteen-night extravaganza leaving from Southampton and taking in the sights of the Mediterranean — was on special offer it had seemed like a no-brainer. By the time Tom had voiced his doubts over it, Hannah had already booked for all of us.

It started off well, although crossing the Bay of Biscay was rough and I spent a fair amount of time lying in my cabin, half regretting the moment I set foot on board. The first docking was in Alicante, and our first day off the boat was a day filled with scorching sunshine. As I look at the photo now, I remember the way the sun had felt as it hit my grey, washed-out skin, remember the relief as my feet hit dry land after three days of feeling nauseous the minute my head left the pillow. Tom and Isla had spent their first three days on deck, enjoying the hot tub and swimming pool, while I was indoors nursing my seasickness on the tiny cabin bunk. They'd both acquired a healthy-looking tan, Isla's hair fading to a brilliant white blonde in the sun. Tom was relaxed and happy for the first time in weeks. He'd been tense in the run-up to the cruise, something I'd put down to the stress of organising a holiday while I was working overtime to pay for it. We hadn't been away since before Isla was born, spending our honeymoon in a tiny cottage in Wales. Isla had come along just six months later, and once we'd made the decision that I would go back to work full-time, I set my sights on becoming a partner at the conveyancing firm, meaning there wasn't much time for holidays. That day we'd strolled along the beach, Tom laughing at the saucy fridge magnets and hideous fake football shirts on sale along the promenade, before finding a little beachside restaurant with a perfect view of the ocean. We were all hot and thirsty, Robert ordering *cervezas* for himself and Tom, while us women tucked into a large jug of sangria — the beauty of the cruise, Robert said, was that no one ever had to drive home.

Tom had pulled Isla onto his lap as we'd waited for the paella to be brought out, the sunlight gleaming off Isla's hair and the white sands of the beach behind them. I'd grabbed the camera just as Hannah had said something outrageous, perfectly capturing the laughter that danced across Tom's face.

'Lovely pic, Claire.' Robert had leaned over me, squinting in the bright sunshine at the photograph on the small camera screen. 'You should enter it into that competition.'

'What competition?' Tom's voice was sharp, no hint of the relaxed, laughing man of a few short moments ago.

'Did you not see the posters on the ship? The cruise line is running a competition for passengers to enter a photograph that sums up their time on the cruise. The prize is a cruise of your choice, up to a certain value. Only condition is, they get to keep the photo, to use for promotional purposes.'

A dark cloud crossed Tom's face as he reached for his beer and drained the glass, nearly upending Isla from his lap.

'Don't, Claire.'

'Why not? Look at the way the light hits — you both look fantastic.' I'd dabbled with photography for years, and was still enough of an amateur to get excited when I took a photo that captured my subjects perfectly. 'And it does sum up our holiday so far, we're having a brilliant time.'

'I said *don't*. I mean it, Claire. Don't. I'll delete the picture.'

'OK, OK. I won't. But I'm keeping the photo, you both look gorgeous in it.'

I remember leaning across the table at that point to kiss him, the taste of beer on his lips as my mouth met his. The photograph was mostly forgotten, buried among the others taken throughout the trip, and I hadn't even thought about it until it appeared on my screen this morning.

'Remember Robert mentioned the cruise line competition?' I smooth my hands over the table nervously, hoping Hannah doesn't notice the tremor in my fingers as I do so. Shame prickles beneath the collar of my blouse, and I realise I don't want to go on, don't want to confess what I did. That this Lydia French using a picture of my husband for catfishing, or trolling, or whatever she's doing could potentially be all my fault.

'Yes, I remember.'

I remember the heat of the sun on our backs as we picked huge prawns from the paella, Tom not quite as jolly as he had been earlier in the day. *I said don't. I mean it, Claire.* Tom getting angry at the thought of the photo being entered into any competition. It wasn't often that I ever went against Tom's wishes, and a shard of regret slices deep into my heart.

'I don't know how to say this . . .' I heave in a deep breath, my chest tight. 'I entered the photo into the competition.'

'Oh Claire, you didn't.' Hannah's face is a picture of disappointment. 'Tom specifically asked you not to.'

'I know — and I hate myself for it now. But I just thought . . .' I shrug, trying to minimise things, even though I can see by the look on Hannah's face that she's disappointed with me. 'I thought he didn't want me to enter it because he was just being difficult. He can be like that sometimes, you know? I was so pleased with how the photograph turned out, there was no way I couldn't enter it. I thought he was just . . .' I shake my head. Tom is never really happy when I photograph him, saying he's not photogenic in the slightest. Not true at all.

'But how would that explain how Lydia French got hold of it? Does she work for the cruise line?' Hannah's brow crumples as she tries to make sense of it all.

'I don't know.' I feel sick, my gut heavy with the idea that I'm the reason Lydia French has this photo. 'All I can think is when I submitted the photograph, I was somehow agreeing to the cruise line using it, even if I didn't win.'

Hannah stares at me, horrified, her hand covering her mouth. 'Oh God, Claire, this is awful. Did you ever tell Tom you submitted it?' The words are muffled, and she almost violently tugs her hand back down into her lap.

'No . . . how could I?' Self-disgust washes over me at the memory of the look on Tom's face when I said I wanted to enter it into the competition. Later that evening, when we returned to our cabin, he had turned to me, wrapping his arms around my waist.

'Won't you let me enter that picture in the competition, Tom?' I had asked, breathing in the scent of his aftershave as he bent to kiss me gently. 'Isla looks beautiful in it, and I captured you both perfectly. We have a good chance of winning.'

'No, Claire.' Tom had pulled away then. 'Just leave it. I don't want our picture plastered all over some cruise line's advertising campaign. This is *our* holiday, all about *us*. Why would you want to send that to complete strangers?' He'd turned away from me, rummaging under his pillow for his pyjama bottoms, and that was it, end of discussion. We spent the rest of our holiday drinking, dancing and having the time of our lives. Later, when we were home, reluctant to let the last feelings of holiday contentment drift away, I emailed a copy of the photograph to the cruise line, thinking that if by any chance we *did* win, I would be able to talk Tom round. I knew it was wrong, but there was a part of me that was proud of the photo and wanted some recognition for it. When I didn't hear back and I hadn't seen any advertisements from the cruise line using it, I pushed it from my mind and carried on without giving it another thought.

'Claire? Are you OK?' Hannah reaches out and squeezes my hand, concern etched on her face, and I realise I'm muttering to myself.

'Sorry, I just . . . I can't believe I did something so stupid. So *selfish*. I should have known if I sent it off somewhere, there could be a chance of it surfacing later on — it's so easy to find things online these days.'

'Do you think that's why Tom's been so weird lately? Maybe if this woman, Lydia French, has managed to find it online, maybe Tom has seen it somewhere too? I mean, you obviously feel like he's not himself at the moment, not that he's said anything to me.' Hannah adds the last sentence in hastily, making it clear that she's just as much in the dark as I am.

'I can't see Tom not confronting me about it if he had seen it — he was pretty quick that day to tell me not to submit it. The competition was *months* ago and we haven't discussed it since. You know what Tom's like — if he knew for definite I had sent the photograph off behind his back, I think he would have said something. He's no good at holding a grudge.' Tom *would* have said something, I'm sure of it.

'You can't beat yourself up about it now.' Hannah grasps my cold hands in both of her warm ones. 'What's done is done. Maybe you're reading too much into this whole post thing — yes, it's out of order that the woman has used your photo, and yes, I would be annoyed if it was one of my kids splashed all over the internet without my permission, but it happens. Hundreds of people get trolled or catfished on the internet every day.'

'You're probably right. If I'm honest, I'm more concerned about Tom not returning my calls and not collecting Isla, but maybe he's just held up somewhere. If he's been delayed at work, maybe something's happened and he can't get out to call me? Perhaps I'm blowing things out of proportion.' Talking myself down, I pull my hands out from Hannah's.

'Go home, Claire. Get Isla some dinner and get her to bed — it's getting late. I'm sure Tom will be home by the time you get back. You two can have dinner together, a bottle of wine, and talk about things. I'm sure there'll be a reasonable explanation for everything.'

I nod, desperately wanting to believe Hannah is right. A spark of hope flares, and pushing back the kitchen chair, I snatch up my mobile phone and call out to Isla to come downstairs. Hannah trails behind me and at the front door I turn back, leaning forward to peck her cheek.

'Thanks, Hannah. Sorry for bending your ear.'

'Honestly, Claire, it's no trouble — it's what friends are for! Just let me know when you hear from Tom — or better yet, get him to call Robert. You never know, he might open up to him.' Hannah waves me away and I walk my daughter back down the path towards home, where I'm almost certain Tom will be waiting for us. At least, I hope he is.

* * *

Back at the house, Tom's car is still missing from the driveway, but even so, I call out to him as I let myself in. There's no reply.

'Where's Daddy?' Isla appears at my elbow, her bag of precious things clutched tightly under one arm. 'You said he would be back by now.'

'I'm not sure, sweetie.' I hesitate, not sure what to say next. 'Perhaps he's busy at work. I expect he'll be home soon.' Isla runs straight upstairs to her bedroom, grumpy with me for cutting short her play date with Brody and Matilda when Tom isn't even home yet. I leave her, too tired to deal with an argument, and knowing she'll come round soon enough — she's like Tom in that her anger is always short-lived and she never manages to hold a grudge for long. *Although, maybe I'm wrong about that.* There is a niggling voice at the back of my mind, trying to tell me that maybe Tom *can* hold a grudge — maybe he's found out that I sent the photo into the competition, and this is his way of teaching me a lesson.

It's now well past the time I would usually have expected Tom to be home even if he had a late viewing, and concern is starting to weigh heavy, sitting like a lead ball in my stomach. I head for the kitchen and pull out the tray of chicken nuggets that Tom has prepared for Isla's dinner. *Did he make these knowing he wouldn't be home tonight?* Twenty minutes later, distracted by my own thoughts, I pull the food back out of the oven just before it burns and call Isla down to eat. Once she's settled, I sneak out into the hallway to call Tom one more time, something sharp twisting in my gut as his mobile goes straight to voicemail. Has he turned his phone off? Or is it simply out of battery? I don't leave a message, instead deciding to do what I try *never* to do. I call him at work. The phone rings several times, and just when I think they all must have left for the day, the receiver is snatched up and a deep, 'Hello, Watson Mayfair,' meets my ear.

'Oh, hi . . . Jonah? Is that you?' I'm surprised to hear Tom's boss on the other end of the line. 'It's Claire Bennett, Tom's wife.'

'Claire. Hi.'

'I'm sorry to call this late in the day . . . I was wondering if Tom was still at the office, or if you knew what time he'd left this evening? It's just, I thought he was picking up Isla, but it turned out he wasn't and . . . never mind, I wondered if you knew if he was on his way home?' I stop, aware Jonah must think I'm a madwoman, rambling on about Isla.

'I was about to ask you the same question.' Jonah's tone is brusque in a way I've never heard him use before.

'The same . . . ?'

Jonah sighs, 'Where is he, Claire? I've been rushed off my feet all day trying to rearrange his viewings. He's made us look bloody unprofessional.'

'But he left this morning . . . he said he had three viewings today.' I don't know what Jonah is saying, can't wrap my head around things.

'And he didn't show up for a single one! That's what I'm trying to tell you, Claire. Tom hasn't shown up for work at all today.'

CHAPTER 6

Stuttering some excuse about getting the wrong end of the stick, I thank Jonah and hang up. I don't know what to think. As far as I was aware, Tom left this morning to take Isla to school and then head into work for a ten o'clock viewing with his client. But now, Jonah is saying that Tom never showed up for any of his viewings today. Add into the mix Tom's distant behaviour lately and the strange post on my social media, and I'm starting to feel like things really, really don't add up.

Moving to the kitchen, I check on Isla, hurrying her through the last few bites of her dinner before impatiently bathing her and getting her ready for bed. As I tuck her in after a story, she snuggles deeper under the duvet.

'Mummy? When is Daddy coming home?' I knew she'd ask again, but I was hoping Tom would have returned home before it was time for Isla to go to bed.

'I'm not too sure, darling.' Tom and I have always agreed we would never lie to our children, something I've always been very strict on after my own upbringing, and I hesitate for a moment before I speak. 'He's not feeling too well at the moment — he's very tired, so he's taking a little holiday.' The lie tastes bitter on my tongue.

'Has he gone to the hospital like Pearl's granny? She was tired and they took her into the hospital.' Isla pushes the covers back and stares me right in the eye, as if she knows I'm lying.

'No, sweetie. He's not in the hospital — I promise.' Somehow, I maintain eye contact, fussing with her fringe and stroking her hair away from her face. 'Come on, time to go to sleep. Daddy will be back soon, I'm sure.' I kiss her and close her bedroom door silently, a sharp pain tugging at my heart. I can only hope Tom *will* be back soon.

Downstairs, I pace, anxiety over Tom's lack of contact making the tension headache that crept up on me at Hannah's pound at my temples. I'm fed up of waiting for him to contact me, fed up of relentlessly checking my phone. How could I have been so stupid? If I had just listened to Tom and not gone behind his back to enter that bloody photograph, maybe he would be home with me now. Maybe this Lydia French wouldn't have tried to track him down. I sit on the edge of the sofa, jittery with anxiety, only to get to my feet and start pacing again moments later. *Has he just taken some time out?* If Tom *was* worried about something, why didn't he talk to me? Tom has always been the strong, silent type, reluctant to talk about the things that matter. God knows I've tried to get him to open up. I know he's an introvert, quiet, happier in his own head most of the time, but surely he must have known he could tell me if something was bothering him? On the rare occasions that we do argue he much prefers to brush things under the carpet rather than talk them through, and while I find it frustrating, I've learned that the harder I push him, the more he clams up. *But this isn't an argument, Claire. This is something else.*

Whatever it was that made him quiet and jumpy around Hannah last week, we could have talked about it — I've always made it clear to Tom that he can talk to me about anything. Maybe I'm making a big deal about nothing. Maybe I'll hear his car at any moment, and he'll come falling through the door, tired and rumpled but with a smile on his face and a reasonable explanation as to why things haven't gone as they usually do today. Maybe we'll open the wine and he'll tell me what happened to stop him from going to work — *Honestly Claire, you won't* believe *what happened* — and then he'll tiptoe in to kiss Isla before we head towards our own bedroom. I'm going round in circles trying to work things out, but there's a nagging sensation in the pit of my stomach that tells me Tom hasn't left of his own accord. He wouldn't have left Isla — not without a good reason. He might have left *me* — and if I just look at how he's acted around me lately, it could happen — but he would never leave Isla. He wouldn't just go, not without saying something, I know he wouldn't. I know *him*. And that, in conjunction with the photo on my timeline, makes me feel sure that this woman, Lydia French, has something to do with it all.

Dragging my hands through my hair I begin to pace again, trying to figure out where to go from here, when a thought strikes me. A few months previously I had gone through a stage of leaving my phone in random places — a combination of a busy work schedule, back-to-back meetings until well into the evenings most nights, and a nasty bout of bronchitis — so I had downloaded the 'findmymobile' app onto my phone. There was an option to add family members so I had added Tom, thinking he would be able to find his mobile if he lost it, never once thinking that I would be using the app to find *him*. I pull out my phone and open the app. It takes a few moments but before long a tiny, pulsing blue dot appears showing me where Tom is, and instead of the relief I should be feeling, there is only confusion. The dot is hovering over our house. Frowning I peer out of the front room window, looking for his car. His parking space on the driveway is still empty, the paving slabs nearest the hedge darkened with moss. Tom isn't here, but his phone is. I turn away from the window, scanning the sitting room, but there's no sign of his mobile and I move quickly to the kitchen, checking the worktops, the drawers, even the fruit bowl to see if he's left it there by accident. *Nothing*.

Hurrying up the stairs, I head for our bedroom just in case he did come home during the day and accidentally left his phone behind, even though deep down, I know I'm starting to clutch at straws. Warily, I push open the bedroom door to find things just as I left them this morning. He hasn't been home at all, despite the blue, pulsing dot on my phone screen telling me he's here. Heart sinking, I lower myself onto the edge of the bed, my mind racing as I try and untangle exactly what's going on, and what to do next. Without his phone, I have no way of contacting Tom. Do I just wait to see if he comes home later on tonight? What if he *doesn't* come home? The thought hits me like a blow, my breath catching in my throat as things suddenly feel horrifyingly real. The fact that he hasn't come home, his phone has been left behind, that it's past Isla's bedtime and there's been no word from him all add up to something I don't really want to admit, and my palms start to sweat.

Do I report him missing? Is he even missing? Maybe all of this is a coincidence — maybe he just took off for the day, played truant and went to the beach or something, and he's lost track of time. I know we've had our ups and downs lately — we've both been tired and busy, Tom quieter than usual and he's obviously had something on his mind, but even so . . . wouldn't he have told me if he needed some time out? I know there are things Tom doesn't like to talk about, like his parents, but I thought I knew everything I needed to know about him. He's complex and precise, a stickler for detail, a lover of routine, which makes his disappearance today all the more unusual. I thought I had seen inside his many layers, all the different parts that make him the person he is — I thought he'd been as honest and open with me as I am with him. *Was it all a lie? Has he been keeping secrets, hiding things from me?* I think again of the blue glow of his phone screen on his face when he thought I was asleep, and wonder what he was doing. What he was hiding. *And what about Lydia French?*

Mind whirling, I lean forward, pushing my hands through my thick, dark blonde hair, my elbows resting on my knees, when something catches my eye. Tom's mobile peeps out from under the bed, the corner just visible from where the foot of the bed meets the carpet. I pull it out, holding it lightly in one hand, knowing now that something really is amiss. I'm not imagining things, and the sense that something really isn't right is overwhelming, fear rapping a sharp fist against my rib cage. Tom must have knocked the phone from the bedside table this morning when he got up, and he left in such a hurry there's every chance he didn't even realise it was missing, but that was hours ago. Surely by now he would have noticed? Especially given the way he's been glued to it lately.

I swipe across to access the phone, typing in Tom's passcode. His screen fills with a picture of me and Isla, taken on that very same cruise last summer, and something tightens in my chest. In a similar pose, Isla sits on my lap, one hand shielding her eyes from the sun as we sit on a lounger on the top deck of the cruise ship, our hair blowing back in the breeze. There are the missed calls from me, two from Gwen, several from Tom's office, and one from Hannah after I had left her house earlier, presumably to let Tom know I was looking for him. Feeling grubby, as if I'm snooping, I go into his messages, to see if there are any clues there as to where he might be. I hesitate for a moment, suddenly sick with fear that there will be evidence of Tom having an affair before I force my eyes down to the screen. There are several messages from Hannah, asking about everyday random stuff: Can Tom pick up Brody when he gets Isla from school? Can Tom help with the tombola at the school fete? One from the school reminding him that Isla has a club on Friday afternoon. Then, a message from an unknown number, sent late last night. It was sent after midnight, long after Tom and I had gone to bed. It simply reads, *I KNOW EVERYTHING.*

CHAPTER 7

My pulse crashes in my ears and there's the strange sensation that the floor has just fallen away beneath me as I read and re-read the message. This must have been the reason Tom was checking his phone last night after he thought I had gone to sleep. The words are like a physical blow to the stomach and I run my tongue over my teeth, my lips numb with shock. Who sent Tom this message? And what the hell is it supposed to mean? I have no idea how long I sit there, perched on the end of our bed, staring at the message on Tom's phone, an icy finger snaking down my spine with every read of it. *I know everything.* About what? I rack my brains, trying to come up with some logical reason as to why someone would send this text, trying to explain it away, but I can't. Scrolling through the other messages, I search for some sort of explanation, some witty bloke banter from one of his friends, a prank from someone who thinks they're funny, but there's nothing. The text is the only form of contact from the unknown number — there are no calls made or received according to Tom's call log, and Tom hasn't replied to the text message. This, combined with the post from Lydia French and Tom's failure to follow his usual routine, has me convinced that things aren't as clear-cut between Tom and myself as I was led to believe. As much as

I want to believe he has just taken a day off, away from the pressures of work, it's looking less and less likely.

With shaking hands I type out a single, brief sentence to the number. *WHO IS THIS?* I pause for a moment before adding, *WHAT DO YOU WANT?* I don't say anything more — just sit back and wait for a reply, the churning in my stomach making me nauseous. After a few seconds, I check the phone again to see if there has been any response, but there's nothing, the status still on *delivered*. Impatiently, I check the phone volume is turned up and bounce back into the messages box. Still nothing. Flicking back to the call log screen, I recall Hannah's words about Tom receiving a call on Thursday, while I was away. I scroll down, but all the numbers are numbers I recognise, programmed into Tom's phone by name. Frustrated, I flick my thumb angrily at the screen and watch as the names blur past, before coming to a stop. At the bottom of the screen is a button marked 'blocked calls'. Pressing it, I wait as the screen changes, and a single number appears in the blocked calls list, all calls logged between four and four thirty, last Thursday afternoon. This must be the so-called insurance company who contacted him on the day Hannah was with him — Hannah said he was jumpy after, which makes me think there is more to it than a simple insurance call. With a spurt of optimism and shaking fingers, I unblock the number and call it, the ringing in my ear shrill and insistent.

'Blackthorn Insurance, how can I help you?'

'Insurance? You are an actual insurance company?'

'Yes ma'am, do you have a claim you wish us to investigate?'

'What? No, I'm sorry. Wrong number.'

Swearing softly under my breath, I hang up, disappointment squeezing at my insides. I thought I was onto something, that whoever called held the key to where Tom might be, because now — I look at the clock, watching the hands inch towards ten o'clock — I'm starting to believe there's every chance he's not coming home.

* * *

As the clock hits ten o'clock exactly, I bite the bullet and call the police. Stepping out into the hallway, I hover over the keypad of my phone, unsure as to whether to call 999 or 101, before plumping for 101. Technically this isn't an emergency. Yet.

'Hampshire Police. Can I help you?'

'It's . . . it's my husband. He hasn't come home.' My throat wants to close over at saying the words out loud, and I swallow thickly as the police operator tells me she'll need to ask me some questions.

'What's your husband's name?' Her voice is calm and steady, whereas I have to take a deep breath before I can speak, my chest tight, as though there isn't enough air in the room.

'Thomas Malcolm Bennett.'

'Date and place of birth?'

'Fourteenth of May 1990, Archmouth in Cornwall.'

'Can you give me a brief description of him — any distinguishing marks, tattoos, things like that?'

'Errr . . . he's medium build, maybe six foot one-ish? Caucasian, blue eyes, dark hair kind of swept back off his forehead . . . he doesn't really have any distinguishing marks. No tattoos.'

'And what was he wearing today, when you last saw him?' My brain freezes for a moment, as I try and remember what Tom was wearing this morning.

'Umm . . . a light-blue polo shirt!' I almost shout it, as a picture of Tom, flipping pancakes at the stove this morning pings into my mind. 'A blue polo, tan chinos and . . .' I think for a moment, seeing Tom reaching for his car keys as he went to leave. 'And a Harrington jacket. Black, with a tartan lining.'

'Excellent. Do you know what his plans were for today?'

'Well, just the usual. I thought he was going to work, and then to collect our daughter from school, only he never showed up at work, or at the school.'

'And he didn't mention anything else? No plans for anything other than his usual routine?'

I think about Isla, sliding into the passenger seat and saying, *'Didn't Daddy tell you?'*

'My daughter did mention that Tom said he might not make the school run — but I think she's getting confused. She's only seven. Tom has plans for a conference in Birmingham next week, so I think maybe he mentioned that, and Isla got the wrong end of the stick.'

'Hmmm,' the operator says, and I screw my face up as my frustration rises. 'And what about your home life? Nothing out of the ordinary there?'

'Not between us, but there was something. There was a post on my timeline this morning, from a Lydia French. It was a photograph of Tom and Isla, with a piece about how she was looking for her husband and daughter.' My voice rises and I take a breath as panic bubbles under my skin. 'What if she's got something to do with him not coming home?'

'Please, Mrs. Bennett, you need to calm down and let me finish asking the questions. What about his state of mind? Are there any mental health issues that we should know about?'

I tell her there's nothing, and she rambles through the last of the questions as I pace the floor, wanting them to just *get out there* and look for him. Finally, after her last few questions about the car Tom was driving and the address of his workplace, she tells me that someone will call me back, and sure enough not long after the phone rings. I go through the entire thing again, answering the same questions, giving the same answers.

'Right. OK, Mrs. Bennett. Unfortunately, there's not a lot we can do.'

'What do you mean, "not a lot you can do"? He's missing, for God's sake. He didn't turn up at work and now he hasn't come home. He should have been home ages ago.' Disappointment leaves a metallic taste in my mouth, so sure was I that the police would go straight out and start looking for him.

'He's not missing in the eyes of the law, Mrs. Bennett. He's an adult, of stable mind. You said yourself he told your daughter he might not be back in time to collect her from school today. Are you sure there hasn't been any kind of domestic dispute? Have you contacted his family?'

'He doesn't *have* any family — only us. He's an only child and he hasn't spoken to his parents for years, long before he met me. And yes, I'm sure — there hasn't been any kind of domestic dispute. Tom and I . . . we don't argue.' As I say the words, I know that's not strictly true, but while we've had a few problems lately, we haven't really argued and there's nothing that warrants Tom not coming home without a word.

'What about the photograph, this Lydia French?'

'We'll circulate his photograph and get in contact with the National Missing Persons Helpline, but in all honesty, Mrs. Bennett, unless the circumstances surrounding your husband leaving change in some way, we won't be able to undertake any further enquiries at this moment. If you haven't had any contact with him after a week or so, give us a call back.'

Resisting the urge to throw my phone across the room, I jab at the button to hang up before sinking onto the sofa, head in my hands.

* * *

I don't know how long I sit there before an insistent buzzing rouses me and I glance up to see Gwen's name on my phone screen. There are several missed calls from her. *Shit. I forgot we were supposed to meet for dinner tonight.* Sighing, I answer.

'Gwen?'

'Claire — where the bloody hell are you? You were supposed to be here hours ago.' Gwen's tone is clipped; she hates waiting for anybody or anything.

'Oh God, Gwen. I'm sorry.'

'What's going on? What's so important that you've left me sitting in the pub like a muppet on my own?' In the background I hear music and the muted sounds of conversation, alongside the ring of a fruit machine.

'It's Tom. He's not home.'

'What do you mean he's not home? Do you need to see him before you leave? Just call him. Oh — do you need to sort out a babysitter? I could come to yours instead, it's half ten already. No point in getting dinner now.' Realising Gwen doesn't grasp what I'm saying, I try again.

'I mean, he's not come home. At all. Like, I've been calling him all day but he hasn't taken his phone with him. He didn't turn up to collect Isla from school, and when I called . . .' I break off for a second as my throat closes over and the first prick of tears stings my eyes. 'He never turned up for work. I don't know where he is, and I don't have any way of contacting him.'

'Oh, Claire.' Gwen's voice takes on a sombre tone. 'You didn't get hold of him in the end?'

'No. I haven't spoken to him all day.'

'Shit.' I hear the background noise fade, as though Gwen has stepped outside the pub. 'Has he taken any of his stuff with him? I don't want to upset you, Claire, and forgive me if this comes across as a bit harsh, but . . . is there any chance Tom might have left you? You did say things have been a bit strained between you lately.'

'*No.* I mean, we've had a couple of silly arguments and he's been a bit distant but nothing serious. Nothing he would leave me over.' I don't know why, but it hadn't even occurred to me that he would have taken anything with him, perhaps the idea he would leave me too unbelievable — or just something that I didn't even want to contemplate. I tell Gwen, 'No, I definitely don't think he's left me,' and explain about the photograph appearing on my timeline that morning.

'That's a bit weird,' Gwen says, 'but it doesn't necessarily mean anything sinister — like you said, it could be a troll. You definitely didn't row?'

'*No*, Gwen, we didn't row.'

'It sounds like maybe he just needs a bit of time out. His job can be quite stressful, you know that. Maybe he's gone to

'. . . I dunno, play golf or something? You said he forgot his mobile, maybe that's why he hasn't called you.' Gwen's voice is calm, practical, and I cling to the thought that if Gwen isn't panicking, maybe I don't need to just yet. Until she speaks again. 'Either that, or maybe he had a car accident or something? Although I'm sure if that happened someone would have found a way to contact you . . .' She trails off, and I say nothing, disappointed that not even my own sister seems to be taking this as seriously as I am. 'Claire, are you really worried about him?'

'Yeah,' I manage, my pulse pounding in my ears. 'I really am starting to worry — I get it if he wants some time alone away from me, but what about Isla? Would he just take off and leave her?'

'Did you call the police yet?' Gwen asks, her voice sober now with no hint of the mockery at the start of the call.

'Yeah. They basically said he's an adult of sound mind and he can do what he wants. They're not interested.'

'You know what I would do, Claire? I'd go to the station and demand to see someone, not let them fob me off with a phone call.'

Reassuring her that she doesn't need to come over, I hang up on Gwen and pace the living room, my mind working overtime. Gwen is right — if something had happened to Tom, like a car accident, someone would have found some way to contact me. He always carries his ID, so even if he couldn't contact me himself, someone would have tracked me down. I ring the local hospitals just in case, but none of them have any record of a Tom Bennett being brought in. That only leaves me one other option. I race upstairs to our bedroom, silently berating myself for not checking if anything was missing before. His side of the closet is in chaos, something I've always struggled to marry up to the man I know so well. Tom is meticulous, organised and methodical. He doesn't smoke, barely drinks and has never even had a speeding ticket — I find it hard to match his untidy, jumbled wardrobe with his usual, tidy nature. Rattling through the hangers, I try to deduce if anything is missing. It's impossible — he has so many clothes that I'm not sure even Tom could see if anything was gone. I check the en-suite, but everything I think Tom would use is all still there — if anything, this has highlighted to me that although I think I know everything there is to know about him, there are so many little things we fail to take notice of in everyday life. I couldn't tell you if his favourite shirt was missing, or the aftershave he wears for best. I realise I don't know where to turn — I can't think of anyone other than Gwen or Hannah who might know where he is. I have no clue about his routine — no idea if there's a favourite place he goes to be alone, a favourite park or beach that he uses as a sanctuary . . . I'm so used to him being *there*, and the realisation that I don't know him the way I thought I did is terrifying. Sitting on the bed, I press my hands over tired eyes, desperate to hear from him just once; one text message is all I want, just to let me know he's OK, even if he does need some time out away from us. *And what about Lydia French?* the niggly voice at the back of my mind asks. I recall Gwen's last words to me during our phone call, when I told her the police didn't want to know.

'You know what I would do, Claire? I'd go to the station and demand to see someone, not let them fob me off with a phone call.'

She's right, the way my calm, zen sister so often is. I get to my feet, trying to shake off the wobbly feeling left by the adrenaline that pumped around my body and the overwhelming fear that something dreadful has happened to my husband. I need to go to the station and speak to someone face to face. There has to be someone there who would be willing to help.

CHAPTER 8

Gwen arrives within twenty minutes of me calling her back, the faint scent of wine on her breath.

'Isla's in bed and you know she sleeps like a log, so you shouldn't need to worry about her waking up. I won't be long, OK?' I push my breath out in a long stream in an attempt to squash the anxiety that courses through my veins.

'Claire . . . calm down. It'll be OK — there'll be some sort of explanation. Tom loves you. He'll be back. I'm sure of it.' Gwen pulls me into a hug, and I throw out a wobbly smile, breathing in the familiar scent of clay dust and sandalwood on her skin. Despite the fact that I'm two years older than Gwen, she's always been the one to prop me up when things get tough. She never seems to get flustered or overwhelmed, and if there's one thing I need right now, it's someone with a clear head.

Nerves jangling, I drive too fast through the near-empty streets, and as I reach the police station in the centre of our small town, I almost bottle it. The idea of walking into the police station and demanding to see someone after they've already told me they won't help me look for Tom makes it feel all the more real — that by saying the words out loud, face to face with the authorities, he will officially be a missing person. Pausing at the entrance to the station, I take another deep breath, almost dizzy with apprehension as I walk slowly towards the front desk, ignoring the fella sitting next to the door singing softly to himself while a fug of whisky rolls off him. A tall, dark-haired police officer stands behind the desk with his back to me, rifling through a filing cabinet that sits against the back wall, a dying spider plant on top of it. There is something vaguely familiar about him, but before I can put my finger on what it is he turns round and I realise. *Shit. It's Adam.*

* * *

Adam, as in my *ex-boyfriend* Adam. I had no idea he was back.
 'Claire?'
 'Adam. Hi.' I swallow hard, my tongue sticking to the roof of my dry mouth, as I try to gauge his reaction towards me while simultaneously squashing down the bubble of panic that's lodged in my throat.
 'Oh God, Claire. It's been ages. How are you? What are you doing here?'
 'Yeah, I'm good. Well, no, not that good. Pretty awful actually. I need help, Adam. That's why I'm here. I really, really need some help.' My nerves jangle under my skin as if a panic attack is just around the corner, and I draw in a deep breath, trying to swallow down the hysteria that threatens to bubble over. Adam eyes me from the other side of the desk.
 'Really? So . . . you're here to report something?' His voice is cool, and I remember his tone from when we'd argue about stupid, silly little things. To anyone watching he's coming across as purely professional, but I know that tone of voice. I remember it from the last months of our relationship together, when things were turning sour faster than milk left out in the sun.
 'Look, Adam . . .' I find myself wringing my hands together, as I lean forward and lower my voice. 'I know I'm

probably the last person you expected to see today but . . . it's Tom, my husband. He's missing.' Straightening up, my belly clenches with fear as I say the words out loud. I look at him in desperation, praying he'll agree to help.

'Missing?' Adam's brow crinkles, but his tone is warmer. 'OK, Claire, come this way and we'll have a chat.' He steps out from behind the front desk and gestures towards a door on the left, opening it into a small interview room. Taking a seat, I decline his offer of tea or coffee and launch into the details of everything that has happened today, from Tom leaving as usual this morning, until his failure to come home tonight. Perspiration dots my forehead and I swipe it away as I tell him how I called Tom's work only to be told he hadn't been in. I brush over the fact that he's seemed preoccupied and distracted lately — I don't want Adam to jump to the conclusion that Tom has left me and run off to make a new life, because I'm pretty sure that's not the case — instead saying he's seemed a little tired lately. I make sure to mention the social media post with his picture on it and the mysterious text on his phone, picking at the skin around my fingers anxiously as I speak, ignoring the sharp nip of pain as I rip it too far, blood beading my cuticles.

'OK. Claire, the first thing I'm going to tell you is that whoever you spoke to on the phone is right — there's nothing more we can do just now, not unless something else comes to light.' I open my mouth to speak, to say I *know* something isn't right, but Adam holds up a hand to stop me. 'Tom's an adult — he's more than entitled to take himself away for a few days, if that's what he wants. He might just need some space — I know you'll probably hate to admit it, but everyone needs a break from their partner every now and again.' *Like we did* is the underlying message that comes through loud and clear.

Adam's voice is soothing and I remember all the times he talked me down when we were together — before exams, when I took my driving test, finding out the truth about what really happened when my dad left, and a hundred other times when I was stressed and he made me see sense. We were good together, before I broke his heart.

'The text and the social media post . . . they're not threatening. I hate to say it, but it might just be something he's not telling you. I'm sorry, Claire, but there's nothing I can do to help.' Adam stands, brushing his hands over his trousers.

'Really, Adam?' There's a stab of disappointment in my gut as I ignore the hand he holds out for me to shake. My own palms are damp and I wipe them surreptitiously on my trousers. 'You really won't help at all? You won't even ask a few questions — try and find out if this Lydia French is who she says she is?' I stop for a moment, a thought striking me. 'Is it because it's Tom?'

Adam stares at me hard, an icy glint in his eye, before slowly shaking his head. 'Jesus, Claire. I can't believe you'd even say that. I won't help because I can't — Tom is more than capable of taking care of himself. He's a responsible adult, and if he wants some time out then you can't stop him. There's nothing I, as a police officer, can do for you right now. Give it a few days at least, see if he comes back of his own accord. If you don't hear anything by then, then come back and we'll file a missing person's report.' He pushes the door open, and I follow him out to the main reception area, unable to even look at him. I can't bring myself to return his goodbye. Instead, I head straight back to the car, back home to Isla. And to an absent Tom.

***

Gwen offers to stay the night, but I decline. I take both Tom's mobile phone and mine to bed with me, Tom's screen remaining stubbornly black and silent. I toss and turn all night but there's no message from Tom, and no response from the unknown number that I texted earlier. At around 5 a.m., I give up trying to sleep and make my way downstairs for coffee, Isla appearing in the kitchen doorway long before I would have gone to wake her up.

'Is Daddy home yet?' She totters on bare feet over to the table, pulling herself up onto the chair and wriggling to get comfortable. My heart sinks at her question and I sip my coffee, the bitter taste coating my tongue, as I try to buy myself a few extra seconds before I speak. 'Mummy? Is Daddy back?'

'Not yet, sweetie.' I struggle to keep my voice steady, but she just reaches for the cereal box on the table and waves it at me.

'Can I have some of this?' she asks, and I pour a bowl out for her. 'Do you think Daddy will be back tonight?'

'I don't know, Isla, I hope so. Now, come on, eat up. We need to get ready for school.' Her bottom lip wobbles a little but she says nothing, instead starting to pick at her cereal, while I kick myself for being so abrupt — Tom normally deals with things like this, the things that unsettle Isla, and I'm not confident I'm dealing with it at all well.

After leaving the house at the last minute in the hope I can avoid any awkward questions from the other school mums about Tom's absence, I squeeze the car into a space at the bottom of the hill, before handing Isla her school bag. Hannah is standing on the pavement waiting as we get out of the car.

'Morning, Claire.' She offers up a sympathetic smile, her dark eyes full of concern. 'I take it Tom hasn't come home yet?'

'No, and he hasn't called either. I've reported him missing to the police but they don't seem to be interested. He's an adult and he can do what he wants, apparently.' I give a tiny shrug, attempting to disguise my worry.

'Oh, Claire, I don't know what to say to make it any better.' Hannah lays a hand on my arm and gives it a reassuring squeeze. 'Listen, if there's anything at all I can do to help, just say the word.' We walk up the hill together, the girls running ahead until we reach the classroom. Reassuring Isla that I'll be there to pick her up — on time this time — I wait for her to reluctantly go into class, before leaving Hannah talking to another mum at the gate. On the way back to the car, I take the opportunity to call Gwen.

'Clairebear. Any news?'

'Nothing. He hasn't called, texted, no contact at all.' I swallow hard, the granite lump stuck in my throat again.

'Jesus. I thought he'd be back by now. Look, darling, have you called into work? I don't think you should go in today. You sound exhausted.'

I'd forgotten all about work. Me, Claire Bennett, who works every hour under the sun in the hopes of impressing the other partners so much that they'll invite me to join them. *What a waste of time*, I think now. Tom is more important than billing hours.

'I'll call in now. You're right, I need to take some time — just until I can figure out what's going on . . . I don't know what to do, where to go . . . I'm a mess, Gwen.' I lean against the car, hiding my face from the mothers that walk past, chattering nineteen to the dozen, not wanting them to see the despondency on my face. Saying goodbye to Gwen, I feel discombobulated, realisation dawning that my ordinary, everyday, routine life has been turned upside down and I have no idea how to fix it.

I fumble my way through a telephone call to the office, laying on a pretty convincing raspy-voiced act of someone who may have Covid, and ask Jasmine to take on my cases in my absence, stressing that I don't know how long I might be out for. By the time I get home I'm mentally and emotionally drained, the struggle of keeping it together in front of others taking its toll on me, so my heart sinks when the doorbell rings. I consider ignoring it, but the idea that it might be Tom — *maybe he lost his keys?* — propels me to the front door. The person standing on my doorstep is the last person I'm expecting to see.

'Adam?' My heart leaps into my throat. 'Oh God, is it Tom? Have you found him?'

'No, I'm sorry, Claire. I told you, we can't do anything for you, not unless circumstances change.' Adam peers behind me into the depths of the house. 'Can I come in?' I stand to one side, pointing him towards the living room where he takes a seat on the couch, awkwardly perching on the very edge of the cushion.

'So, if you're not here to help, then why are you here?' Realising I'm still standing, almost looming over Adam, I lower myself into the closest armchair to the couch.

'Look, it's not that I don't want to help you, Claire, it's just that as a police officer I can't. I explained that to you last night. The reason I'm here now is to offer you my help *as a friend*. I've got annual leave booked, so I just thought . . .' Adam tails off and, as I look him over, I notice he's wearing casual clothes — jeans and a rugby top, with Adidas trainers on his feet, nothing like the smart clothes he was wearing at the station last night. 'I can help you as a friend, but *only* as a friend. Nothing in an official capacity. I can't look up information or use the police computer — I'll lose my job. And you need to remember that Tom might have left of his own accord — and if that is the case, I won't be able to help you get him back. But in the meantime, if you want someone to be there, for a bit of guidance and support, well . . . I'll help.'

'Really? Adam, that would be fantastic — I just have no idea where he is . . .'

'As a friend though, Claire,' Adam interrupts. 'Please remember that — please don't ask me to do anything that might jeopardise my job, OK?'

'OK, OK. Thank you, Adam — I don't even know where to start. And you know I hate to ask you for help, after the way things were left between us . . . I just want to find Tom — Isla needs her dad. We need him here, with us.' Aware I'm starting to babble, I take a deep breath and pause. 'I understand, Adam, about the job, I do. But where do I go next? What do I do?' Relief washes over me. Relief that Adam doesn't hate me, and relief that someone is willing to help me track Tom down and find Lydia French and whatever she has to do with my husband, because after a sleepless night of tossing things over in my mind, I've convinced myself she definitely *is* connected to all of this.

CHAPTER 9

Adam is, as ever, the voice of reason, and I wonder briefly what would have happened if I hadn't met Tom — maybe neither of us would have come back to Easthampton, and we'd still be living in London, bringing up our children together. But then there wouldn't be Tom or Isla, and the Bennett family wouldn't exist. Even so, there's still a twist of guilt at the way I treated Adam. We'd dated since school, and throughout university, both of us moving together to London when Adam joined the Met and I joined a solicitors office as a junior conveyancer. Things had been fine — good, I suppose — until I met Tom when I came back to visit my dad in the hospital, after he got sick. Adam had been working, so I'd come back on my own. I'd gone for a drink after a long day watching my dad struggle on, feeling low and, if I'm honest, resentful about the fact that Adam hadn't taken the time off work to come with me. The moment I saw Tom in the pub where Adam and I had spent our teenage years illegally drinking cider, it was like I'd been hit by a bolt of lightning. He caught my eye and smiled, as if appreciating what he saw. He looked at me in a way that Adam hadn't for a long time.

Tom approached me and asked if I was OK — to which I lied and said yes — and then brought me a glass of white wine. I should have refused it, should have gone back to my old bedroom in my parent's house to wallow alone, but there was something about this man that made me stay. Tom was bright and funny, there was a spark about him that I'm not sure Adam had ever had. Long hours at work meant Adam and I were often ships that passed in the night, more like roommates than lovers, and when we did spend time together our conversation was mostly full of sniping remarks and bitter words. Tom, on the other hand, made me laugh when it was the last thing I felt like doing, and the way he looked at me as I sipped that crisp, dry wine made me feel as though I was something special, not a woman with a sick father, a stale relationship and a bone-crushing weariness that I wore like a cape.

I didn't mean to say yes that night when Tom asked if he could walk me back along the river to my parents' house so I didn't have to walk it alone. I didn't mean for the breath to stop in my throat, to lift my face to meet his lips in a kiss that turned my legs to jelly. I didn't mean to tell him about my dad being ill, how alone and afraid I felt about it all while he just listened, one hand reaching out to close over mine. I didn't mean to agree to meet him for dinner the following evening either, before I returned to London. It just happened, and when it did, it made me realise how much I'd lost with Adam.

Watching my dad fade away showed me that life was short, and that what I had with Adam wasn't enough. I couldn't imagine spending the rest of my life the way I was with Adam. I needed something more, and Tom was it. It only took three months of me fighting my attraction to Tom before I told Adam I was leaving him. Three months of illicit text messages that I tried my hardest to ignore, messages where Tom told me how he couldn't stop thinking about me, how much he wanted to touch me, be with me — a stark comparison to Adam's lacklustre replies and the sight of his back as he rolled away from me in bed. Three months of whispered phone conversations and snatched cups of coffee after I visited my dad, Tom's fingers snaking out to touch my wrists, my hands, my hair, like he was an addict who couldn't keep away.

It was as though the lightning that struck me that first night had ricocheted off his body onto mine.

Now, I offer to make Adam coffee and we move through into the kitchen. I switch the kettle on and go to the fridge for milk, the magnet notepad stuck to the front catching my eye as I rest my hand on the door handle. 'MILK' is written on it in Tom's familiar hand, to remind me to pick some up yesterday on my way home — only, understandably, I forgot. My heart twists at the sight of his sprawling, sloppy handwriting, and I get that airless feeling in my chest again.

'No milk — is black OK for you?' I reach for mugs, avoiding looking at the front of the fridge, not wanting to see the reminder of my missing husband.

'I've never taken milk in my coffee, Claire.' Adam gives a quick, sad smile as I turn to face him, gone before I'm even sure it was ever there. 'Let's go back to the start. Think about places he might have gone.' Brisk and no-nonsense now, Adam stops me as I try to interrupt him. 'I know, Claire. I know you don't think he's left of his own accord, but until you know otherwise this is all you have to go on. He might have come across this Lydia French before he met you. If you can figure out who she is, or where he might have met her, then you've got more chance of finding her, and maybe finding Tom at the same time. Are you even sure that she's got anything to do with it?' I go to remind him about the social media post, but he holds up a finger and carries on speaking. 'Is there a time in his life that was important to him? People that he's close to? What about his parents? His family?'

'That's just it — I don't know. He fell out with his parents years ago . . . his dad died and then he fell out with his mum. Tom hasn't spoken to her since he left for university. It was just him, no brothers or sisters. I don't know the whole story behind it; he says he finds it too upsetting to talk about. All I know is that they've never resolved whatever they fought over. She never even came to our wedding.' The first time I'd asked Tom about his family we'd only been dating a few months and were still in that phase where you greedily drink in every fact you learn about the other person. He'd shrugged my questions away, turning it back on me, and although I'd tried probing him on it since — especially when Isla was born, and I thought he might consider a reconciliation — Tom refused to discuss what happened, and was adamant that being involved with his mum would only cause more heartache.

'What about his friends?' Adam asks. 'Is there anyone he's close to now that he might have gone to?'

'Only Robert and Hannah — and they haven't seen him. You don't realise what Tom's like, Adam. He's really . . . introverted. He doesn't need to surround himself with loads of people. There's just me and Isla, Hannah and Robert, and Jonah at work. I've spoken to Hannah and Jonah and neither of them have seen or heard from him. I don't know where else he would go.' I take a deep breath, trying to neutralise the panic clawing at my insides.

'What about before he met you — you say he doesn't speak to his mum, so maybe he hasn't gone there. And he left when he went to uni? So, what about people he might have been close to there?'

My heart gives a little leap — *yes*. Tom has talked about uni to me — he's talked many times about the friends he made there and how much he enjoyed it. To me, that's where Tom's life really began — in all the time we've been together he's rarely spoken about his life before, but Bristol he does talk about.

'There was someone,' I say slowly. 'A lecturer of Tom's at Bristol that he became really friendly with. They've stayed in contact ever since, although it's mostly via email. He still teaches there, but I've never met the guy.'

'Can you remember his name? Maybe find an email address for him? See if you can remember the names of anyone else he was close to there — does he have a diary, or an old address book that he might keep phone numbers in? Maybe that's where he came across this Lydia French. See if anyone there knows who she is. You know where he grew up, right? So, try there too — maybe he's decided it's time to reconcile with his family? Maybe Lydia French also grew up there.'

'West. His name is Greg West.' My head spinning at Adam's barrage of questions, I unlock Tom's phone and scroll through his contacts, but there's no number for Greg West, and I remember that he and Tom mostly emailed. Pulling up the Mail app, I search for his name but nothing comes up. There are emails from Jonah and others at the estate agency, spam from a couple of clothing stores Tom has bought from, and a link to an article on the benefits of a Mediterranean diet from Gwen, but nothing at all from Greg West. 'There's no contact in here.' I pause for a moment, my mind racing. 'I could go there — to the university. Ask around, see if I can speak to Greg.' A jolt of excitement runs through me. Finally, I have something I can use, something I can actively do to try and find Tom.

'Go there? Are you sure that's a good idea, Claire? It's a long shot, isn't it?' Adam bites his lip, doubt crossing his face. 'I was thinking more along the lines of making a few phone calls. Wouldn't that be better?'

'I need to do *something*, Adam!' The words come out strained and I take a deep breath, lowering my voice. 'If I call, what's to stop them just hanging up on me? I know you mean well, but I feel like I should be doing something, something *active*. Not just sitting around making phone calls. And if Greg West does know something about where Tom is, it'll be harder for him to lie to my face than over the phone.'

'Well, if you think that's the best way to go about it . . . but Claire, you need to bear in mind . . .' He gives me a long look as he breaks off, clearly not in agreement with me that a trip to Bristol University is the best way to go.

'Bear in mind what?'

'You need to bear in mind that maybe Tom doesn't want to be found, OK? He might not want to come home. And if he doesn't, you can't make him.' There's a stilted tone to Adam's voice now, and I realise he probably feels uncomfortable talking to me about all of this — about the fact that my husband, who I left Adam for, might now have left me without a word. I give Adam my word that I'll bear it in mind and thank him for his help, before showing him out and promising I'll keep in touch.

I'm still convinced something more sinister has happened to Tom, that he wouldn't voluntarily leave me. We have a good marriage; we're happy together. We don't really argue, don't really even disagree about things — not very often, anyway. Yes, we've been a bit niggly with each other the last few weeks but every couple has those ups and downs; we just need a bit of time to relax together, that's all. And the post from Lydia French... even if Tom has left me voluntarily it doesn't explain Lydia French posting that picture. Tom wouldn't cheat on me — *would he?*

* * *

Shaking away thoughts of affairs or cheating, I pull out my mobile and call Gwen. She answers on the second ring, sounding slightly breathless.

'Claire? Is he home?' The words tumble out of her mouth in a frantic rush.

'No, he's not. I have spoken to Adam though.'

'*Adam?*'

'He was actually really helpful, even though he agreed that the police can't officially look for Tom. Listen, I was wondering if I could ask you a favour.'

'Of course. I thought you were calling to tell me he was back — I thought I saw him earlier, you know? I stopped off at the mini supermarket for milk.' At her words, I twist round to look at the magnetic notepad on the fridge before turning my back on it again. 'I thought he was outside. Obviously, it wasn't him, just a man with a similar build.' Gwen gives a sad little laugh and I realise she's feeling Tom's absence almost as much as I am. 'What did you want to ask me?'

'I was just wondering if Isla could stay with you for a night tomorrow? I think I know where to start looking for Tom, but I'm not happy about dragging Isla along, just in case it doesn't come to anything.' I feel panicky at the thought of letting Isla out of my sight if she's not at school, knowing her face is in the photograph as well, but I know she'll be safe with Gwen.

'Of course, Claire, you know it's no problem. I love having Isla. You reckon you know where to start looking for Tom? And what about this Lydia woman?'

'I'm going to Bristol Uni — remember Greg West? Tom's old friend? You must have heard him speak about him. He still lectures there. I'm going to head down there first thing tomorrow morning and see if I can speak to him, see if he knows where Tom might have gone.'

'Blimey, Claire.' Gwen's voice is filled with doubt. 'It's a long way to go on a hunch, isn't it? Couldn't you just call him?'

Gwen sounds just like Adam. Fighting back frustration, I say, 'I know it's a long shot, but, like I said to Adam, if he knows something it'll be difficult for him to lie to my face. Gwen, I have to try.' I stumble over the last word and clear my throat. 'The police think he's left me, Gwen. I can't believe he would do that to Isla . . . and I can't just sit here and wait for him to contact me. If I go there I might be able to find someone who knows him, who can help me find him. I need to *find him*.' My voice finally cracks and a hot tear slides down one cheek, salt seeping into the side of my mouth.

'Oh Claire, I don't think he's left you . . . he loves you both too much to just walk away. You have to do what you have to do, I get that.' Gwen sounds subdued. 'Just keep me posted, won't you? And don't worry about Isla, I'll have her for as long as you need.' I feel the heavy weight of responsibility on my shoulders at her words — knowing it's all on me to get my husband back. I have to find him, before Lydia French does.

CHAPTER 10

I have a little while before I need to leave to collect Isla from school, so I decide to make the most of my time by searching through Tom's things to see if I can find anything with any contact details for his lecturer friend from Bristol. The house feels silent and unwelcoming, eerily quiet without any talking or laughing, and I realise the majority of my time spent at home is with Tom and Isla — they get home long before me every day, and by the time I get back from work the house is warm and full of life, the air filled with the mouth-watering smells of Tom's homemade dinners or the scent of laundry drying. My heart aches as I climb the stairs and enter the bedroom Tom and I share. I head straight for the top drawer of the desk in our room. The one that belongs to Tom. The one where he keeps his old paperwork, diaries and other admin — I've never looked at it, despite the temptation. We're both respectful of each other's privacy, and I've never had any reason to go through his things before. He made it clear to me from the first day we moved in together that he isn't someone who finds it easy to lay himself bare, and he would appreciate it if I would respect his privacy and vice versa. I've never had any reason to doubt him . . . until now.

Heart thumping, as though Tom will walk in and catch me at any moment, I push my nerves away and open the drawer, pulling out a stack of papers neatly clipped together. Rifling through, there's nothing. Digging my hands into the rest of the papers, cringing inwardly at what he would think if he saw me now, I root through right to the back of the drawer, my fingertips brushing something square tucked away against the back of the desk. I pull the other papers — including a passport, which, on inspection, appears to be his current one — out of the way, and reaching in, I grab the corner and pull the object out. It's a diary, but I'm not sure why he would tuck it away like that — it's an old one, the gold embossing on the outer cover reading '2010'. Flicking it open, I see there's nothing written in it — a few notes here and there, reminders for Tom to do certain tasks, to make certain appointments — nothing of any interest. Nothing that warrants it being hidden away out of sight. It must have ended up shoved to the back of the drawer and forgotten about. I flip through the pages to the back, settling on the address and telephone numbers page. There is the name 'Roman' scrawled across one line, with a mobile number underneath. Of course, Roman is Tom's friend from uni, the only one he seems to have stayed in contact with other than Greg West. I've never actually met him, but Tom often talks about him. On the following line, 'Mum' is written in Tom's sprawling writing, the words scored into the paper as though he was gripping the pen tightly between his fingers, a harsh imprint pressed into the pages underneath. *Maybe this is why it was tucked away out of sight.* There is a telephone number attached — a landline with a Cornwall dialling code — and I hold the page down with one hand as I dial the number on my mobile with the other. Swallowing, my mouth dry with nerves, I wait for the call to be connected. I know it's a long shot — Tom hasn't spoken to his mum in years, he doesn't even speak about her to me, almost as though she never existed — but I have to try. It turns out I don't need to worry. A robotic voice tells me the number

I've dialled is unavailable. I redial, trying it again in case I misdialled, but no, the number is disconnected. Deflated, I turn back to the page with Roman's number. Dialling, I wait anxiously, almost half convinced that this will be a dead end too, but the call connects, and it rings for a few moments before a generic voicemail cuts in. I leave a message, trying to keep myself from rambling, telling Roman who I am and asking him to call me urgently. I make no reference to Tom not coming home, worried that if he is with Roman it may put him off calling me, and I hang up, feeling drained. I spend the rest of the afternoon pacing, repeatedly checking both my phone and Tom's, but there's no call back from Roman, and no word from Tom.

I'm the first in the playground at three o'clock, eager to make sure Isla can see I'm there as soon as she leaves the classroom. I spy her blonde head before she sees me and wave, until she looks over and runs to me.

'Mummy!' She throws her arms around me and I squeeze her tight, before taking hold of her hand and leading her down the hill to where I'm parked. Although when she first leaves school she seems OK, she's quiet in the car, a solemn look on her face. As we pull into our road, she visibly perks up and starts peering out of the window, and my heart sinks as I realise what she's looking for.

'I can't see Daddy's car, Mummy.' She turns to me, her bottom lip wobbling. I can guess her next question. 'Is he home yet?' I pull onto our drive, in the space where Tom would usually park and roll to a stop, gently tugging the handbrake up.

'I'm sorry, darling, he's not back yet.' Isla's eyes fill with tears, and I blink rapidly, my own eyes stinging. *Don't fall apart, Claire.* 'Hey, how would you like to go for a sleepover at Aunt Gwen's tomorrow night?'

Isla shakes her head, her blonde ponytail bouncing on her shoulders. 'No, Mummy, I don't think I want to.' A single tear rolls down one of her cheeks and deep in my chest I feel my heart crack. Unclipping her seatbelt, I gesture for her to climb over and sit in the driver's seat with me.

'Baby, I really need you to be brave for me right now, OK?' Settled on my lap, both of our knees pushed to one side by the steering wheel, I drop a kiss on Isla's head. 'I need you to have a sleepover at Aunt Gwen's because I'm going to look for Daddy. We need to find him, don't we?' She sniffs and nods. 'Can you be brave for me?' She nods again and I hold her tight, wishing more than anything Tom was there, with us.

* * *

Despite an unsettled night with Isla, who cried out for her dad in her sleep more than once, I'm awake before dawn the next morning. Rolling over to reach for Tom as inky darkness gives way to pale fingers of light streaking the horizon, my hand meets empty space and I remember he's not there. Barbed wire wraps its way around my heart, the gap where Tom should be causing me physical pain. Stumbling out of bed, I can't help but venture into Isla's room, desperate to reassure myself that at least she's still here. The duvet scrunches up around her waist where she's tossed and turned in her sleep, her blonde hair spread across the pillow. Tugging the duvet further up her body, I tuck her back in and leave her to sleep for a little while longer, then, swallowing down the lump in my throat, I head for the shower.

After a pot of strong coffee and breakfast for a reluctant Isla — who still isn't happy at the idea of spending the night away from me — I pull up outside Gwen's rose-covered cottage, Gwen waiting in the open front doorway. Panic seizes me in a vice-like grip once more when I say goodbye to Isla, and as Gwen pulls me in to a tight hug, I whisper into her ear.

'Don't let her out of your sight — please?'

'I won't, I swear. I'll watch her go into the classroom when I drop her off at school and I'll be the first one in the playground when I pick her up. Claire . . .' Gwen pulls back, running her eyes over my face. 'Be careful, won't you? If this Lydia French woman really is involved then maybe Tom has got himself—' Gwen breaks off as I give her a sharp look and gesture to Isla with a discreet nod.

I lower my voice. 'It'll be fine. I'll come home with Tom, and then everything will be OK.' *I have to believe that.*

Kissing Isla goodbye one more time, I promise to keep Gwen updated before getting in the car and starting the long journey to Bristol. The weather is beautiful — the sun already beating down on what promises to be a glorious day — which will hopefully mean no traffic on the roads at this early hour. I've already checked the maps on my phone and it's 100 miles and approximately two hours to get to Bristol from Easthampton as long as I don't hit any major traffic jams. It's crossed my mind that once in Bristol, I'm already over halfway to Tom's hometown of Archmouth, but I shake the thought off, hoping I'll get the answers I need. Tom doesn't speak much about his home life before he left Archmouth, all talk about his family strictly off limits despite the many times I've tried probing him. Instead, he prefers telling stories of his days at Bristol Uni, regaling me and Gwen with drunken anecdotes around the dinner table, usually after a few drinks. He always says he hopes, when it's time, Isla will choose somewhere further afield for university than Easthampton, somewhere where she can shake off the shackles of our parenthood and find out who she really is. Easthampton is a small town, the kind of place you either escape the moment you can, or you rot there, from birth until death, so in a way it's odd that both Adam and I both found ourselves back there. It's the kind of place where, while it's not quite an 'everybody knows everybody' town, it's small enough that if you wanted to find someone there you could, quite easily. Claustrophobia claws at my insides, my hands slipping on the steering wheel as a wretched panic takes hold at the thought of Lydia French hunting Tom out in our small town, of someone Tom vaguely knows innocently pointing her in his direction.

I spend the rest of the drive trying to picture Lydia French. What she looks like, how she behaves. Is she some femme fatale, beguiling and bewitching who has stolen her way into Tom's heart and taken him from me? No. The moment I think it, my instinctive reaction is that Tom wouldn't do that to me, to Isla. What then? The alternative turns my blood to ice in my veins — is she someone nasty, vindictive, involved with the wrong people? Does she believe Tom has wronged her in some way and she wants revenge? Honestly, neither of these visions sit well with me, and I don't recognise Tom, my Tom, the Tom who lies beside me every night in either scenario.

Forcing Lydia French from my mind as I hit the M4, I try to remember the tales Tom has told me about his university days, going back over the stories in my head to see if I can remember him mentioning anybody in particular, other than Roman and Greg West. People who I can check with at the university. I know it's doubtful there'll be anybody there who remembers Tom, but maybe they have some sort of register or database of alumni, something I can search for any name that might look familiar.

The journey is long and I find my mind wandering as I drive, from Tom's old uni friends, to thinking of the night before Tom went missing. It was a perfect evening, the kind that seemed to have been missing in our lives for too long recently. I'd known things were looking up between us when I'd opened my laptop bag to find a neatly packed lunch, complete with a note in Tom's handwriting saying, 'EAT ME'. I'd smiled as I pulled the note out, relieved to see he was behaving more like his old self — it had been weeks since I'd found one of his notes in my bag, when they used to be a regular occurrence. I had raced home early that night — he had texted me after lunch to say he was cooking, and he was expecting me at seven o'clock sharp — excited to get home and find my husband, my *real* Tom, not the cold, distant Tom I'd come home to night after night for the past few weeks.

And when I got home, he *was* my Tom. He pulled me into an embrace when I walked in, dropping my laptop bag at his feet. He kissed me and I breathed in the scent of him — sea salt and something woody that was uniquely his. I was happy that evening and so was he, he told me as we curled up next to each other in bed after steak and wine, and sex that was just as good as it was in the beginning. *So, where is he?* My heart squeezes at the thought of him never coming home. He told me he was happy that night, so why would he leave of his own accord, without saying a word? *He wouldn't* is the phrase that loops in my mind as I drive, barely concentrating. *He wouldn't leave without saying goodbye.*

CHAPTER 11

A little after ten o'clock I squeeze into a space in a public car park a fifteen-minute walk or so from the university campus. It feels odd to be in a place where Tom spent so much time, and as I walk I find myself wondering if he walked this way... did he grab a coffee from this particular café? Did he sit on a bench in this park and watch the world go by? I walk briskly, almost too fast, as my breath catches in my throat and a stitch pierces my side, but I'm anxious to get there — anxious to start talking to people, trying to find answers. Finally, I'm starting to feel as though I'm actually doing something to try and find Tom. My pace slows as I reach the reception building, my heart still thumping hard in my chest, but whether that's from the walk or nerves, I don't know. Pushing open the door into the building, I'm faced with a stern-looking woman with glasses perched on the top of her steely-grey hair, glaring at me over the top of her computer screen.

'Yes? Can I help you?'

My mouth goes dry as I realise my mind has gone blank, and I have no idea of how best to ask my questions, or even what question to start with. I was so busy imagining Tom in the places I was passing as I walked, I didn't think far enough ahead to consider what I was going to ask first. I tuck my hair behind my ear with a shaking hand and try to smile at the receptionist.

'Good morning, I was hoping you might be able to help me,' I stall, trying to form a coherent sentence in my mind. 'I'd, err . . . I'd like to speak to Greg West in the English department, please.' My skin prickles, sensitive, as though all my nerve endings are exposed as I wait for her to answer.

'Do you have an appointment or . . . ?' She pulls her glasses down from her head to her nose so she can look at me properly. I give her a story about wanting to catch up with my old professor, telling her I was an English student at the time Tom would have been here. Realising I have no clue where to find the English department, I fumble a question along the lines of whether the lectures are still held in the same place. She gives me a sharp glance, before directing me to the English department and warning me to be quick as lectures are due to begin in thirty minutes. I walk briskly towards the building, trying to look as though I know where I'm going, hoping and praying Greg West will be able to give me some idea of where Tom might be. I know it's a long shot — almost a dead end before it even starts — but what else can I do? I can't just sit around and wait, hoping Tom will eventually make contact. *I don't even know if he can contact me.* Who knows? If Greg doesn't know where he is, maybe he'll be able to give me the name of someone Tom was friends with besides Roman, someone I can track down to see if they've had any recent contact with him. Someone who might know of a connection with Lydia French. Maybe he'll even remember Roman and be able to give me some idea of where he is now. I know I'm grasping at straws, but I'm willing to take any scrap of information I can find at the moment. He's been gone for forty-eight hours already with no contact. *If he's even still alive,* a spiteful voice whispers at the back of my mind. I shake it off, unwilling to let myself entertain that possibility. Spying an older man fiddling with papers on a desk through the window of the first room I come to, I give a brisk knock and push the door open, startling him.

'Hello — can I help you?'

'I'm looking for Greg West?'

'That's me.' He looks at me warily, seeing as my face is not obviously familiar to him as a student. In his late forties or early fifties, he has salt-and-pepper hair and fewer lines on his face than I do.

'Hi, I'm Claire Bennett, Tom's wife.'

'Tom?' Greg's brow creases and he lays the paperwork down on the desk.

'Tom Bennett,' I say. 'You taught him, back in 2010 or 2011?' The smile on my face wavers as Greg West shakes his head. 'The two of you stayed in contact after Tom graduated. He gets an email from you every few months or so. I'm so sorry we've never met in person before, but Tom did explain to me that your wife has been unwell . . .'

'Wait. Wait a second.' Greg holds up a hand and I trail off. 'Tom Bennett? You say I've stayed in contact with him for years?'

'Yes,' I say eagerly.

Greg shakes his head again, his face grim. 'I'm so sorry, Mrs. Bennett, I have no idea who you're talking about.'

I search his face, looking for tells that he's lying, but all I see is confusion. It's as though the floor has disappeared beneath my feet and I reach out a hand to grasp the table and steady myself. 'What? No, you do know him, you email each other, you have done for years.'

'Trust me, I don't know your husband. I've never stayed in contact with a student after they've graduated. And as for an ill wife . . . I've never even been married.' He peers at me closely. 'I think perhaps you should take a seat.'

Gratefully, I slip into the closest chair, my teeth feeling oddly numb. 'I'm sorry,' I say, as hot tears spring to my eyes. 'I thought . . .' Why would Tom lie to me about this? I realise now that I never read the emails from Greg West that Tom claimed to have received, I was never there when he took his calls.

'Don't apologise,' Greg says, not unkindly. 'I'm afraid I don't know your husband, or why he would say he knows me, but obviously you're here for a reason.'

I pull a tissue from my handbag and dab at my eyes. 'This is going to sound crazy . . . but my husband . . . he's gone missing and I'm trying to go back, retrace his steps if you like, to see if I can find anyone who might possibly know where he is. Yours is the only name I had, the only person he said he was in contact with from his past. Even if you didn't stay in contact, you might have taught him? You might know someone who was friends with him back then.'

Greg West pushes the papers on his desk to one side. 'Blimey. Umm, well . . . I can take a look for you. I've taught hundreds of students though, so I might not be much help.'

Grateful he's even going to entertain the idea, I dig in my bag with quivering fingers for a recent picture of Tom that I keep there, another photo of him and Isla together, their cheeks smashed against one another, cheesy grins on their faces.

'Thank you. I'd really appreciate any information you can give me. This is Tom. Do you recognise him?' I feel sick as I wait for him to look at the photograph.

West takes the photograph from me, pulling a pair of glasses out from a drawer and perching them on the end of his nose. He sees me watching and smiles wryly. 'Vanity,' he says. 'I try to go without, but I can't see a bloody thing up close, truth be told.'

I give an impatient smile and wait anxiously for him to finish looking at Tom's picture. After what feels like an eternity he hands it back to me.

'I'm sorry,' he says with a shake of his head, and I feel a crushing sense of disappointment. 'I don't remember him at all. The only other person who might have done is the other lecturer who was here at the same time.' I perk up at the news that someone else might remember, but his next words come as a blow. 'Although he won't be able to help. He was diagnosed with dementia around five years ago — he's in a care home now, apparently he doesn't really remember anyone anymore.'

'What about a boy called Roman? I don't have a surname but he would have been in the same year — possibly even the same lectures.'

'I'm sorry, I really can't remember. It was a long time and hundreds of students ago.'

Although I knew it was a long shot before I even got in the car this morning, my heart sinks. I thank Greg for his help and dejectedly make my way out of the lecture hall towards the entrance gates. Passing the sign for the admissions office again, I decide to make a quick detour, to double-check if the admissions woman can give me any more information about anyone who was at the university in 2010. This time when I enter, she smiles.

'Did you catch up with Greg?'

'Yes, I did, thank you so much for your help.' Now that I've spoken to Greg West, I feel even more confused over why Tom might have lied about knowing him. Maybe he admired Greg as a lecturer and wished he'd stayed in touch with him? 'I'm sorry but I wasn't exactly honest with you earlier.'

'Oh?' The smile slips slightly.

'I know I said I wanted to catch up with my old lecturer . . . but the truth is—' I pause for a moment, knowing that saying the words aloud again will scratch at my throat like brambles — 'my husband is missing. He's been gone since Tuesday morning, with no contact at all.' I blink as I feel the familiar fizz of tears behind my eyelids.

'Oh gosh. You poor thing.' The woman, the lanyard around her neck naming her as Mrs. Randall, pats my hand, a sympathetic smile on her face. 'And you think he . . . might have come *here*?'

'To be honest, I have no idea. All I know is he's gone . . . and we have a seven-year-old daughter waiting for him at home. Tom would have graduated in 2011 . . . I was hoping maybe someone would remember him, or the names of his friends. Anything that could give me something to go on, I suppose.'

At the mention of Isla, Mrs. Randall's hand flutters to her chest. 'Look, I shouldn't really do this — it's supposed to be confidential. But I could take a look at the intake list for his year, if that would be any help to you at all?'

She's flustered, anxiously checking over her shoulder to see if anyone has overheard us. I lay a warm hand on top of her cold, thin one and squeeze it gratefully, a flicker of excitement burning low in my belly. Maybe this trip won't be such a lost cause after all, maybe I was right to come here rather than make a phone call.

'Could you really do that? That would be amazing.' I have to know if there are any familiar names on that list. If Lydia French's name is on that list. With one more brief glance over her shoulder, Mrs. Randall agrees to print me a copy to look over.

'Don't tell anyone I gave it to you. And I can't let you take it away. But if it helps you find your husband . . .' She presses her mouse button and somewhere behind her I hear a printer whirr into life.

'Thank you. You've no idea how much this could help me.'

She hands over the list and I quickly scan down the names. There is no Roman. There is no Lydia. I re-read, wanting to make doubly sure that what I've read is correct. Because there's no Tom Bennett either.

'Is that everything, dear?' Mrs. Randall looks at me anxiously, clearly wanting me — and the list — out of the way before anyone sees us.

'There's just one thing . . . if I could get you to quickly check it for me?' Despite the heavy sensation pressing down on my shoulders, I try to smile but it falls flat before it reaches my eyes. She nods. Anything to get me out of here, now she's broken the rules.

'Could you check for a Tom Bennett? That's his name ... my husband, I mean. I can't find it on the list — maybe I got the year wrong? He might have been a year or two either side. I'm sorry, I know you've done more than you should have already.'

Mrs. Randall obliges and I can feel my pulse loud and insistent in my ears as she types Tom's name into her system. I anxiously tap my fingers on the desk. After a few minutes she looks up.

'I'm ever so sorry. Are you sure he definitely attended this university? It's just that, well ... there is no Tom or Thomas Bennett on our system at all. Tom Bennett never attended this university in 2011 or any of the years either side.'

CHAPTER 12

Squinting into the bright sunshine outside, I fumble my way out the door, barely remembering to thank the admissions officer for her help. My mind is reeling from the discovery that Tom never attended the university — that a whole section of his life has been a lie. He never knew Greg West, hasn't kept in contact with him all these years like he said. Head aching, I make my way back towards the park and find a bench in the shade of a large oak tree. The warm sunshine that put me in such an optimistic mood hours earlier now beats down, an unrelenting wave of heat that adds to the ache in my head and the churning in my stomach. I sink onto the bench, my mind whirling. *Tom never went to Bristol University.* A flicker of anger sparks into life somewhere deep inside my belly as I hear Mrs. Randall's voice in my head, telling me there is no record of Tom Bennett at all. Tom lied to me and that was the one thing he promised never to do, especially after we were married and I told him what had happened between my parents. I pull out my phone to call Gwen, needing to share what I've discovered with the one person who wouldn't know how to lie if you paid her.

'Gwen, it's me.'

'Claire! Are you OK? Is there any news?' Gwen's tone is muffled, and I can hear the thunder of water in the background. I can picture her, phone clamped between jaw and shoulder as she washes red, sticky clay from her hands. 'Did you find Tom?'

'No — and I haven't heard from him either.' I pinch the bridge of my nose between my thumb and forefinger, trying to hold back a tidal wave of sobs. 'Gwen . . .' It's no good, the dam breaks and tears spill over the edge of my lower lashes. 'Tom . . . he's just like Mum.'

'What? What do you mean?' A note of alarm creeps into Gwen's voice and I imagine her starting to pace, her long skirts swishing about her legs, the way she always does when she's worried.

'I mean, he lied to me. He never came to the university. I checked the records. His name doesn't appear on the database once. Greg West isn't friends with him — he's never even met Tom.'

'Are you sure it's not just a mix-up . . . maybe you got it wrong?'

'I didn't get it wrong, Gwen!' I cry, my voice rusty with tears. I ignore the wary glances being thrown my way from passers-by. 'He lied — he's just as bad as Mum. Only this time it isn't Mum lying to me about the reason Dad doesn't live at home anymore, this is my *husband*, lying about a whole part of his life that I believed was true. He told me stories, Gwen, talked about friends . . . all of it was a lie.' I slump back onto the bench, an ache in my heart to match the one in my head. Tom has just trampled over everything we had together. 'He barely told me anything about his life before he met me, and everything he did tell me I kept close. They were precious, the few things he did open up to me about, and now I don't know if I can believe anything he said.'

'There might be a good reason for it,' Gwen says cautiously, as though she expects me to jump down her throat again. 'At the moment, don't get too focused on the fact that he's lied to you . . . you still need to find him, and that has to come first. You can talk about his reasons for lying once you've got him back at home.' I don't speak, not able to trust myself not to say something I regret. 'What will you do now?'

'I don't know. Go back even further, I guess.' Deflated, confused and with a thick, dark cloud of betrayal hanging over me, I shrug, my shoulders heavy. 'There's no point in me hanging around here. There's nothing to show he's ever been to Bristol in his life.'

'It doesn't mean he's lied about everything though, Claire. He's never lied about the fact that he loves you and Isla. Listen, Claire, I need to leave soon to pick up Isla — there's that class party after lunch. She went into school fine this morning, and this afternoon we're going to go to the Common and fish for sticklebacks.'

Oh God, Isla. In my shock at finding out Tom lied to me, I had forgotten about my daughter. *What kind of mother am I?* 'Gwen, I'm sorry.'

'Sorry? What the bloody hell for? Isla is going to have a whale of a time here, I'll make sure of it. And Claire?' Gwen says, just before I hang up. 'Tom's not like Mum, OK? Whatever he's done, whatever he's said, you and he will never be like Mum and Dad.'

I slide my phone back into my pocket, my anger at Tom's deceit bubbling away under my skin. I'd grown up from the age of ten believing my mother when she told me that the reason our dad walked out on Gwen and me was because he met someone else and no longer wanted to be in our lives. I spent the rest of my childhood hating my dad for leaving us, when, years later, I overheard a conversation between my mother and my aunt that revealed to me that my mother had lied to us. Our dad didn't leave us — she threw him out, because she had had an affair and thought the grass was greener. Tom had promised me after we were engaged that he would never lie to me and that he would always talk to me if he ever felt the way my mother did. And now, it seems, he's gone back on his word. OK, he never talked a lot about his university days, but there were tall tales, anecdotes that have been absorbed into our family storybook — we would laugh about some of the things he got up to, like the time he lost his shoes to the River Avon and had to walk home barefoot in the rain. He said his love of poetry came from Greg, his friend and tutor, a man who taught him not to just read the words but to listen to the rhythm of the poem, to hear it as music. Was all of this a lie? Did he just make up stories to trick me, to create an illusion of a life he never led? Deep in my thoughts, I startle as my phone chirps in my pocket. I pull it out, squinting at the screen where the sharp sunlight hits it, momentarily obscuring the caller's name. My heart beats faster, as I think for a moment maybe it's Tom. Maybe he's calling to tell me he's home and ask where I am.

'Hello?'

'Claire? It's Adam.'

'Oh, Adam. Hi.' Disappointment washes over me, even though I didn't really believe it would be Tom. I squash it down and try to focus on what Adam is saying.

'Are you at the university? I just wondered how you were getting on.' There is the slightest hint of irritation in his voice and I know he's annoyed at me for not calling, after haring off to Bristol when he thought a phone call would suffice. I can hear voices murmuring in the background and realise he must be out somewhere, unable to properly vent his annoyance.

'I didn't. I mean, I went, but I didn't get on very well at all.'

'Shit, Claire. I did think you heading off over there would be a waste of time. What happened?'

'He lied to me, Adam. He never went to Bristol University at all.' I almost spit the words out, the bitter taste of Tom's duplicity like ash in my mouth. There is silence at the other end of the phone as Adam takes in what I've told him.

'Never? He never attended at all? Are you sure you didn't get the dates wrong?'

'No, Adam, I didn't get the dates wrong. I saw Greg West too, the English lecturer who supposedly taught him. The guy Tom said he'd kept in contact with since he graduated. West'd never heard of him and didn't recognise his photo. I asked them to search the admissions roll to see if he was there and there's no record of him at all. He never went there, Adam. Now what do I do?'

'He definitely told you Bristol University? There's no way you could have made a mistake?' Adam's voice is sympathetic, and I wonder what he's really thinking about all of this.

'He definitely told me Bristol.' I tell Adam the story Tom told me about drunkenly losing his shoes in the River Avon, and Adam lets out a non-committal hum.

'I'm sure there's a reason, Claire; we just need to find out what. Look, I don't know Tom — and I only know the old you, Claire — but you *do* know him. Do you think he could have lied to you? Or do you think there could be some sort of explanation, no matter how random it might be?'

'An explanation? What explanation could there possibly be, Adam? He's lied to me — *he never went there!*' I stand and start to walk away from the bench, towards my car, blinking back more tears of frustration. 'I believed him when he told me he went there, that he had a life there. So now, finding out it was all fake, how can I think anything other than that he's a liar? I need to find him and quickly. I need to know what's going on and why he's lied to me — about something that didn't need to be lied about. I want to know why he hasn't come home. I want to know why he couldn't just be honest with me.' Anger subsiding, I feel sick at the thought of something happening to Tom, even though I'm furious with him for lying right now. 'We were happy, Adam, as happy as we possibly could be, and now it seems like there's so much that I never knew.' Adam makes all the right noises, before quietly asking me what my next plan of action is. I tell him I'm going back to the very beginning. I'm going back to Archmouth, Cornwall, to the village where Tom grew up, and I'm going to get some answers.

CHAPTER 13

I force myself towards a café on the corner, even though the smell of fried food wafting from its open doors makes my stomach turn, knowing I need to eat before I start the long journey down to Cornwall. I barely ate this morning when I fixed Isla some breakfast, too anxious to get on the road, so despite my stomach churning and the sour taste of Tom's lies on my tongue, I buy a BLT and a latte.

Tom's passion for Bristol and his life at university there was one of the reasons I fell in love with him, if I'm honest. I remember the pair of us sitting in the park on a hot summer's day, not long after I first met him. I had told Adam, my stomach churning with guilt, that I was helping Gwen move into her cottage but instead I sneaked away to meet Tom. While Adam was at work in Central London, both of us were stretched out on a picnic blanket in a park close to Easthampton, talking about our lives before we met, the things we loved, the people who meant a lot to us. Tom was so passionate about his university life, his face so animated as he spoke, that I remember thinking, *If he's this passionate about a city he loves, how amazing would it be if he felt like this about me?* There was something raw and exciting about Tom, something I'd never found with dependable, reliable Adam. A blade of grass was lodged in Tom's hair and I could smell the faint scent of wine on his breath as he laughed, and I remember thinking he was the one. He was the one I wanted to be with for the rest of my life.

I mentioned to him several times over the course of our marriage about going to Bristol, spending a long weekend there and catching up with some of his old uni friends, hinting at how I'd like to meet them, but he always brushed me off, saying people had moved away and had families, that nothing would be the same. I'd tried to encourage him, to say it didn't matter where people lived now, friendship was friendship, but he'd resisted until I'd eventually accepted it, understanding that perhaps he didn't want to tarnish his memories. Today, I realise why he never wanted to go there, and the sting of betrayal and humiliation cuts deep.

* * *

Back in the car, windows open to air out the stifling midday heat, I pull out an old map that sits in the glove box of the car. It's been there for years, moved from car to car as we've upgraded them, lying in the dark compartment unused. Usually I would use the satnav or my phone to get directions, but today the map feels right. I know deep down it's a stalling tactic on my behalf — that I want to delay the trip to Cornwall because I'm scared of what I might find. What if I get there and find him but Tom tells me he's not coming home? What if I get there and he's with Lydia French, and he's left me to be with her? What if she's holding him in some homemade prison, forcing him to become part of her sick fantasy, in which he is *her* husband not mine? What if he's not there at all? Forcing the dry remnants of the sandwich into my mouth, rinsing it down with lukewarm coffee, I refold the map and stash it back in the glove box. It's time to find some answers.

The drive is another long one, and once again I find my mind wandering, thinking up more and more outlandish reasons as to why Tom lied to me about going to Bristol University, and why he hasn't been home for two days. There is a constant churning in my stomach as I try to rationalise both Tom's absence and his reasons for lying, but try as I might, I can't reach any satisfactory result. There doesn't seem to be any obvious reason as to why he would tell me he went to Bristol University when he didn't. No reason why he would tell me he was friends with Greg when Greg has never met him. It's as though someone has cut the ropes on me, and now I'm free falling. I find myself craving the sound of Isla's voice, the sound of something constant and real, so, finding a garage, I pull in and dial Gwen's number, even though she's probably at the class summer party.

'Claire?' Hope fills Gwen's voice and I close my eyes briefly.

'Gwen, I'm sorry to call again. I know you're probably at the party with Isla,' I say hurriedly. 'Can you call me back when you guys get home? I miss her.' Maybe hearing Isla's voice will ground me, remind me that I haven't imagined the happy family I thought we were, that we are still there, somewhere.

'I was just going to call you.' Gwen sounds hesitant and my heart skips a beat. 'The school called as I was on my way to the party. I've just collected her to bring her home.'

'Why? What's wrong? Is she OK?' Fear makes my mouth dry and I struggle to swallow.

'Oh God. Sorry, Claire, I didn't mean to panic you. She's fine, she just has a bit of a tummy ache, that's all. She didn't want to go to the class party, so I thought maybe she'd be better at home with me. Is that OK?'

'Yes, yes, of course. Can I speak to her?' It feels like an age before Isla comes on the phone, but the sound of her voice when she speaks is so normal, so *Isla*, that I almost want to cry.

'Hello, darling, how are you feeling?'

'I've got a tummy ache, so Aunt Gwen said I could come home from school. Are you with Daddy? Is he coming home?' My heart breaks as I realise the source of her tummy ache.

She's not poorly, she's just missing her dad, and now her mum is halfway across the country too.

'Not yet, baby, but I'm working really, really hard to find him.' Isla promises to be good for Gwen and I promise to be home as soon as I can in return.

Two hours later I find myself heading down a small country lane, following the signs for Archmouth, and a few minutes later I reach the village where Tom grew up. Picturesque and pretty, on the main road into the village there is an abundance of thatched cottages, surrounded by climbing roses and the refreshing scent of the sea on the air. It's tiny, much smaller than Easthampton, and hope surges through my veins. This really does look like the kind of place where everybody knows everybody. A large green with a border of bright flowers dominates the heart of the village, as narrow roads twist off in all directions from the centre, leading to smaller, terraced houses painted in pastel colours, the age of the buildings given away by the way they lean against each other and the way the salt has stripped paint from the woodwork in places.

I park the car next to the village green and stretch as I get out, pushing my hands high above my head and ignoring the curious looks I attract from a woman walking her dog across the grass. Being a stranger, I've obviously piqued her interest. Tom always said people in his village couldn't keep their noses out — that was part of the reason he left and never returned. Taking this as a good sign that someone *somewhere* will remember Tom and his family — possibly even point me in the right direction of where they live, if they're still here — I head towards the local shop that sits opposite the green. A small, traditional-style shop — no sign of a Co-op round here — it sits on the main street and is hopefully a hotbed of gossip. A bell tinkles overhead as I enter and an elderly gentleman looks up from his position behind the counter. He doesn't look particularly welcoming and I pause for a second at the entrance, apprehensive about asking this surly-looking old man for information, and nervous about what he might tell me, especially after my discovery in

Bristol. Making my way down the aisle towards the till, a girl in her mid-twenties with a huge, pregnant belly and a toddler in a pushchair in front of her avoids eye contact with me, instead concentrating on the tins of custard on the shelf at eye level. I pick up a newspaper and lay it on the counter.

'Lovely weather out there.' I smile awkwardly, trying to break the ice, but the shopkeeper doesn't seem inclined to talk, ignoring me as he taps the amount I owe into the till. Tom was right, they really don't like strangers round here — either that or my agitation is rolling off me in waves. I try again. 'Not a cloud in the sky.'

'Hmmm.' He holds out a withered hand for the money.

'Archmouth is a beautiful village. Have you lived here long?' I hold the change slightly out of reach in the hope that he won't avoid my question.

'All my life, Miss. Now, do you need anything else?' A quick flick of the fingers in my direction and a shuttered look draws down over his eyes. *No conversation, please.*

'Sorry.' Undeterred, I drop the coins into his hand and plough on clumsily, hoping that if I can just engage him in conversation he might be able to tell me where I can find Tom's family, who can hopefully, in turn, give me some sort of insight or clue as to where he might have gone, and whether Lydia French is involved. 'You don't happen to know where I can find the Bennett family, do you? Only, I'm not in the area for long and was hoping to catch up with them.' The lie sticks in my throat, and I almost choke the words out. He makes a chewing motion and I think he must be deciding how to answer, before I realise that he's moving his false teeth around in his mouth, not intent on giving me an answer in the slightest. I wait a moment, but he stays silent.

'Sir? I'm sorry to have bothered you but . . . the Bennett family? Do you know where I can find them? It's important and I'd be really grateful if you could help at all.'

He gives a start, as if I have disturbed him from a daydream, not at all as though he'd spoken to me just moments before. 'Bennett? No, sorry, can't help you.'

Swallowing back my frustration, I thank him, pick up the paper, force out a smile and leave. I'd really hoped that someone like that, a figure of the community who must hear all the goings-on in a small village, would have been able to help. Outside, the sun is beating down hotter than ever, and despite the proximity to the sea, there's no breeze. I stuff the paper angrily into the bin that sits outside, my nails digging into the palms of my hands in frustration, as the young woman with the baby comes out of the shop.

'I wasn't listening intentionally in there, honestly, but you're looking for the Bennett house, is that right? Mr. Gorman isn't very helpful, I'm afraid. He doesn't really like strangers, none of them do, not round here.' Big blue eyes peep out curiously from under the woman's thick-cut fringe, which sticks to her forehead slightly in the heat. Resting her hands in the small of her back, she puffs a little breath upwards, as if to shift her fringe but it doesn't move. 'Sorry. This heat is unbearable, especially with this one on board.' She gestures to her huge, round stomach.

'I remember those days,' I say, the memory of Isla twisting and turning in my belly sharp in my mind. 'That's right, I'm looking for the Bennett house — do you know where they live?' I leap onto her words, hopeful that finally I might be on the right track. The woman leans down to hand the toddler a lolly, eyeing me closely as she straightens up.

'That big house on the corner, as you come into the village. That was the Bennett house. Not sure if you'll catch anybody there now though, to be honest. There's lots of stories about that house.' She blushes slightly. 'That's what my mum says, anyway. I don't know what actually happened, but . . . anyway, that was their house. You can walk it from here.' She gives me a shy smile and turns to walk away.

'Wait!' I call, a thrill leaping in my gut at having the next step to go on. 'Thank you . . . you've been a great help.'

She smiles at me again and gives a little wave of her hand as she crosses the street, steering the stroller with expertise.

CHAPTER 14

It's only a ten-minute walk from the green to Tom's family home, and I wonder what the woman meant about there being lots of stories about it. It's not at all how I imagined it. Tom described it as a 'country cottage' on the rare occasion that he ever spoke about it, but the reality is a five- or six-bedroom house built of grey stone at the end of a long drive, set in immaculately manicured lawns. There is a single car on the sweeping turning circle at the end of the drive, a relatively new Mercedes. You can smell the money surrounding this place a mile off, and I wonder what could have been so bad that Tom felt he had to leave and not come back.

My heart in my mouth, I walk slowly up the drive towards the house, perspiration tickling the back of my neck and my shoes crunching loudly on the gravel underfoot. This is, potentially, my first meeting with my mother-in-law, a woman that Tom turned his back on years ago. Tom has never gone fully into detail about what happened between him and his mother after his father died, choosing only to tell me that he was better off without her. He didn't invite her to our wedding, even after I tried to persuade him that perhaps it was time to let bygones be bygones. Whatever had happened, you only get one mother.

The more I questioned Tom the more he refused to discuss it, in true Tom fashion. Even when I told him I found it strange, all he would say was he felt no desire to have her there. Finally, on the verge of a huge row in which Tom told me I was disrespecting him, I dropped the subject, secretly hoping Tom would change his mind. When it came to the day itself, I could kind of understand where Tom was coming from, as thick tension between my own parents threatened to ruin our day.

Thinking all this through as I walk slowly towards the house, I realise this is likely to be another dead end. Tom is probably not here. After everything he's said about his mother — or rather, the lack of things he's said about his mother — Tom would have to be desperate to come back here. Or maybe, I think to myself, this is the one place he thinks I'll never look for him. Maybe his mother knows the story behind Lydia French — maybe they grew up together, and his mother knows where to find her.

Reaching the solid oak front door, I lift the brass knocker and let it thud back down three times in quick succession. A few minutes later the door is wrenched open.

'All right, all right, keep your hair on.' A petite woman in her late fifties with coiffured hair and wearing a pink workout outfit stands before me. 'Can I help you darling?'

'I hope so. Are you Mrs. Bennett?'

The woman laughs, a deep, throaty laugh scented with the rasp of a thousand cigarettes, and I can't help but warm to her — if this is Tom's mother she is not at all what I was expecting. 'No, my love. Is that who you're after?'

'Yes. Does she live here? A girl in the village said that this was the Bennett house.'

'This is the Bennett house, or it was, anyway. I'm sorry, sweetheart.' She lays a manicured hand on my forearm, laugh dying away as she senses my confusion. 'They've been gone a long time. Ever since . . . well, from what I heard they had a bad time and they left the village. We moved here a while ago and they were gone then.'

My heart sinks. So, the house is known as the Bennett house, even though they've been gone for years — a typical example of small village life. Another dead end.

'Do you know where they went?' I try to keep the desperation from my voice, but even I can hear it leaching through, lacing my speech with a frantic air.

'I'm sorry, darling, I don't. Are you all right? You look ever so hot — do you need a glass of water?' Her voice is kind and I blink back tears of frustration and disappointment, my stomach sinking down to the thin-soled sandals on my feet. Thoughts skitter across my mind, thoughts of Tom lying injured somewhere, his brain fuddled by amnesia, Tom being held somewhere against his will, desperately waiting for me to come and rescue him. I shake my head, trying to force these ideas from my mind; I'll go crazy if I let myself believe that any of these scenarios are real.

'I'm fine, thank you. You have no idea where I can find them?'

'No. No one in the village has heard from them since they left. It's like they vanished off the face of the earth.'

Just like Tom. 'Why did they leave? Can you tell me what happened?'

'Oh, this place is full of rumours.' The woman gives a rueful smile and I wonder how different things would have been if this *had* been Tom's mother. 'I don't know the full story, but I gather they lost their son and found it too painful to stay here.' She rests her hand on mine, patting it gently. 'It might be better not to rake over old coals — sometimes the past is best left there. I'm sorry.'

I nod, unable to raise even the smallest of smiles, wanting to tell her that raking over old coals is the only option I have right now. Instead, I thank her for her time before walking slowly back to the car, trying to decide how I can possibly return home without Tom.

CHAPTER 15

It's later, but I don't know how much later, the lack of light making it impossible to tell how much time has passed. I have slept, in a fitful, dozing kind of a way, the position I'm forced into meaning that I can't properly sleep, the cold from the hard, filthy floor still seeping constantly into my bones, making me feel achy and shivery as if I'm getting the flu. My mouth is dry, so dry that I think I can feel my tongue cracking, and that, combined with the heavy, thick fog that fills my head, makes me think that whoever brought me here must have given me something, a drug to make me docile. How else would they have got me here? I'm young, strong. I wouldn't go without a fight. I try to plough through the mud that fills my brain, trying to remember what happened. The last thing I remember is the sun, hot on my back as I walked... where? Where was I going? I want to weep with frustration, but I'm so dehydrated I have no tears. I yank uselessly at the cuffs that bite into my wrists, pulling them down as hard as I can, that maddening clunk of the metal on metal ringing out over and over, until I have to give in, the pain in my wrists too much to bear. Something warm trickles along the inside of my wrist, the stinging sensation accompanying it making me want to cry. Blood. I'm bleeding. I try and shift round onto my other side, the weight of my own body making my right hip ache and groan. I manage it, even though it intensifies the pain in my shoulders slightly. Why is this happening to me? The fog in my brain thickens until exhaustion takes over and I try to sleep, dreaming of home, of family.

CHAPTER 16

I shudder as a chill runs down my spine. There's no way Tom would intentionally leave his daughter, not the Tom I know. Ignoring the whisper at the back of my mind telling me maybe I don't know him the way I think I do, I check his phone just in case he's received any further messages but there's nothing, and still no call back from Roman.

'Did you find them?' A voice from behind the car startles me and I see the young woman with the pushchair come into view.

'What? No. No, I didn't find them.' I tug at the car door handle, anxious to get back on the road towards home to see Isla. 'They left a long time ago, apparently.' I pause, wondering if I should push on. I drove all this way, I can't leave without trying. What do I have to lose? 'Do you know anything about it?'

'No — my mum said something bad happened to them and they left. I'm sorry, I didn't realise you were actually looking for the Bennett family, I thought you meant whoever lived at the house now.' She gives me a shy smile, rocking the buggy to and fro in an attempt to get her child to sleep, her swollen belly meaning she has to lean forward in order to be able to reach the handles comfortably. Despite my frustrations, I smile back. I had been just as attentive to Isla when she was little, and for a moment the longing for my child is almost painful. Maybe when Tom comes home we could talk about trying for another baby, it's been a while since we discussed it . . . but I stop myself. I need to find him first, and find out exactly why he's been lying to me, before I can leap ahead to thinking about our future, if we even have one after this.

'It's not your fault. Everything seems to be a bit of a dead end at the moment, really.'

'Did you try the library?' She points to an old building set back on the hill leading into the village. 'They keep old newspapers and stuff there. It might be worth a try, although I don't really know what you're looking for. Stories stay alive for a little while in tiny places like this, but if they're not exciting enough they soon die out. If my mum doesn't know about it, then it's probably not worth knowing, to be honest.' She turns away and starts to push the stroller towards the coastal path, before she stops and turns back to me. 'Oh, and just one other thing. Be careful what you say — people can be funny round here, you know? They don't really like talking to strangers.'

Thanking her, I climb back into the car and head straight towards the old library, not sure why it didn't occur to me in the first place. The modern age has us all so reliant on mobile phones and Google that I didn't even think about the library.

It's cool inside, the quiet hush and the smell of old books on the air a refreshing change from the dusty, bright sunshine outside. It's not busy and I find myself sitting at an old microfiche machine, a file of cards dating from early 2006 next to me, the seats either side of me remaining empty. A teenage girl sits at a dated computer, and I don't see any others available, so the microfiche is my only option. My plan is to go through the years until I find something, *anything*, that can tell me why Tom's family upped sticks and left what by all accounts appears to have been a comfortable life in the village. I decide to start in 2006 as I figure that's around the time Tom would have left school and started thinking about going to university. Of course, now I know Tom didn't go to Bristol University, but why would he make that up? It figures there must be some truth to it somewhere along the line, so it's entirely possible that he did leave the village in 2008 when he turned eighteen, just not to go to uni. I met him in Easthampton in early 2016, when he was twenty-five, so I have approximately eight years to look through before I catch up with him. Sighing at the enormity of the task ahead, I start to scroll through the files, eyes peeled for any mention of the Bennett family or the name French.

I have a couple of false starts when the name 'Bennett' stands out at me from the page, but it turns out to be nothing related to their disappearance — they seem to have been a fairly prominent family in the village, regularly allowing the use of their house and the surrounding grounds for village functions. I imagine it must have been quite the talking point when they disappeared. They just vanished with no clue as to where they might have gone. Under normal circumstances, I wouldn't have given a second thought to any of it, but this might be my only chance to find Tom.

Several hours later, I'm thirsty, my head aches and my back is in agony from hunching over the microfiche all afternoon. I've scrolled through what feels like thousands of pages of newspaper articles, and I could probably tell you everything you ever wanted to know about Archmouth — everything, that is, apart from where the Bennett family went. Staggering out into the still-bright sunshine despite it being almost six o'clock, I realise the building next to the old library is the registry office. My eyes ache with the effort of concentrating on the long drive and hours of microfiche, but even so, I check the sign outside. It's open until 6.30 p.m., so I push the door open and make my way inside. They evidently don't have many people popping in unannounced and the receptionist looks up in surprise as I enter, giving me a welcoming smile before she makes it perfectly clear that 6.30 p.m. is closing time.

My plan is to go back even further, to see if I can find any registration of Tom's parents. It's another shot in the dark, but I'm hoping at least one of them grew up here — maybe the big stone house is a childhood home? It's big enough and old enough to possibly have been handed down to them, an old family estate, maybe? I know I'm clutching at straws, but with no help from the police I'm desperate to find Tom as soon as possible, the threatening text and the post from Lydia French hanging over me like a sword, poised to topple at any moment. Every time I think of the words on Tom's phone screen telling him someone 'KNOWS EVERYTHING', my stomach flips and the bubble of panic that threatens to overwhelm me rises to the surface, forcing me to take deep breaths in order to keep things together. Despite Adam's warning that Tom might not want to be found, my gut tells me Tom hasn't come home because he can't — not because he doesn't want to.

'Hi.' I smile as I approach the front desk, a wobbly smile that feels more like a grimace. The receptionist is in her early sixties, with soft, greying, curly hair, and the glasses on a chain around her neck remind me of Mrs. Randall at the university. Remembering what the young girl said to me about being careful what I say, I decide not to mention that Tom is missing, not wanting to put her off helping. 'I'm looking for some information on births, deaths and marriages. Do you have a register I could look through?'

'A register? Oh gosh, no.' The receptionist shakes her head regretfully. 'There's no register, not a physical one anyway, not here. Most of it is all done online now. I can give you some website addresses that might help, but if you want copies of certificates, you'll have to order them. It only costs about ten pounds, but it takes a little while for them to come through.'

Her words pebbledash me with disappointment. I had hoped I would just walk in, look through a book and somehow find whatever it is I'm looking for, and now it seems I'm stuck at a dead end again.

I blink, damping down the frustration I'm sure must be written all over my face. 'Thanks anyway. I don't actually know the names of the people I'm looking for, if I'm honest with you. All I know is they used to live at the big house on the edge of the village, and their surname was Bennett.' I half turn away from her, ready to go back outside and rethink my plans.

'Oh!' The receptionist lets out a little gasp of recognition and I turn back to where she stands, a hand over her mouth.

'Do you know them?' I ask, a faint fluttering of excitement in the pit of my stomach. Maybe this isn't such a dead end after all.

'Oh, everyone knew them. But I shouldn't really talk about it.' She pushes her glasses onto her nose and busies herself with the computer mouse, but there's a gossipy air about her, the feeling that she spends too many hours in here alone without anybody to talk to.

'That's a shame. I believe they were close to someone I know. They lost touch and I was hoping I could track them down.' I cross my fingers behind my back. 'The only thing is, I'm not too sure of their names — all I know is they lived here, and then they left after something happened to them.' The nape of my neck starts to itch as sweat prickles there, and I wish I'd tied my hair up. The receptionist stares at me over the top of her glasses before she slides them off, leaning closer to me.

'Really? Oh, that is lovely of you — although I'm not surprised your friend lost touch with them; they left such a long time ago, and didn't seem to keep in touch with anybody.'

'Can you tell me a bit about them?' I hold my breath, waiting for her to tell me to mind my own business, but I'm hoping my gut feeling that she's a gossip is right. My pulse triples and I can taste it on the air, the truth about what happened to Tom's family.

'It's not my place to talk about it,' she says, giving a little sniff, her mouth folded into a thin line. 'We don't gossip in Archmouth.' The excitement dies a little — I can almost see the answers being tugged away from me, locked back in their box to be kept secret for another decade.

'Please? I won't tell anyone you told me, I wouldn't want to get anybody into trouble.' I feel her waver as she looks down at her computer screen, avoiding eye contact. 'It's not a friend I'm asking for . . . it's my husband.' I meet her eyes, letting her see my desperation. 'He's missing. I'm trying to find him and I think the Bennett family might be able to help.'

'Oh, you poor, poor thing,' she breathes, hand fluttering to cover her mouth. 'Missing? And you think the Bennetts might know something?'

'I'm hoping they might be able to point me in the right direction to find him,' I say, allowing the little ball of hope in my chest to grow wings. The receptionist glances over her shoulder, even though the place is empty, before leaning over the counter conspiratorially.

'I'll tell you, but only in the hope that it helps you find your husband. It's such a sad story,' she begins, and I wait anxiously for her to continue, my nerves stretched taut like piano wire. 'Debra was only young when she and Alan got together. Twenty, I think she was, when they got married. It caused a lot of friction — her family were the ones with the money, and they didn't really approve, even after the wedding.'

I picture them on their wedding day, thinking how different it must have been to ours, wondering if Tom's grandparents had put aside their differences for that one special day. I remember how excited I was on my wedding day to Tom, less than a year after we first met. Standing at the top of the aisle, waiting to walk on my father's arm towards my future. The nerves that made my hands shake and my stomach swirl as the music started, Tom turning to look over his shoulder, his face lighting up at the sight of me gliding towards him in an elegant cream silk dress, towards the start of our new life together. *Whoever would have known what was around the corner?* Swallowing hard and pushing away the memory, I smile impatiently at the receptionist, but it seems she's going to tell the story her way.

'Her mother wasn't happy about things *at all*,' she goes on, rubbing at a spot on her glasses, 'but it soon all sorted itself out once the baby came along. Her mother fell in love with that little boy the minute she laid eyes on him.'

'Tom? The little boy was called Tom, wasn't he?' I ask, eager for her to confirm that I do have the right family.

'That's right. Tom. Tiny little thing, he was. And then, of course, everything went wrong. They tried to make the best of things but they just couldn't get over it. Debra was ever so depressed, she stopped leaving the house, and then they just upped sticks. There one minute, gone the next. But that was years ago — around 1990, it must have been — and I'm not sure anyone from Archmouth heard from them again. It was a terrible business.' She sighs, lost in her own memories. Beginning to pace backwards and forwards in front of the desk, I wait for her to continue, the truth at my fingertips. I stop in front of her, pausing to lift my hair away from my neck, my hands starting to shake as the adrenaline begins to pump. *I'm so close to finally getting some information — so close to finding someone who might know where Tom could have gone.*

'But where did they go? Did they go to live with family, or did they leave on their own? I need to know where they are now . . . please . . . if you know . . . I'm desperate.' My voice cracks and then something she said swims to the forefront of my mind. I hesitate for a moment, my brain ticking over. *1990? Tom would have been a tiny baby when they left.* 'Do you know what happened? Was it something to do with Tom?'

'Tom?' The woman gives me a sharp, sideways look. 'Well, of course it was something to do with Tom. That's why they left. Tom died when he was three days old.'

***

Sweating, with the sour taste of bile hitting the back of my throat, I thank her for her time, apologising for bringing back any bad memories. I head towards the library, my head a tangled whirl, my stomach churning. I can't believe what I've just heard. Is this a joke? A cruel prank? Reaching the thick oak doors, I push hard on them but to no avail — it's past closing time and the library is all shut up for the night. Sinking onto a bench outside the ornate building, I pull up Google on my phone. Now I know what I'm looking for and the timeframe I should be looking at, it's much easier. I type *Archmouth Post* into the search engine, my knee jiggling as the website for the local newspaper slowly loads. Checking my coverage, still surprised to see two bars of signal in such a rural village, I click on the *archives* button and enter the dates I'm looking for. It takes two agonising minutes for the page to load, and I get a rush of adrenaline when I see it. I was almost half convinced that I had read things wrong, that it never really happened, or that the archives wouldn't go back that far, but no. The lead story for 20 May 1990 is the death of baby Thomas Malcolm Bennett, who died from complications after being born prematurely, complications the hospital failed to pick up. My lips numb with shock, I scan my eyes over the story again — Malcolm is Tom's middle name, and his birthday is 14 May — the newspaper reports this baby was born on 14 May and died three days later, on 17 May, just as the receptionist told me. The world spins, the concrete footpath seeming to tilt beneath my feet. The Bennetts did move away to escape the pain of losing their son — but where I thought the pain of losing their son was Tom choosing to move away and live a life they weren't a part of, their pain was the death of their son, something that could have been avoided, it seems. It also seems that my husband is not Tom Bennett. And I have no idea where — or even who — he is.

CHAPTER 17

My back twinges at the thought of another long car journey back home to Easthampton, but I jump behind the wheel, my brain on a constant loop. As I drive, the roads emptier now it is late in the evening, I find myself asking the same questions over and over. *Where is Tom? Who is Tom? Why did he lie to me?* How is it that he could walk out of the house at eight o'clock on a Tuesday morning and not be seen for almost sixty hours — no phone call, no messages, no contact at all? I feel the pressing urge to speak to Isla again but Gwen will be getting her ready for bed, and anyway, what do I say to her? She's bound to ask if Tom is with me if I tell her I'm coming home — how do I tell her I haven't found him yet? I could try contacting the police again, but what's the point? They weren't interested when they thought he'd left me before I discovered everything he'd told me was a lie, why would they be interested now — now I've found out he isn't who he says he is? I feel queasy every time I hear the registry office receptionist's voice in my mind telling me, *Tom died when he was three days old,* my stomach rolling and saliva filling my mouth. What if I never find him? What if this is it — Tom never comes home again, gone for good? I have to pull over as my stomach gives an almighty flip, vomit burning the back of my throat. What does Lydia French have to do with this, if anything?

My phone rings insistently over and over again as I drive, but each time I snatch it up from the passenger seat to see if it's Tom calling, it's either Adam or Gwen and I can't face talking to either of them just yet. After the seventh call I angrily hurl it onto the back seat, pressing my foot to the floor to get home as soon as possible with no regard for speed cameras or other motorists until, halfway home, I'm overcome with exhaustion and have to pull into a lay-by before I end up killing myself or someone else. The information I've discovered over the course of today has made a confused, jumbled mess of my brain and that, combined with the hours spent driving, means I can barely keep my eyes open long enough to park up safely. Two hours later I jolt awake, dreaming of Tom's fingers brushing my face, close enough to touch. Swiping at my cheek I disturb a tiny money spider crawling over my skin. The sun has disappeared over the horizon and I shiver in the inky darkness, the white glow of the moon streaking the road in front of me. Goosebumps ripple over my arms and I start the car, turning the heater up.

It takes a little over two hours to complete the rest of the journey home, and I'm conscious of the minutes ticking away like sand in an egg timer. Swinging onto the drive a little after one in the morning, I park the car haphazardly on the drive and bolt into the house. It's been a hideously long day, and between the tiredness fogging my brain and what I've uncovered in Bristol and Cornwall, my skin feels sensitive, my bones aching as though I have the flu. I slam the front door closed behind me, resting against it, as I tilt my head back and try to fight the tears that spring to my eyes. Everything that I thought I knew was a lie. Tom is not who he says he is. The only part of his life before us that he ever really opened up about is fabricated. I realise I've spent the past eight years living with someone, making a home, a family, a life with someone whose real name I don't even know. What does this mean for us? Are we even legally married? He's not even here to answer my questions. I turn his phone on again and re-read the message from the unknown number. 'I KNOW EVERYTHING.' *Well*, the thought drifts through my tired mind, *I'm glad you do, because at this moment in time I know precisely nothing*. Angrily, I bash out another text in reply, demanding answers, but the phone stays silent.

A long, hot shower does nothing to improve my mood, and despite the late hour I don't feel tired anymore, so I make my way downstairs in jogging pants and open Tom's expensive whisky. Fuck him, he's not here to drink it. My phone pings with a text — Adam, asking me to let him know I got back safely. Slugging back a shot of the fiery whisky, wincing at the burning sensation as it makes its way down my gullet, I ignore the text and throw the phone back down on the table. What am I supposed to say to Adam? That on top of not knowing *where* he is, I don't even know *who* my husband is? I pour another shot, knock it back and repeat. It doesn't take long for the whisky to go straight to my head, given that I haven't eaten since yesterday lunchtime and the most I usually drink is a bottle of wine shared with Gwen over lunch. *Fuck you, Tom.* I will find out who you are. A wave of fury washes over me, sparked by the burn of the drink. I won't sit back and let this happen to me. I *will* find Tom, whoever he is. I know deep down, even if he *was* lying to me the whole time, Tom does love me, and he wouldn't leave without good reason — for Isla's sake, if not for mine. All my doubts over me being the breadwinner while Tom became a part-time stay-at-home dad after Isla was born faded within weeks of going back to work. Tom adores the time he gets with Isla, leaning fully into his role as the main carer. He even waved me away when I suggested Isla went to after-school club and he went back to the estate agency full-time, telling me he loved being home with Isla, and he wouldn't want things to change until she started high school. There's never been any doubt in my mind that Tom adores our family. And besides, no one could fake it for that long . . . could they?

Attempting to take the stairs two at a time but underestimating the power of the whisky, it's more of a stagger as I make it upstairs and throw open the door to our bedroom. Heading straight for the wardrobe, I pull out Tom's clothes, tossing them into a bundle on the bed, trying to see if I can figure out if anything is missing, my booze-fuddled brain convincing me I must have missed something. Sod his requests for privacy and respecting each other's wishes — he didn't think about that when he was telling me stories, making me believe in a whole different Tom, a Tom who doesn't exist. Sweaters, shirts and trousers pile up in a heap on the bed, soon joined by a tangle of loafers, sliders and trainers as I yank them from the bottom of the wardrobe. I pull out each pair, holding every shoe upside down in a vain attempt to uncover anything that might have been hidden inside. From time to time, I swig whisky directly from the bottle, having long dispensed with a glass, the dirty tumbler now buried somewhere underneath the mountain of clothes. Finally, the wardrobe empty with no secrets uncovered, exhaustion overwhelms me and I sink into the pile of Tom's clothes, the scent of his aftershave tickling my nose. All night, I dream of him. I'm chasing him, but at every turn he runs faster and faster, and I'm left empty-handed and alone.

CHAPTER 18

I'm woken the next morning by a hand shaking my shoulder as I struggle into consciousness, the stale taste of whisky on my tongue and furring my teeth.

'Tom?' I squint in the early-morning sunshine, aware that I'm terribly thirsty and my head aches with the sounds of a marching band hammering its way through my skull. *Ugh*.

'Sorry to disappoint you.' Adam leans over me, Gwen peering over his shoulder. I struggle into a sitting position, my clothes crumpled and slept in, my usually sleek bob a tangled bird's nest.

'What are you two doing here?'

'Gwen was worried — we both were — when we couldn't get hold of you last night. She called me to say you'd told her about Tom, and that you were going to head down to Archmouth to try and find him. We both kept ringing and ringing you, but no answer. After you didn't respond to my texts, I drove over and your car was here, so I knew you'd made it back all right, but then Gwen couldn't get hold of you this morning. We thought we'd better come over and make sure you're OK. Good job we did, by the looks of it.' Adam looks around the room, wrinkling his nose and surveying the damage I did in my drunken state last night. I dig in my pocket and pull out my phone, which has several more missed calls on it.

'I'm sorry, guys, you didn't need to come over. I'm fine.' I look at Gwen sheepishly, stifling a nauseous burp as I haul myself upright. 'Isla — where is she? Is she OK?'

'She's at school, Claire. And she's fine.' Gwen hands me two paracetamol and a glass of water with an arch look and I take them from her gratefully. 'You, on the other hand, are not. You look like shit. What went on here last night?' She perches on the bed next to me and the toppling pile of Tom's clothes and I gulp greedily at the water. Despite my protestations, I'm glad the two of them are here as the memory of yesterday's discoveries hit me with a thump, my stomach clenching.

'I got drunk . . .'

'Yeah, no shit.' Gwen waves the quarter-empty whisky bottle at me as Adam shushes her and a wave of nausea rolls through my belly at the sight of it. I'm not sure I'll ever be able to drink again, let alone whisky.

'I think I was entitled to have a drink last night after what I discovered yesterday, in Bristol and then . . .' I trail off, remembering I haven't told them the biggest news yet, my discovery in Archmouth — further evidence of Tom's lies.

'That doesn't necessarily mean anything,' Gwen butts in. 'I was thinking about it after we spoke yesterday . . . You've got a degree, Claire, maybe he felt like he had to tell you he went to uni? Maybe he thought he needed to make himself more than he actually is, for you to want to be with him when you first met.'

'Tom wouldn't do that. Come on, Gwen, you know him.' I feel a prickle of unease at discussing the time Tom and I first met in front of Adam. 'He never feels like he needs to be something he's not. And anyway, it's not just that.' I go on to tell them how I went to Cornwall, tracing Tom right back to where he was born, and the shocking discovery I made at the registry office.

'Shit. That's really heavy stuff, Claire.' Raking her fingers through her hair in a gesture that we both inherited from our mum, Gwen looks as confused as I feel, whereas Adam sits quietly, his face sombre.

'Now I see why you opened the whisky. It must have been a real shock. You should have answered the phone, Claire. We could have helped you. You didn't need to get drunk and do all this.' He gestures to the wreck that is my bedroom, the clothes scattered all over the place.

'I was just looking for . . . something,' I say feebly, the effort of holding off my hangover making me feel sick. 'I don't know what, just something that would give me some sort of clue as to who he really is. I don't even know his real name. Why would he lie to me about something as important as that?' I feel it again, that sharp pain in my chest, and wonder if this is what a broken heart feels like.

Adam is quiet for a moment, his face pensive as he rubs a hand over his dark beard, and I wonder what he's thinking. Does he think I deserve this, for the way I left him for Tom? The old Adam wouldn't have felt satisfaction over something like this, but I don't know him anymore. Not like I used to.

'Well, you didn't get very far with your search,' he says eventually, raising an eyebrow and giving me a glimpse of the old Adam. 'Tom must have had his reasons; we just need to figure out what they were. I've seen this before on a previous case I worked on. It sounds like he searched for a child born around the time he was who would have passed away at a very young age. This means he could take on their identity — apply for identity documents et cetera in that name. He could start again. Become someone else.'

A strange look crosses Adam's face and he looks as though he wants to say something more, but decides against it. Sympathy over with, he stands and briskly rubs his hands together and I imagine this must be what he's like at work — no-nonsense and unflappable. 'Obviously you'd gone through the wardrobe before you passed out. Go and get in the shower.

Gwen will make you some toast and then we'll tear this place apart to see if we can find anything. There must be something somewhere that will point us to who Tom used to be.'

I give him a grateful smile and allow Gwen to pull me to my feet. My head pounds and my stomach churns, the whisky threatening to make a reappearance, but I have to pull myself together if I'm going to get my husband back.

CHAPTER 19

Systematically, we make our way through the clothes flung over the bedroom, checking the pockets and shaking them out to make sure we don't miss a thing. It seems I didn't do the thorough job I thought I had in my whisky-infused frenzy last night, and Adam creates a small pile of all the items we find in Tom's pockets, but it still doesn't amount to much. There's a crumpled five-pound note left in the pocket of a tan leather jacket, one I remember him wearing on a trip to the pub just a few weeks ago, and a couple of old receipts left in a pair of jeans. Gwen checks through the en-suite and the desk and I pull out the drawers in the chest, uneasy and jittery as I root through Tom's underwear in the hope that he's left any kind of clue about Lydia French or his life before he met me tucked away where he thinks I'll never find it. It's slow going and the hangover isn't helping — my head is still pounding despite the paracetamol and the cups of tea Gwen has made. By two o'clock, we've found nothing useful and I'm close to tears, the air in the bedroom getting thinner and thinner, the room becoming more and more claustrophobic with every pocket emptied. We start to hang the clothing back in Tom's wardrobe, when a frown creases Adam's brow. He's holding the tan leather jacket, his hand deep inside one of the inside pockets.

'Claire?' Adam pulls out a tiny, screwed-up piece of paper. 'We missed something.' He untwists the paper, smoothing it out on the surface of the bedside table.

'What is it?' I peer over his shoulder. 'A phone number?' Now flat, the crumpled paper shows a mobile number scrawled across it, in a hand that isn't Tom's. My heart starts to bang in my chest — it could be nothing, but after what I've uncovered about my husband over the past couple of days there's a chance it could mean *something*. I pluck the piece of paper from the table, digging in my pocket for my phone.

'Claire, what are you doing?' Adam asks as Gwen leans over my shoulder, a frown to match Adam's tugging her brows into a sharp V.

'Calling it.' I dial, my hand shaking slightly in anticipation. 'It might be nothing, but it might not be. Maybe he called this person before he left . . . maybe they know something.' Yet another long shot, but when you're grasping at straws even the tiniest blade will do. The call connects, and taking a deep breath I ready myself to speak, to ask the person on the other end of the line if they know Tom, only to hear a generic voicemail message click in.

'Voicemail.' I say despondently, my hopes raised only to be dashed again. Adam rummages under the pile of clothes left on the bed, pulling out Tom's mobile.

'This is Tom's, isn't it?' He holds the phone out to me. 'Why not check the number on his phone? Maybe if he did know them he might have saved it.'

Yes. I take the phone from him, carefully typing in the number. There isn't a match with any of his contacts, nor with his call log . . . but there is one match.

'This is the number,' I breathe out shakily. 'Look — this is the number that texted him that night, the night before he went missing. The number that texted him, "I know everything."'

'Claire—' Gwen lays a hand on my arm as I sink down onto a cleared space on the bed — 'try not read too much into this . . .'

'Gwen — he knows them!' I wave Tom's phone at her. 'He knows the person who sent him that message. He must do if he has the number in his pocket.' My mind whirls and I have to consciously think about my breathing, the air in the room thick with tension.

'Maybe he did,' Gwen says rationally, 'but it doesn't mean they have anything to do with him not coming home. He might not have known them at all. He might have received the text and made a note of the number.'

'Or,' Adam says, scratching at his chin as he thinks, 'maybe this is something to do with Lydia French — maybe she's the one who sent him that message?'

CHAPTER 20

On discovery of the mobile number, I'm sure Lydia French is somehow involved in Tom's disappearance. For Tom to have this number tucked away in his jacket pocket, to then have received that text, then Lydia French's post shows up on my timeline, with *my* photo, on the very day that Tom disappears ... it all just seems too coincidental not to be related somehow. While I've been showering for the second time today — leaning wearily against the wall as hot water thunders above me, trying to clear my head and pondering how the phone number, text message and Facebook post could be linked — Tom's wardrobe has been put back neatly, and it crosses my mind that he won't recognise it when he comes home. *If he comes home.* Gwen dusts her hands off and closes Tom's wardrobe door.

'Sorry, Claire, I'm going to have to go soon,' Adam says. 'I promised I'd meet a friend this afternoon.' He pauses, something that looks worryingly like pity written over his features. 'There's nothing else here. He hasn't left you anything. I don't know what else you can do. I'm sorry.'

I nod, wondering briefly who he's meeting, who is more important than this. 'Thanks for your help, Adam. Does any of the stuff I've found out over the last twenty-four hours mean your lot will want to get involved now?' I look up at him hopefully, but he gives a small shake of his head.

'I'm sorry. We could look into the stolen identity, but it's going to be difficult to know where to start without the faintest clue where Tom really came from. I hate saying it, but it's looking more and more like he wanted to leave. The fact he's changed his name before doesn't look good — how do we know he didn't do this to someone else? Another girlfriend?' He doesn't say the word *wife* and for that I'm grateful.

'But don't you think it's strange Tom receives that message, and then the very next day he disappears? And what about the sponsored post from Lydia French? And the fact that she has his photo? She wants to find him badly enough that she's prepared to pay for advertising for God's sake!' Realising I'm shouting, I lower my voice. 'She referred to Tom and Isla as *her husband and child*. Surely that has to mean something?' That now familiar lead weight of fear turns in my gut, an icy fist that threatens to squeeze the life out of me.

'She could have got the photo from the cruise line. There's nothing illegal about posting a picture on social media, unfortunately, nor for paying for an advert, or for referring to someone as something they're not. I don't know, Claire, I really don't. Maybe he does know her, from sometime before he met you?'

'And the text? The one that said, "I know everything"? Plus the fact he hasn't even checked to see if Isla is OK?' I feel as if I'm going over old ground, repeating the same things over and over in an attempt to convince Adam — and myself — that Tom wouldn't just up and leave like this.

'The text wasn't threatening him. OK, it's a strange thing to send to someone, but I'm sorry. I'm just calling it the way I see it — sometimes it's hard to accept that someone simply doesn't want to be with you anymore.' His words bite, just as they're meant to. 'Claire, I have to go. Let me know if you turn up anything else. I've already said I'll help. For you. And for your daughter.'

'Thanks, Adam, but I'm already sure he hasn't left of his own accord. He wouldn't do that. He might have lied to me, he might not be who I thought he was, but he wouldn't do that to Isla. He'd never leave her.'

'As far as the police are concerned, you two have had a domestic and he's left you, maybe even for this Lydia French.' Adam ignores my wince at his harsh words. 'There's no evidence pointing to anything else. I'm sorry.' Knowing he's only trying to prepare me for what he thinks is the worst, I squash down the anger rising in my chest as Adam turns to leave, and then moments later there is the distant slam of the front door. Gwen sits down on the bed beside me.

'Sorry, Claire. I don't know what to say.'

'What can you say? I know Adam thinks Tom's left me voluntarily, Gwen, but I know *inside* that he hasn't. I know he's lied and things aren't what I thought they were, but my gut is telling me that Lydia French has got something to do with it and I need to find out what. It's no coincidence that that picture appeared on my timeline, and then that same day Tom didn't turn up at work, didn't come home. He's been distracted lately, Gwen, like there's something on his mind. Even Hannah commented on it. He's keeping his phone next to him, like he's waiting for a call. Maybe she already found him and she's been hassling him? Maybe Adam is right, and she's the one who sent him that text message. *She's* the reason Tom is missing — I can't stop until I track her down and get to the bottom of it all. She could be the reason he changed his name in the first place. What if she's some kind of crazy ex-girlfriend, and she's stalking him? I just need to find Tom and get him home. Then we can discuss all the other stuff I've discovered.'

'Claire, I hear everything you're saying, and I understand your frustration, but . . . aren't you worried that Tom might be having an affair with this woman? Occam's razor says the simplest explanation is usually the right one and this . . . *is* the simplest explanation.' Gwen's voice cracks as she speaks, and

I know deep down she doesn't really believe Tom could have an affair either.

'No, Gwen. I'm sure. It's not just an affair.' *Just an affair.* The very thought of Tom with another woman makes me want to be sick. 'It's something more. I can feel it.'

Gwen nods slowly, running her hand over the duvet, smoothing out the wrinkles. 'Look, Isla's club finishes in an hour . . . Do you want me to . . . ?' Gwen trails off, and I'm aware of my unbrushed hair and holey jogging bottoms.

'Do you mind picking her up? I just feel . . .' I look around the bedroom. There must be something that can point me in Tom's direction. 'I'm not finished here, not yet. I'll come by yours this evening.'

* * *

Gwen stands to leave, reaching for her bag. 'Listen, Claire. I don't know what to think, but I do know Tom and I don't think he'd just up and leave without some sort of explanation. Not without Isla.' She shrugs, clearly just as confused as I am. 'I won't mention any of this to Mum just yet, shall I?' Gwen seems to know instinctively that I don't want Mum involved. She'll just panic, and I can't trust her to keep calm in front of Isla. Isla's worried enough already without my mum flapping around her making it worse.

'No, please don't say anything, not yet anyway. Give me some time to track Lydia French down and find Tom. Tom knows her from somewhere; I just need to figure out where. I don't want Mum getting involved in it as well, you know what she's like.' I stand, grateful for Gwen's support. 'We're not like them, Gwen . . . me and Tom, I mean. We're not like Mum and Dad. We don't hide things from each other.' Even as I say it, I know it's no longer true — Tom has quite clearly hidden things from me. Gwen comes towards me, throwing her arms around me, not even flinching at the smell of whisky that still seeps from my pores despite two showers.

'Keep me posted, OK? I can take care of Isla as long as you need me to — you know she loves staying at my house. I don't want you to worry about Isla on top of worrying about Tom.' She pulls back and kisses me on the cheek. 'You'll find him, I know you will. We'll get this all straightened out.' I manage to raise a small smile as she leaves, but I'm not so sure.

CHAPTER 21

Once Adam and Gwen have left I get straight back to it. Although we've pulled the bedroom apart and checked all of Tom's wardrobe and drawers, there are numerous cupboards downstairs I need to search to see if he's hidden anything there, if there any clues at all left to find. A thorough search of the rest of the house turns up nothing of any interest, nothing that could point me in the right direction, and I find the only place left to look is up in the attic. Neither of us is a fan of going up there. Tom doesn't like the dust and spiders that congregate seemingly deliberately by the trap door, sending down small showers of grit and spidery legs onto the face of whoever has the misfortune to open it. I don't like the thick darkness that threatens to envelop you up there, that brief moment before the overhead bulb sparks to life where you can't see your hand in front of your face.

Already sure this will be a wasted exercise, I pull the trap door handle down hard, the inevitable shower of dust sprinkling down over me as I pull out the ladder. Holding my breath, I fumble for the light switch, blind for a moment before bright light illuminates eight years of collective rubbish, stuff we've placed up here and never used again. I start on the left and work my way round, opening boxes and rooting through black sacks of items we thought we couldn't live without, but haven't actually used for years. I find old baby clothes of Isla's, carefully folded and wrapped in tissue paper to keep the moths from them, and a box containing all my old uni stuff. Now I realise I never found it strange that Tom didn't have that box, the box all graduates seem to have of old textbooks, notes, and stolen ashtrays from pubs that you were never going to frequent again. I just thought that was typical Tom — organised, thorough, not one to hang onto things just for their sentimental value. Now, obviously, I realise Tom's box probably never existed.

Upending a plastic storage container reveals all my old maternity clothes, packed away after Isla was born to be saved for the next pregnancy. Only the next pregnancy didn't happen, though not for the lack of trying. We both wanted more children after Isla, but it just didn't ever seem to happen. I asked Tom to visit a fertility clinic to see if we could get to the bottom of it, but he wouldn't ever discuss it, only to say whatever happened was meant to be, despite my wanting answers. The older Isla got, and the further I went in my career, I eventually stopped bringing it up, even though there is still a part of me that wishes I'd pressed harder. Pushing aside thoughts of babies and family, I work my way around the attic, only to be left empty and disappointed when my search, as suspected, brings up nothing.

Wearily, I make my way back down the ladder, covered in dust and cobwebs, my arms aching from hefting the heavy boxes and the remnants of last night's whisky still sloshing queasily in my belly. There's no sign of anything to show Tom isn't who he says he is. Back in the bedroom I check my phone, but there's still nothing from him, only a text from Hannah, asking if Tom has turned up yet.

I'm drained, the emotions of the past seventy-two hours leaving me exhausted, and wanting nothing more than to sleep and wake up to find it's all been a bad dream. As if to prove to myself this is really happening, I pull Tom's phone out of my pocket and re-read the message that sits there spitefully, almost taunting me.

I KNOW EVERYTHING.

I don't know where it comes from, but a tidal wave of anger washes over me, causing my pulse to triple, beating loud and insistent in my ears, my fists clenching. Heat rises in my face as realisation hits — everything I have worked for, everything I thought was true and good in my life is a lie. Tom is the only one who has the answers to all of this and he's not here. If he were here, I would slap him. I would pound my fists against his broad chest until he told me the truth. It all comes back to Tom, or whatever his real name is, and events from his past, no matter which way I look at it. Whether he's left of his own accord or not, neither I nor Isla deserve to be put through the hell we're going through right now.

Furious, I yank open the bedroom drawers, pulling everything onto the floor, sure that somewhere in there, there must be something. Kicking at the various garments I've thrown across the floor in frustration, I pick up the paperback lying face down on Tom's bedside table, the spine broken and cracked, and hurl it across the room, pages scattering as they fly free from the old glue binding. Slumping against the wall, exhausted and furious as my breath rattles in my chest, my hangover thumping an insistent beat at my temple, I press my hands into the carpet — and that's when I see it. Two dents, either side of the feet of Tom's bedside cabinet, like it's been moved. As I peer closely at the thick carpet fibres, I can see a series of dents, as though the cabinet has been moved about regularly. I know I haven't moved it, and Adam and Gwen definitely didn't, so it can only mean Tom must have done. Aware it might just be a case of him moving it to vacuum around it, I pull out the bedside cabinet drawers, rifling again through old receipts, paracetamol bottles and various leads to old devices, all the same items that were sitting there two hours ago when Gwen did the same thing, but there is still nothing.

Shoving the drawers back into place, I place a hand either side of the cabinet and push it towards the window, leaving a fresh patch of carpet exposed beneath it. Only, it isn't quite a clean patch of fresh carpet. Falling to my knees, I peer closely at the pale blue pile. A line has been carved very carefully into the carpet, making it easy to pull back both the carpet and the underlay beneath. Fibres catching under my nails, I peel back the thick woven material and rubbery underlay to reveal the wooden floorboards underneath, one of which is loose. Peering closely into the space I've created, I can see the nails in the boards have been removed. The gap between them is big enough for me to slide the tip of a finger in and gently prise the board loose, my heart hammering in my chest as a splinter pricks at the end of my pointer finger. Pulling the floorboard free, I reach into the small void it has created and feel about inside the cavity, my fingers rasping against the side of something solid and square. With a bit of manoeuvring I manage to wiggle it free, my mouth suddenly dry. It's a cardboard box, slightly smaller than a shoebox, made up of plain white card with no logo or picture, nothing to identify where it might have come from, the lid held in place with three or four rubber bands. I put it to one side while I replace the floorboard and carpet, stalling the moment where I discover whatever the box holds.

Picking up the box, I sit on the bed and gently run my hands over it. I want to think it was left there by a previous occupant, that it has nothing to do with what has happened in our house over the last two days, but we laid this bedroom carpet not long after Isla was born. That, and the fact my hands come away clean when I remove them from the box, with no dust or dirt clinging to them, says this box has been handled regularly and that, as I've never seen it before in my life, it can only belong to Tom.

Fighting the urge to fetch the bottle of whisky that Gwen spirited away downstairs, with that claustrophobic feeling filling the air again, I carefully pull off the bands securing the lid. Part of me doesn't want to open it, the other half wants to rip off the lid and plough through the contents. I rake my hands through my tangled hair and smooth it back down again before, unable to put it off any longer, I tip the contents of the box onto the bed. There are a few trinkets — a plastic bracelet of the kind worn by little girls; a watch, the brown leather strap old and cracked, the time forever at six thirty-two; and a handful of old cardboard beer mats, the card fuzzy with age. Things that on the surface don't have any significance at all to anyone other than Tom. There is nothing relating to either myself or Isla, no photos or cards, so I can only assume everything in this box relates to Tom's life before we came along. Reaching out, I pick up the small plastic beaded bracelet. It's something Isla would wear and I roll the brightly coloured beads between my fingers before throwing it onto the bed, unable to place the uneasy feeling in my stomach.

Going back to the box, I lay out all the other items from it in a straight line across the bed. Only two other things stand out as being significant. The first is a thick wedge of bank notes, tightly rolled and secured with an elastic band, the red kind used by the postman. Puzzled, I pull off the band and the notes spring out into a furled comma on the palm of my hand, several dropping to the carpet. I bend to pick them up, already mentally starting to count. There are a few twenty-pound notes, but the majority of them are fifties, and as I flick through them I get a terrible sinking feeling. There must be thousands of pounds here, more than Tom could ever save up on his part-time wages. We have a joint savings account, one that hasn't been touched by either of us since the boiler exploded last winter. I don't understand where the money has come from or why Tom would hide it from me. *And why*, a voice whispers at the back of my mind, *has Tom left that money here? Surely if he was planning to leave, he would have taken the money with him?* I swallow hard and re-roll the bank notes in their elastic band, throwing them back into the box as though they will burn me. The bank notes hidden under the floorboards seem to me to be another red flag that Tom hasn't left of his own accord — he hasn't come home because he *can't* come home. The second item, the thing I think will kick start my search again, is a photograph.

The photograph must have been taken in the early 2000s. It has that sheen on it that you don't seem to see anymore, not now everyone prints their own digital photos. It shows a young Tom, maybe aged around fourteen, standing at the edge of a cliff, his arm around a girl maybe a couple of years younger than him. His hair is lighter and longer, blowing around his head in the sea breeze. Tom faces the camera straight on, a smile on his lips, as the girl gazes up at him, a look close to adoration on her face. The sight of Tom — a younger, plumper Tom — hits me in the guts like a fist. I've never seen a picture of him as he was in his teens — he said he left all the photos behind when he left his mother's house, that they were only photos and they didn't mean anything. Obviously, this one did. Peering closely at the photo, I can just make out brightly coloured beads around the girl's wrist, a match to the bracelet in the box. *Could this girl be Lydia French?* Flipping it over, I see there is writing scrawled across the back of it in faded blue biro. Tom's hand, only that too has a younger feel to it, the letters less spiky, scrabbling across the page in even more untidy than usual backward-sloping letters.

Me and Harriet, Jack's Place, Lockwood Bay, 2006

Lockwood Bay. I saw signs for the bay as I was driving to Archmouth. I was on the right track earlier, only I didn't follow the coast far enough round. Checking my watch, I realise it's six o'clock, too late now to make the journey back down to Cornwall. As if also realising the time, my stomach growls in protest and I remember I haven't eaten anything since Gwen made me toast some eight hours ago. Getting to my feet, I tuck the photo carefully into my jeans pocket and head downstairs, snatching up my car keys and hurrying towards Gwen's cottage.

CHAPTER 22

'Claire! I was about to call you.' Gwen ushers me into the warmth of her little stone cottage, where Isla sits at the kitchen table, colouring in. Isla looks up as I enter, a smile rippling across her face as she climbs down from the table and rushes towards me.

'Mummy,' she says, as I crouch to greet her, her arms going around my neck. She smells different, like Gwen's peach shampoo with a hint of the incense Gwen burns around the cottage. 'Is Daddy home?'

'Sorry, darling, he's not back yet.' I press my cheek against her hair, her voice muffled as she presses her face into my shoulder. 'I tried, I really did, but I couldn't find him. I'm still looking.'

'But you *promised*!' Isla pulls away, her voice threatening to become a wail. Her cheeks are pink, and I half expect her to stamp her foot. Lifting her into my arms, I carry her to the table and settle her on my lap, where Gwen places a bowl of Thai curry in front of me.

'Listen, Isla . . . listen to Mummy.' I force myself to be firm as she relents, pressing her head against my chest. 'You know how Daddy always loses his keys? And then Mummy always finds them? What does Mummy say to Daddy every time?'

'She says, "Oh, Tom, you just weren't looking in the right place!"' Isla sounds calmer now, her voice brightening.

'That's what's happening now. Mummy is looking for Daddy, but she just didn't look in the right place this time.' I draw in a deep breath, hoping this will be enough to quell her anxiety. 'So, I'm going to keep looking. I always find things in the end, don't I?'

Gwen gives me a quizzical look, and I discreetly shake my head, nodding towards Isla. 'Let Mummy eat, and then I'll take you up to bed, OK?'

Gwen makes herself scarce while I eat, and then I put Isla to bed into the small back bedroom in the cottage. Accepting the small glass of red wine Gwen hands me, I tell her what I found under the floorboards.

'What are you going to do?' she asks, her brow crinkled with concern. 'Do you think this is connected to Tom's disappearance? And why didn't he take the money with him if he planned to go?'

'Exactly.' I take a tentative sip of the wine. 'At least now I feel like I have something to go on. I saw the signs for Lockwood Bay in Archmouth . . . I'll go back to Cornwall and actively start searching to see if anyone remembers him there, see if I can find Harriet. Yes, it's another long shot but if it comes off, I'll hopefully be one step closer to tracking him down. And then all this will be over.' And maybe my marriage will be too. 'I won't go alone.' Pulling my phone out, I dial as Gwen frowns at me. 'Adam? I found something.'

CHAPTER 23

The sound of a heavy door being pushed open, creaking on its hinges, and the pinpricks of light forcing their way through the tiny holes in the fabric covering my eyes, pull me from the fitful doze I eventually managed. My heart thumps in my chest and my mouth feels even drier, if that's at all possible. Thirst rages in my dry throat, and I have no idea how long I've been here. Every bit of my body aches, the cold seeping up through the thin fabric of my jeans and soaking into every part of me, a cold so damp and all-consuming that no amount of shivering can quell it.

For a moment, fear renders me speechless, and a surge of panic washes over me. Then, 'Hey.' My voice is a cracked whisper. 'Hey, please. I need water.'

A shuffling movement that is almost impossible to pick out in this dim light, and then a small bottle of water is placed into my desperate hand. I'm still chained to the metal pipe and I have to bend my wrist to accept the drink. The bottle cap is off, cold rivulets running over my wrist and hands, making my throat close with the desperate need to drink. I try and manoeuvre the bottle to my lips, but it's impossible. I want to cry, but no tears come, the thirst an unbearable burning in my throat.

'Please,' I beg, choking on the words. 'Please give me some water.'

A hand takes the bottle and holds it gently to my lips, where I suck greedily, the liquid pouring down my throat like nectar. It spills over my chin, soaking the fabric of my t-shirt, but I don't care, even as the water hitting my stomach makes me feel nauseous. The bottle is taken away and replaced by cool fingers pushing something into my mouth — peaches, fresh peaches sliced into tiny pieces, followed by small chunks of bread. Not a lot, but enough to keep me alive. My captor pushes the bottle back against my lips, and as I drink, a familiar scent fills my nostrils and my nausea intensifies. As realisation dawns, I struggle, twisting my head away and knocking the water bottle away from my mouth, sending icy-cold liquid cascading down my torso.

CHAPTER 24

Waking early the next morning, the enormity of what I've uncovered over the past few days hits me. My husband is missing. Some woman I've never heard of is claiming him, and my daughter, as her own. And I don't even know my husband's real name. He is not the person I thought he was and I don't know how I feel. Realising I might have bitten off more than I can chew, I pick up the photograph and stare hard at the picture of a young Tom, wishing I knew whether I've uncovered all of his secrets. I was so sure I knew him better than anyone else and now I'm left questioning everything. The only thing I am still one hundred per cent certain about is he wouldn't leave our daughter, not without good reason, and this gives me the conviction I need to reassure myself he hasn't just upped and left. Something more sinister is going on and without the aid of the police, I'm the only one who can find him. Rolling over, I inhale the faint scent of Tom, embedded into his pillow. I feel emotionally battered and I'm more than a little apprehensive over what might be waiting for me, or not, in Cornwall. I'm an intelligent woman; I know there's a slim chance Tom *has* left me. But there's a chance he hasn't, and he's in trouble.

An hour later, I'm back on the road to Cornwall, only this time Adam is sitting beside me in the passenger seat, wearing an old Nirvana t-shirt I recognise. It could almost be us ten years ago — he even still wears the same aftershave. He leans forward to pull out a bag of sweets.

'I can't believe you still keep your emergency boiled sweets in the glove box.' He plucks one from the bag and holds it out to me, trying to diffuse the cloud of tension that fills the small space. I'm grateful to him for coming along, but last night's discovery of the photograph and the untouched bundle of money has left me with a heavy weight on my shoulders. Where did the money come from? Has Tom got himself involved in something bigger than he can control? Sneaking a glance at Adam's familiar profile now, I have to fight down the urge to wonder what it would have been like if I'd never left. If I'd have woken up today to a normal day, a normal life.

'I'm sorry, Adam. I know you weren't expecting to spend your week off helping me. Especially after . . . everything.' I pop the sweet into my mouth, relishing the flood of saliva it brings to my dry throat.

'Look, Claire—' Adam twists in the seat to look at me — 'let's get this out of the way. I'm not going to lie to you. You hurt me badly. In fact, I'm going to be honest with you, you broke my heart and it took me a long time to recover. But I'm over you, over us and what we had. I still care for you — of course I do, we spent years of our lives together — but you're with Tom and I've moved on. We grew up together, Claire. We have a history, we have *memories*, that neither of us will ever have with anyone else and because of that, I'll help you. Any time you need me, I'll always be there.' I can feel his gaze searching my face and I briefly tear my eyes from the road, my heart thumping hard against my ribcage. 'I'm here to make sure you don't do anything stupid in Cornwall. To stop you from haring off over things that might not lead anywhere.'

'Thank you. I really do appreciate—'

'Shut up, Claire. I've said my bit. Let's not make this awkward. Let's just get there, OK?' His grin is infectious and I smile back, pressing my foot further to the floor.

Lockwood Bay is exactly what I pictured for Tom when he told me, very occasionally, about where he grew up. Driving carefully through the village that precedes the bay, a tiny place called Morton, I realise it closely matches the description of Archmouth, enough that Tom could get away with describing things and I could be fooled. I follow the winding roads right up to the edge of the bay, where at the top of the cliffs there's a lay-by for parking with only a few cars tucked in off the road, their occupants already on the beach. The weather is wilder down here on the edge of the South West coast, and the heatwave of the previous few days seems to have abated. Grey clouds roll in over our heads and as we leave the car the wind picks up, a sure sign that wetter weather is on the way. My hair tries its best to escape the elastic tie holding it back, and I tut impatiently as the wind whips my fringe into my eyes, Adam pulling his jacket tighter around his body. We make our way cautiously around the car and follow the dirt track leading towards the edge of the cliff, Adam stumbling slightly on the stony path. A surfer jogs lightly past us, wetsuit clinging to his body and surfboard tucked under one arm, and I watch as he starts to descend the cliff following the tiny, narrow dirt track that leads all the way to the bottom.

Fishing the photograph of Tom out of my pocket, I study it carefully, trying to see if there are any clues as to where Jack's Place might be. Adam peers over my shoulder, running his finger lightly over Tom's face, a thoughtful look crossing his features. He looks as though he wants to say something but thinks better of it, and gestures towards the clifftop, where handmade signs litter the road running along the top of the sheer drop, pointing the way to the Beachside Café, Wally's Surf Shop and other businesses that run along the beach. But I don't see one for Jack's Place. Walking towards the next track leading down to the beach, Adam points out a sign for Lockwood Bay Holiday Park.

'Claire — look. There's a holiday park. Maybe someone can tell us how to find Jack's Place. Locals will be working there — surely one of them must know where to find it?'

A spark of hope leaps in my chest and we turn towards it. There must be somebody available at the holiday park — it is nearly the summer holidays, after all. Walking through the tall iron gates, we follow the signs to the reception area, but the place is deserted — no one on reception and no sign of life anywhere, the whole place neglected and run-down, so much so that I'm not even convinced the park is actually open. Not the good start I was hoping for.

'There's no one here, Adam. It's a waste of time.' Frustrated, I make my way back towards the road, hoping we might spot a cleaner or at least one member of staff, when an older couple stroll hand in hand towards the gates.

'Excuse me!' I give them a dazzling smile, turning on the charm. 'You don't know where we can find Jack's Place do you?'

They turn to one another, slightly puzzled, before the woman pushes back the hood on her rain mac to reveal a head of tight grey curls. 'Sorry, we're just here on holiday. We're the only ones in the park by the looks of it, although I shouldn't complain. Did you try asking at reception?'

Disappointed, I thank them and grasp Adam lightly by the arm, ready to turn to leave, before the lady's husband speaks. 'Hang on a minute though, didn't we see a sign?' He scratches thoughtfully at a patch on top of his head where the hair is thinning, as though teasing the memory from his mind. 'Yes, we did, Sharon, don't you remember? If you cross over the road here, back towards the cliff edge, there's one of those dirt tracks that leads down to the beach. I'm sure, about halfway down, there's a rusty old sign that says *Jack's Place* on it, with an arrow pointing down towards the beach. I might be wrong, mind you, it's an old sign and I didn't really look closely at it. Just mind yourselves on that path — you don't want your wife taking a tumble.' He winks at Adam, and Adam glances down at me with a smirk.

Brushing off his comment about being Adam's 'wife', I thank them again, fired up by the idea of a potential lead, and Adam grasps my hand, jogging lightly across the road to the track. No wonder we couldn't see the sign if it's halfway down the path to the beach. It's a twisty, steep track, made up of gravel and dirt, and slippery underfoot. About halfway down, my thighs already burning at the thought of the walk back up, I spot the rusty sign, half hidden by the bushes and weeds growing up the side of the cliff. It does indeed say *Jack's Place*, the sign weathered and pimpled with rust spots, and it points further along the dirt track, down towards the beach. As we make our descent, our feet slipping and sliding on the more treacherous parts of the path, Adam speaks.

'I wonder what it was about Jack's Place that made Tom keep the photo?' He holds out a hand to me as my trainers slide out from under me, the sandy gravel that litters the path making this a particularly dangerous part. I hold onto him for balance, my hand lightly gripping his forearm. 'Or was it nothing to do with Jack's Place at all, maybe it was to do with the mysterious Harriet?'

'I have no idea, to be honest. I didn't even know he had the photo. I thought he'd left everything behind when he left his family home after the row with his mum.' The walk down the steep path has me puffing slightly, whereas Adam doesn't seem to be out of breath in the slightest. 'Whichever it is, it's been enough for him to keep the photo, hidden away where I couldn't find it.' I don't mention the money I found in the box to Adam. Not yet, not until I at least have some idea of where it might have come from. The idea of Tom keeping secrets from me when I thought I knew everything there was to know about him stings like vinegar in a paper cut — sharp and insistent, bringing tears to my eyes.

We walk the rest of the track in silence, the weight of Tom's secrets hanging over me. I don't want to talk about it, don't want to discuss the fact that the man I thought I knew has turned out to be someone completely different. After ten minutes of navigating the winding, gravelly path, we reach the beach, Adam's hand still resting on my arm as we reach the more stable part of the track. I glance down and he follows my gaze, before pulling his hand away and tucking it into the pocket of his shorts. At the bottom of the track, steep steps are carved into the rock face that lead straight down onto dry, golden sand, reminiscent of holidays to Greece or Spain. There's a shop and a surf school next to the rock face, so, slipping off my trainers, I walk towards them, Adam tugging off his own shoes and kicking up a shower of sand as he hurries across the beach to catch me up. The surfer that dashed past us earlier stands outside, his surfboard leaning up the cliff as he polishes it, all his attention focused on the board.

'Excuse me?' I tap him lightly on the shoulder and he spins to face me, blinking as though I've pulled him out of a daydream.

'Hey . . . you after surfing lessons?' He flicks dirty-blond hair out of his eyes, his voice filled with a honey-rich West Country burr.

'No, afraid not. Sorry. I'm looking for Jack's Place. The sign further up the track said it was down here on the beach.' I surreptitiously brush at the sand that has flicked up onto the backs of my legs, making my skin itch.

'Jack's Place?' He gives me a puzzled look before flicking his eyes over Adam, who gives him a cool stare in return. 'What do you want with Jack's Place?'

'I . . . I'm looking for an old friend, actually.' I wonder for a moment if this boy could help, before shaking the idea away. The kid looks as though he might have been five or six when Tom left, he'd never remember him.

'Right.' Catching Adam's hard stare, he shrugs and turns back to his board. 'It's up there, past the old boiler. It's on the only part of the beach that doesn't disappear at high tide. You can't miss it.'

I nod my thanks to him before he gets completely engrossed in his board again, and we follow the beach around the edge of the cliff face. My feet sink into the soft, dry sand, making my calves ache, and I move further down the beach onto the firmer, damp sand, the waves washing perilously close to my feet. We need to round two points of rocks before reaching Jack's Place, as it looks as though it's tucked into the cliff further along the beach. Taking the hand Adam holds out, I let him help me clamber over the slippery, seaweed-drenched rocks, my trainers swinging by the laces around my neck.

'I hope this is worth it,' Adam says, as my feet slide out from under me completely and I land with a slight thud. I ignore his helping hand and haul myself to my feet, brushing the damp sand from my shorts.

'It will. It has to be. Let's face it, it's the only lead we have.' Gingerly, I lift a foot to step onto the next round of rocks that jut out into the water, greener and more slippery than the last rocky outcrop.

'Just—' Adam grabs at my shirtsleeve to stop me — 'don't be disappointed if you don't find what you're hoping for, that's all.' He searches my face, his green eyes meeting mine in a firm look.

Impatiently, I tug my sleeve out of his hand. 'I won't. Come on, the sooner we get there, the sooner we find Tom.' I climb up on the rocks and start to make my way across, checking behind me every so often to make sure Adam is following.

Passing a rusty old ship's boiler that has found itself shipwrecked and abandoned on the shore of the bay, I know we must be nearly there. Clearing the wall of seaweed-covered rocks jutting out towards the sea, I catch my first glimpse of Jack's Place and my heart sinks.

Where Jack's Place once stood is a dilapidated, charred ruin. What was a sturdy wooden porch that must have held tables and chairs is a black hole, shards of metal and wood sticking up dangerously in places, just waiting to pierce skin. The roof has collapsed in on itself and the only thing that seems to have escaped unscathed is a metal sign, the paint worn and peeling. It's screwed into the rock face, *Jack's Place* painted in red on a white background, still just about legible.

'Oh, Claire.' Adam's voice is low as he takes my hand, linking our fingers in an old, familiar gesture. 'I don't know what to say.' I stare ahead unblinking at the devastating view of what was my only lead in finding Tom.

'Sorry, Miss.' A hand lands on my shoulder and I turn to see the young surfer behind me. 'I didn't think. I probably should have told you the place burned down.'

Dropping Adam's hand, I blink back tears of disappointment as another dead end smacks me in the face. I'm starting to feel as though Tom has disappeared off the face of the earth, never to be seen again. Every avenue that I pursue to try and trace him, or Lydia French, blows up in my face.

'No problem. It's fine . . . it's just . . . it's fine.' My throat swollen with unshed tears, I pat him clumsily on the shoulder and turn to make my way back up the beach.

'Claire — wait!' Adam shouts to me and I stop, having almost forgotten he was here. 'Are you OK?' His brow is furrowed, his hair whipping around his head in the sharp breeze rolling in off the sea.

'To be honest, Adam, I don't know. How can everywhere I turn end up being a complete dead end?' I swallow hard, blinking back the tears that sting my eyes. 'How can he just disappear off the face of the earth?' Kicking at the sand in frustration, I march past the wide-eyed surfer, back up the beach towards the track that leads back to the road. Adam runs round and plants himself in front of me, reaching out to grip me by my upper arms.

'He hasn't — listen to me, Claire.' Adam stares into my eyes. 'He hasn't disappeared off the face of the earth, we're just not looking in the right places.'

I shake my head at him, marvelling at his will to try and find a man he probably despises. Searching for my husband, despite the way Adam and I parted, despite the way I treated him. Maybe everything that's happening to me now is all I deserve.

CHAPTER 25

Once back at the car, the rain that has been threatening all day starts to hammer down, bouncing off the roof and the windscreen, the wind whipping along the coastline and rocking the car slightly with its force. The sense I'm being thwarted at every turn, and not just by the weather, is huge and I lean my head against the headrest and close my eyes, at a loss as to where to go next. The passenger door opens and I turn to Adam as he slides into the passenger seat, his hair a mess from the rain lashing down outside.

'Sorry, Adam. I've dragged you all this way for nothing.' I want to cry with frustration but pride won't let me. Adam combs his hair back with his fingers and gives me a reassuring smile.

'It's fine, Claire. I told you, I'm happy to help.' He pauses for a moment. 'I know you're getting desperate. I'm here, and I said I'd help you, so don't apologise. You've nothing to apologise for.' The atmosphere in the car thickens slightly and Adam holds my gaze for a moment before looking away, peering out of the car window at the stormy weather outside. I'm not sure how to respond, so I don't say anything.

'Come on.' He turns back to me, his cheeks a rosy pink in the warmth of the car. 'Let's find somewhere to get something to eat and then we'll decide what we're going to do next. It's too late to think about driving back tonight — let's see if we can find somewhere with rooms that does food.' The atmosphere lightens, the tension trickling away, and I give a brisk nod before starting the car, ready to leave behind yet another closed avenue.

* * *

We drive back to Morton, a sleepy village with not a lot going on. There's only one hotel and it's a little run-down, much like the holiday park, but it'll have to do for the night as I'm too exhausted to face driving back to Easthampton this evening and I feel the need for a strong drink. We stagger in, windswept and tired, and the manager politely asks if we require a double room.

'Two singles, please. If you have them.' Adam's voice is smooth as he lowers both of our overnight bags to the floor. Thankfully they have two rooms available and, avoiding any potential awkwardness, we head up to the rooms through the bar, agreeing to meet back downstairs once we've freshened up. Sparsely decorated, with peeling wallpaper and a small, grubby window, the hotel room won't win any prizes but I'm past caring. I strip off and take a long hot shower, rinsing away the sand and disappointment that comes from running into another dead end, before pulling my clothes back on and heading back down to the bar. Maybe somebody there can tell me what happened to Jack's Place, or might even remember Tom.

The bar isn't busy when I arrive and Adam sits alone on a stool, a pint of pale ale in his hand. I'm expecting him to be watching the people around him in the mirror behind the bar, an old trick he's always used, telling me he liked to see what people did when they didn't know they were being observed, but he's tapping away on his phone, pausing momentarily to sip at his beer. I smile a little at that memory, realising he doesn't know he's being observed by me, or by the woman sitting in the booth by the lit open fire. I walk towards him and as I approach he swings round to greet me.

'You *did* see me in the mirror, didn't you?' I ask. The smell of his aftershave is familiar, yet not.

'Of course I did. I was a pro at that even before I became a copper. I got you a glass of sauvignon.' He hands me the cold glass, condensation running down and soaking my fingers. Moving to a table at the back of the bar, we order food, a miserable-looking woman slamming the plates down on the table ungraciously.

'So, I was thinking . . .' Adam takes a bite of his steak burger, washing it down with a slug of beer. 'The next step, logically, has to be this village, right? The photograph was taken here, at Jack's, so there's a chance someone here will remember him, especially if you think this is where he grew up.'

'I guess so. I mean, I don't know where else we can go. Jack's Place was the only lead we had — and the girl in the photo, this Harriet. The way she was looking at Tom in the picture . . . she adored him. Tom meant something to her. But I've no idea where to start looking for Harriet, if Jack's Place isn't here anymore.'

'So, let's try asking around. We've got the photo — we can show that around, see if anybody recognises either one of them. It can't hurt, and someone might be able to give us some sort of idea of how Tom came across Lydia French, if that's even her real name.' Adam's words cause my stomach to give a sickening lurch.

'What do you mean?' I push my Caesar salad aside and lay down my knife and fork, appetite gone now. It had crossed my mind, especially after finding out that Tom wasn't Tom's real name, but the idea of Lydia French not being Lydia French is a terrifying one — then I really wouldn't have any kind of lead.

'I just mean . . . maybe that's not her real name. Maybe she's relying on using a false name to trick Tom. Maybe she's got nothing to do with it all. Maybe he's left you. I don't know, Claire, I'm just throwing things out there. I'm a police officer — it's what I do. Throw stuff out there until I find something to go on.' He sips at his beer again, his eyes never leaving my face.

'OK, I get it. But I have to take this at face value, Adam, for now at least. I don't think I can cope with the idea that she's not who she says she is either. Then where do I go?' Panic threatens to grab me by the throat again — panic and desperation. Sensing it, Adam grasps my hand across the table, holding it tightly.

'Listen, I'm just talking. It doesn't mean anything, don't freak out. We will find Tom. It's my job to find people.' I nod slowly, wanting to believe him. 'Trust me.'

We finish our meal together, me forcing down my salad despite the stone lodged in my stomach, and before long Adam glances at his watch.

'Claire, I don't know about you but I'm exhausted. I'm going to go up to the room and do a bit of scouting around online, see if I can find anything in the local newspaper archives that might give us anything to go on, before I hit the sack. Hopefully I can find something, somewhere, that might give us an idea where to start. Are you coming up?'

Wearily, I shake my head. I'm tired to my bones, but I know I won't sleep, not yet anyway.

'I'm going to stay down here for a bit — maybe speak to some of the locals if I get a chance, see if they know who Harriet is.' Adam nods, before heading through the bar to the back stairs that lead to the rooms above.

Without Adam sitting next to me, the locals eye me with suspicion, and no one makes any attempt to engage me in conversation. Moving back to the bar, I keep an ear out to see if anyone mentions Jack and I ask the barmaid if she knows him, but she's either ignoring me or she's so busy she hasn't heard me. By ten o'clock my head is aching, the acidic taste of the dry wine dragging me down into melancholy. Jolted out of a boozy daydream, in which I have found Tom and Isla enjoying the surf on the beach, Tom unaware that I have spent the last three days looking for him, I turn to the man who has plonked himself down on the bar stool next to me.

'Hey.' He gives me a quick smile and gestures to the barmaid. 'Pint of your finest, please, Bella. And whatever this pretty lady is having.' He winks at me and I try to roll my eyes but they don't seem to want to do as they're told.

'I'm married,' I say, holding up my hand as I squint at him.

'No worries,' he says with a laugh. 'I wasn't trying it on, you just looked as though you could do with one for the road, that's all.' He, too, has that West Country lilt to his voice, and I wonder how long it took Tom to iron it out of his voice completely. He doesn't even have that slight Hampshire twang that I have, just a bland, generic southern accent.

'I'm looking for my husband, actually.' I raise my glass to him, all earlier inhibitions gone, feeling a sense of relief that at least one of the locals isn't giving me the evil eye.

'Really? I'm forever trying to lose my wife.' He gives a little chuckle.

'He's missing. He's been gone for four days.' *Four days, fourteen hours and twelve minutes, to be exact.* 'He left the house as usual on Tuesday, and I haven't seen him since. The police don't want to know. They think he's left me, but I know he hasn't. Something's happened to him, something that's stopping him from coming home.' My tongue loosened by alcohol, I take another large sip of lukewarm wine.

'I'm sorry to hear that.' My new friend eyes me closely, clearly not sure whether I'm serious or just some drunken madwoman, and takes a sip of his beer. 'You're not from round here though, are you? So, what are you doing here? Do you think he's here?'

'I don't know. I don't even know what I'm doing. I don't know where he is, or even *who* he is anymore. I thought I could find him but it's all just a . . . bloody mess.' I push the glass of wine away from me and signal for a glass of water from the barmaid. 'Here, look at this.' I pull the photograph from my pocket, turning it over so he can read the scrawled writing. 'It says here, *Jack's Place*. That's where he was. Only, it's bloody burned down, can you believe it?'

'Jack's Place? Yeah, I know it. Down past the surf place on the beach?'

I nod, sipping carefully at the water the barmaid has put in front of me, resisting the urge to gulp it. I'm starting to feel better now I've stopped knocking back the wine, the swirling, sickly feeling in my stomach muting itself to just a mild nausea.

'It burned down, God, must be ten years ago now. Everyone said Jack did it deliberately because Esther walked out on him. Esther was his wife, you know. She left him and six weeks later the bar burned to the ground. I don't think he did it on purpose though, I think he was devastated by her leaving and got pissed. He was drinking a lot by then. He's still down there though, if you wanted to speak to him.'

At first, I think I've misheard him, but he repeats it and my heart starts to beat a little faster. Maybe there is still something to come of this; maybe I can still find Tom.

'He's still down there?'

'Yes. My boy, Bailey, runs the surf shop. He sometimes takes him a lunch when he's not busy teaching.' The surfer. He must be my new friend's son. Shame he didn't tell us Jack was still around six hours ago. 'Jack runs a small fishing charter now from the pier on the next beach over. If you get there early in the morning you should be able to catch him.'

Elated, I buy the gentleman a drink and head straight up to my room to sleep off the effects of the wine. Hopefully tomorrow, I'll find out exactly who Tom really is, and why he's lied to me about his past.

CHAPTER 26

After a fitful night's sleep, I wake early, thirsty and with a dull headache squeezing vice-like at my temples for the second morning this week. Unused to drinking this much, the hangover is fierce and I gulp down the glass of water that tipsy me remembered to leave on the bedside table last night. Necking two paracetamol, I stand under a shower of the coldest water I can bear, pull my clothes on and tiptoe past the other doors until I reach Adam's room. Knocking lightly but insistently, I whisper through the door.

'Adam! Adam, it's me.' There's a rustling, then the door is yanked open and I'm faced with a rumpled, tired-looking Adam, hair flat on one side and pillow creases on his cheek.

'Bloody hell, Claire, what time is it?'

'Quarter to six. Listen, I was talking to a guy last night in the pub after you left. He said Jack's still here. He's on the next beach round, on the pier. I'm going there now — are you coming?'

Stifling a yawn, Adam tugs the door open and gestures to the bed. 'Sit there. I'm going for a shower. And feel free to make some coffee.'

Ten minutes later, Adam emerges from the bathroom looking — and smelling — much fresher. He grumbles under his breath as I hand him a coffee, only giving me a smile once he's taken a large sip. I remember now how he really isn't a morning person. 'Now I'm actually with it, tell me what this guy said.'

As I update him on what my new friend told me, he raises his eyebrows, his interest piqued. Once he's downed his coffee, he follows me out to the car, just as eager as I am to get to the beach and finally meet Jack.

The morning air is brisk and cool, the sky blue but with a misty haze hanging over the sea that will hopefully burn off before long. It's going to be a beautiful day, and the thought pops into my head that Tom and Isla would love it here, before I angrily shake it off. Of course Tom would love it here — he obviously spent time here at some point in his life, and it was important enough for him to keep a photograph stashed away as a souvenir. Adam is silent in the passenger seat, perhaps not quite as awake as I first thought, as I drive slightly too fast through the village, anxious to reach Jack before he heads out in his fishing boat. Passing the lay-by that I pulled into yesterday at Lockwood Bay, I follow the curve of the road round to the next bay and find a small car park. It's a short walk from there down to the beach, past small pastel-coloured houses packed tightly together, all quirky and slightly uneven. Reaching the bay, I pause for a moment and take it all in, sucking in a deep breath of briny sea air.

'Are you OK?' Adam stops alongside me, his hands shoved deep into his jacket pockets. I nod, unable to speak for a moment. This tiny beach, in a tucked away corner of England that I've never considered visiting before, is potentially where my life as I know it unravels completely.

Stepping onto the slightly gravelly sand, we make our way towards the far end of the beach where a small jetty runs out into the sea. This bay is a lot smaller than Lockwood, the sand less fine, and it's enclosed on both sides by a towering rock face, giving it a slightly sinister feel in the early-morning gloom. The mist still hangs over the water at this early hour, creeping its way up towards the shoreline with eerie white fingers, and I shiver slightly as the damp seeps into my bones, the warmth of the summer sun yet to filter though. There is a man on the jetty, fiddling with a rope attached to a small fishing vessel, if it can even be called that. The boat is tiny, barely even able to sit six people, and it isn't in the best state of repair. Cautiously, I make my way across the shingly sand, Adam hanging back behind me, not wanting to startle Jack, if this is indeed him. As my foot hits the wooden jetty he turns and I see an older man, in his sixties maybe, with a thick beard, the face around it tanned and weathered, a lived-in face. Dark, knowing eyes peer out from under bushy eyebrows that match the facial hair below. Eyes that have seen a lot. With his beard, tattered jumper and oilskin trousers, his white hair blowing about his head in the chill sea breeze, he looks the epitome of an old sea dog, even though I know he managed a bar for all those years. He scowls at me as my feet slip slightly on the damp wooden jetty boards and I paste a nervous smile onto my face.

'Good morning... are you Jack?' The jetty rocks slightly under my feet with the movement of the waves below and I feel the warmth of Adam as he comes to stand behind me. Tossing a thick coil of rope over his shoulder like it's nothing, the man turns to face the boat before throwing it onto the deck.

'Who wants to know?' His voice is gruff, unfriendly, and I start to think that perhaps I've made a mistake, maybe this is another dead end. Thinking of Tom, who has possibly got himself into something he shouldn't have done, I straighten my shoulders and fix my eyes on his back, refusing to give in to his hostility despite the crashing of my pulse in my ears.

'Me,' I say quietly, before clearing my throat and raising my voice over the call of the gulls overhead. 'I want to know. Are you Jack? Because if you're not, I'd really like to know where I can find him.' I stare at his back, trying to mask my impatience and the nerves that flutter through my veins. He slowly turns to face me, a matchstick now hanging from the corner of his mouth, poking out from his grizzly, grey beard.

'I'm Jack. Now, who are you?' Finally, a break. Glancing at Adam, relief makes me wobbly, a cautious smile plucking at the corners of my mouth.

'You're Jack? The Jack who owns Jack's Place?'

'*Owned*, Miss. Have you seen the place recently?' Jack switches the matchstick from one corner of his mouth to the other, his gaze hard and steely. 'And I'm still waiting for you to tell me who you are.'

'Claire. Claire Bennett.' I lean forward and extend a hand to him. He eyes it cautiously before he grasps it in his large, callused hand, the nails blackened with grime, and shakes it in a firm grip.

'Well, Claire Bennett, nice to meet you, although that still doesn't tell me who you are and why you're looking for me.' He drops my hand and looks at me expectantly, the matchstick wiggling at the corner of his mouth as he speaks.

'I'm looking for someone. Apart from you, I mean.' His scrutiny has me flustered and I start again. 'What I mean is . . . I'm looking for someone, and I think maybe you can help me, if you don't mind?' I dig in my pocket for the increasingly battered photograph of Tom and the elusive Harriet. Smoothing out the creases, I hold out the photo and after a tiny pause, Jack takes it, squinting slightly as he holds it up to his face.

'Where did you get this, eh?' He eyes me closely for a moment, before going back to the photo, peering at it intently.

'It belongs to my husband.' Pausing for a moment, I take a deep breath. 'He's the one I'm looking for.'

'Oh yeah? Left you, has he?' Jack looks closely at the photograph again, a small frown drawing his thick brows together, the mist that has crept along the jetty leaving tiny droplets of moisture in his hair. I raise my hands to my own head, smoothing my hair down, my hands coming away damp. 'And if he's your husband, who's your boyfriend?' He gestures at

Adam, standing silently behind me. At his words, Adam steps forward, a welcoming smile on his face.

'Hello, Jack. My name's Adam. I'm a friend of Claire's, that's all. I'm helping her look for Tom.' He holds out a hand for Jack to shake and he ignores it, instead turning back to me.

'Sure your husband didn't leave you?'

'Yes, I'm sure he hasn't left me.' Frustrated, I try to get Jack back on track. 'It's a long story, but I found that photograph among his things, and I wanted to see if I could find the other girl, see if she's had any contact recently with Tom. She might know something about where Tom is, or . . .' I stop for a moment, not sure how much I should divulge. 'She might know something, that's all.'

'Yer looking for Harriet?' Jack pulls the matchstick out of his mouth and snaps it in half before tossing it through the gaps in the boards of the jetty to the rumbling waves below.

'You know Harriet?' A spark of excitement ignites low in my belly and I feel Adam start beside me — it looks as though, finally, we're getting somewhere. Jack gives a little laugh, growly and deep in his throat.

'Ha. Everyone knows Harriet, you didn't need to come and find me if you were just after finding Harriet.'

'Sorry — it's just . . . the photo, on the back . . .' Gently, I take it from him and flip it over. 'See? The writing says Jack's Place. I wasn't sure if it was the place or the person that was the most important thing to Tom, and I figured it would be easier to find someone who knew the place, than someone who might know Harriet.' Jack raises a bushy eyebrow at me and takes the photo back for one last look. 'That's Tom there, beside Harriet. Do you recognise him?'

'This was a long time ago,' he says softly, fiddling in his pocket and pulling out a box of matches. He takes one, and slides it between his teeth before putting the box back in his pocket.

'So, you remember it — the photo being taken? You remember Tom, my husband?' I search his face for any sign that he might know something, *anything*. He looks at me sharply and hands the photograph back without another glance, before wiping his filthy fingers on his oilskin trousers. I see the oily prints at the edge of the picture where Jack has held it, reflecting on the shiny surface of the photo, and fight the urge to smooth the grease away on my own shorts.

'I don't remember a lot about that time, if I'm honest.' Any hint of a friendly demeanour has vanished and he's back to being brusque and standoffish. I remember the man in the bar last night, a dim boozy memory of him telling me that Jack's wife left him and Jack drowned his sorrows in a bottle of something strong. Taking care not to crease the photo, I tuck it back into my back pocket, guiding Jack back towards the reason I'm here.

'So . . . Harriet? Do you know where I can find her? Does she still live locally?'

Jack ignores me, seemingly intent on doing something with the boat again, and keeps his back turned to me. I sigh in frustration and try again, pulling my hands through my damp hair.

'I'm sorry, Jack, but Harriet . . . do you know where I can find her? I really do need to speak to her, if I'm going to find out what has happened to Tom.'

He turns back to me, and there is the glisten of tears in his eyes. Ashamed I was so abrupt with him, I give a small smile and wait, hating the thought that I've upset him somehow.

'It was all a long time ago, Missy. Are you sure you want to start raking things up? I don't want Harriet being upset. She's a good girl.' I open my mouth to say that would never be my intention — I don't want to upset anyone, I just want to find Tom — but he interrupts me, his voice gruff.

'She's my daughter-in-law. Harriet, I mean. She comes over to the beach and brings me a meal every evening. If you want to see her, come down here to the jetty this evening at six o'clock. I'll be back by then and she'll be here to give me my dinner. You can only speak to her if she wants to talk to you, mind. I told you, I don't want you upsetting her.'

'Thank you — thank you, Jack. I really do appreciate all your help.' I grasp his hand in mine, not bothered about the oil that sits under his nails this time, and give it a firm shake. 'I'll be back here at 6 p.m. sharp. Oh, and Jack?' Before I leave one more thought occurs to me. 'Do you know someone called Lydia French?' He shakes his head and without a word boards the small fishing boat, unties it from the mooring and sets about getting ready to travel the water. I watch as he negotiates the cross of the waves, the boat rising and falling in a hypnotic rhythm until he's just a tiny speck in the distance.

We spend the rest of the morning wandering the bays and the village of Morton, and I'm unable to settle to anything, the idea that I might actually have some answers by this evening making me restless, fidgety, my concentration span at an all-time low, even after I call and check in on Gwen and Isla. I wonder about the connection between Tom and Harriet. *Friends? Family?* They both look too young for them to have been in a relationship. And where does Lydia French fit, if she even fits at all? Finally, Adam asks me to drop him in the next town so he can find an internet café, or at the very least a coffee shop with reasonable Wi-Fi access, so he can continue his search of the newspaper archives.

I wander the streets, Jack's words about raking up the past weighing heavy on my mind, the day dragging out interminably, thick and slow like pouring treacle. The mist burns off after a few hours and the rain and high winds of the previous day are a faint memory by lunchtime as the sun returns with force, the weather seemingly as changeable as the people who live here. I visit Lockwood Bay again, standing at the top of the cliff, the warm sea breeze raking through my hair. I stand in what I think is the precise spot where Tom and Harriet must have stood to have their photograph taken by an unknown someone, the same thought beating endlessly on a loop in my mind. The idea that I am standing in all of the places Tom must have stood, seeing all the things he must have seen when he was living the truth. Back before his whole life became a lie.

CHAPTER 27

Six o'clock can't come around quickly enough. Visiting all the places Tom might have been has left me with a strange sense of longing as I explore, wishing he could have felt able to share this with me. Battling my confusion over why he felt the need to keep Cornwall such an enormous secret, I head back to the hotel room to freshen up before I meet Adam in the hotel bar. I take my time as I get ready, running the straighteners over my hair, and pulling my make-up from my small overnight bag. There is some part of me, as I lean in towards the small bathroom mirror, eyes wide as I apply three layers of mascara, that wants to look my best when I meet Harriet, a woman so important to Tom that he's kept her photograph hidden for over twenty years. *Tom could be with her now*, I think, my hand shaking slightly as I run a lipstick over my mouth and press my lips together. Eyeing myself carefully in the mirror I swallow down the fear that licks at the fringes of my mind. I know part of me is out to impress Harriet, but another part of me is out to remind Tom — if indeed he is with Harriet — of what he has waiting for him at home.

Satisfied this is the best I can do with what I have, I blot my lips on a piece of tissue and reach out to check Tom's phone, making sure there's enough battery life on it. There are no more messages. Gwen has left a voicemail on my phone while I was in the shower, checking to see if I'm OK. She tells me Isla is fine, and I glance at my watch. There isn't enough time to call her back now, and I stuff the phone into the pocket of my jeans. Thinking about Isla brings back the feelings of guilt and culpability that swamped me after I confessed to entering the photo into the competition — if I had just respected Tom's wishes and kept the photo to myself, there's every chance we wouldn't be in this position now. If I hadn't submitted it to the cruise line, perhaps Lydia French wouldn't have seen it, and would never have been able to use it to track Tom down. *If she's even involved with this*, that little voice whispers at the back of my mind. The little voice that likes to remind me that I never really knew Tom the way I thought I did.

I realise now, thinking back to that holiday, the reason why Tom must have been so tense before we left. We had never had a holiday abroad together before, and the question of Tom's identity has to be the reason for that. He must have been terrified, having to use a passport that, even though it bore his photo, was not in his real name. And if he has been hiding from something in his past, something he didn't want to catch up with him, then of course he wouldn't have wanted his photo plastered all over the place. If Lydia French — or someone even worse — does have something to do with all of this, then I've led her straight to him.

Swallowing down all thoughts of my disastrous decision making, I grab my sweater from the end of the bed and head downstairs to meet Adam. He's waiting for me at the bar, just like last night, in battered Levis and a shirt I bought him ten years ago, and I feel a disconcerting rush of déjà vu. He turns, smiling as he sees me.

'Ready to go and meet Harriet?'

'I think so. God, Adam, I feel ridiculously nervous. What if she doesn't know anything? What if she *does*?'

'Relax.' Adam shrugs on his jacket — also a relic of our time together — and places his hand on the small of my back as he guides me through the busy bar and out to the car. 'It'll be OK. This is the only lead we have, remember? We need Harriet to give us some answers.' Nodding, I step back, double-checking I have Tom's photo tucked safely into my back pocket.

We pull into the tiny car park a little before six, and although Adam makes noises about waiting until Harriet arrives, I already have my seatbelt unclipped before he's finished speaking. Butterflies make a mess of my stomach as we leave the car and walk the short distance to the far end of the beach, where the jetty juts proudly out into the sea. Jack's boat is back in, tied up tightly against the mooring, but there's no sign of either him or Harriet. My heart sinks and I start to think maybe Jack has no intention of introducing me to Harriet, maybe he wants to keep Tom's secrets for him.

'It doesn't look as though they're here, Claire.' Adam turns in a circle, his hand shielding his eyes from the sun as it makes its way down the horizon. 'I hope we didn't miss them.'

'Jack said six o'clock, and it's not quite that yet.'

'Hang on.' Adam holds up a hand. 'Can you hear that?' Following Adam back along the wooden planks of the jetty towards the shingle, I hear the rise and fall of voices, and I realise that to the right, behind the rocks protruding out towards the sea, the top of a beach hut is just about visible. Gesturing to Adam to follow me, I begin to climb carefully over the rocks. The tide is coming in and the waves lap gently at the seaweed that clings tightly to them, forcing me to climb over if I don't want to get wet feet. On the other side of the jagged cliff, the beach hut sits nestled against the rock face, just about escaping the high tide line of a twisting rope of dark seaweed. It's more than your average sort of beach hut — in fact, it's not dissimilar to how I imagine Jack's Place to have been before it was ravaged by flames. Painted a vivid yellow with a white trim, a veranda winds its way round the front and sides, big enough for a small table and chairs to sit on. This is where the voices are coming from, and I clear my throat as we approach in the hope that the two people talking urgently in low voices will notice our arrival.

'Claire. And you've brought your friend.' Jack raises a hand from where he sits in a low chair, matchstick in his mouth, his grey hair wild and frizzy from his time spent at sea today. The woman on the veranda turns from where she leans over him and I stumble slightly as I make my way up the sandy steps to the porch, sure for a moment that I know her. There's something in the way she holds a hand up to shield her eyes from the sun that's so familiar I feel a sharp pang deep in my gut, and then it's gone. The woman is younger than Tom, maybe thirty-two or thirty-three, with a body made of soft, rounded curves. Her hair is long curls, dark and tangled by the sea breeze, and when she meets my gaze full on there's no mistaking who she is. This is Harriet.

'These are the ones I was telling you about, Harriet. These two that came snooping around earlier.' Jack's voice is gruff and she puts out a hand to gently shush him.

'Claire?' Harriet walks across the veranda towards me, her long skirt wrapping around her legs in the mild breeze floating in from the sea, carrying the scent of fish and salt. I smile weakly at her and hold out a hand. It all feels slightly unreal — that just a few days ago I was at home with Tom and Isla, with no idea Tom wasn't who he said he was, and now I'm here after so many dead ends, about to meet someone who knew Tom before, who knew Tom at a time that he doesn't ever talk about.

'Hi. You must be Harriet?'

'Yes, that's me.' Harriet flicks her hair away from her full mouth and gives me a smile, showing even, white teeth. 'I hear you've been looking for me.' She runs her gaze over Adam's face, curiosity burning behind her eyes.

'Well, you and Jack, really. This is my friend, Adam. He's helping me out.'

Adam holds out a hand for Harriet to shake, before Harriet turns to Jack and mouths something at him. He nods, and then she turns back to us.

'Come on, Jack's sorted here for a bit, he's got his dinner and that'll keep him quiet for a time. Walk down onto the beach with me and we can have a chat. You can tell me why you're really here.' She gives me a little sideways glance, evoking an eerie sense of déjà vu, a stirring of a faint memory somewhere, and then she jogs lightly down the porch steps onto the sand. I follow her, aware of my heart hammering in my chest. Adam comes alongside me and gives my hand a quick squeeze, the pressure of his palm against mine reassuring and solid. I'm nervous now I've found Harriet, scared of what she'll reveal to me about the man I've spent the last eight years of my life with, and at the same time worried in case she can't tell me anything and this turns out to be yet another dead end. We walk a little way along the beach, away from Jack's keen ears, before she leads the two of us to a small outcrop of rocks and sits down, avoiding the clumps of seaweed clinging tightly to the stone as she tucks her skirt under her legs. She taps a flat rock next to her and gestures for me to sit.

Adam stands uncertainly. 'Should I leave you two alone for this? I don't want to intrude.'

'No, Adam, don't leave. Is that OK with you, Harriet? I mean, anything you have to say you can say in front of Adam.' I don't want Adam to go — if I'm about to hear something truly awful about my husband, I'm not sure I can handle it alone.

'Up to you, Claire.' Harriet glances at me before smiling up at Adam. 'I don't mind — but then, I still don't really know what you want. Come on, then. Why are you here? Jack was rambling on about something, but he does tend to get a bit confused sometimes, I couldn't make out half of what he was on about. The only thing he was clear on was that you've been looking for me.' Her voice also has that rich West Country rumble to it, like warm butter oozing out from a fresh bread roll, the same as Bailey's, the surfer on the beach.

I wonder again whether this was how Tom used to talk, in his old life, before for whatever reason he reinvented himself as someone else. Adam remains standing as I perch on the edge of the rock, wary of the green, moss-like seaweed clinging to parts of it, making it slippery. Tugging out the photograph, I smooth it flat and pass it over to Harriet. Her face crumples as she takes in the sight of the two teenagers, arms slung casually around each other.

'Oh my God,' she says, her hand pressed to her mouth. She looks at me, tears pooling in her eyes. 'That's Theo.'

CHAPTER 28

Theo. I whisper the name softly to myself, rolling it around on my tongue, unsure as to whether I enjoy the taste of this foreign name on my lips. Tom's name is Theo. It's not the name I would have given him — Theo is exotic, rebellious, a rule breaker. Tom is the polar opposite, steady and dependable, quiet and reserved, always considering what other people think of him. He doesn't drink or raise his voice, and has never even had a parking ticket. I never would have thought Tom could have been a Theo. Equally, Adam obviously didn't either, shock widening his eyes when Harriet calls Tom by that name. A hand on my arm jolts me out of my thoughts and I realise Harriet is talking to me.

'I'm sorry, I was miles away.' I shake my head, feeling disorientated, as if I've been tumbled in the waves that crash against the end of the jetty. 'So, you do know him, the boy in the photograph?'

Harriet gives me a strange look before she speaks, repeatedly glancing down at the picture, which is clutched tightly in her hand as if she's terrified it's going to blow away. 'It's been such a long time, *years*. Do you know where Theo is? Have you seen him?' Her voice is slightly raised and two spots of colour blaze high on her cheeks, her eyes sweeping over my face as if searching for clues. It's my turn to lay a hand on Harriet's arm, as what I'm going to tell her is only going to disappoint her. Adam sees Harriet's distress and swiftly steps in, his calm, soothing voice one he must have perfected over his years in the force.

'We don't know where he is, Harriet. That's what we wanted to ask you — that's *why* Claire was looking for you. To see if you knew where Tom — *Theo* — might be. I'm sorry if we got your hopes up, we didn't mean to disappoint you.'

'I don't understand. Jack said you were looking for me, that you wanted to speak to me about Theo?' Her brow creases in confusion as she looks from me, to Adam, and back again. Jack, the old dog, must have known exactly who Tom was when I showed him the photo; he was just playing his cards close to his chest. Clearly, he didn't want to tell me anything, presumably unsure if he could trust me, especially as I referred to the boy he knew as Theo as Tom. I remember Tom telling me how people where he grew up were suspicious, distrustful of strangers, never willing to give anything away.

'I don't know how to tell you this.' I feel Harriet's pain as keenly as my own, and it's hard to say the words out loud. 'He's missing, Harriet. I'm his wife; we've been married for eight years. He left for work as usual on Tuesday, but he never arrived and there's been no word from him since — he hasn't even called to check on our daughter. I need to find him, anything you can tell me will help.' Looking down, I find I'm squeezing Harriet's hand for dear life and let go abruptly. 'Adam is an old friend of mine who's helping me track Tom down. He's a police officer. Anything, *anything at all*, that you can tell us might help.'

'Theo has a daughter? He's married?' Harriet's eyes are wide, her breathing hitching as if unable to process the information I've given her so far. I feel a flicker of fear, a ball of tension that winds its way around my heart as I realise I still don't know what relationship Tom had with Harriet. 'He's *missing*?'

'Look, Harriet, there's a lot I need to tell you. Is there somewhere a bit more comfortable we can talk?' The sharp corners of the limpets clinging to the rocks are digging into the backs of my thighs as we sit.

'We can go to my house. It's only a short walk from here and then you can tell me everything. I haven't seen or spoken to Theo since 2008.' Tears fill her eyes again and Adam pulls her to her feet, placing his arm gently around Harriet's shoulders. As I follow them both back up the beach towards the road, Jack watches us leave from his porch, tipping his hand towards me in a small salute.

* * *

Harriet's place is one of the small, tucked-together houses that Adam and I passed on the way down to the beach earlier this morning. Painted a light pastel blue on the outside, inside it is higgledy-piggledy, the rooms cosy and full of ornaments and knick-knacks that she's picked up over the years, with piles of books teetering in the corners. She leads the two of us through the hall into the kitchen, a larger area that doubles up as a dining room with enough space for a sofa at one end. It's warm and the early evening sun casts pink and gold streaks across the walls. She gestures to the table for us to sit and fills the kettle. Once the tea is made, she takes a seat opposite me, a determined look on her face, as Adam walks about the room, peering at the photographs that litter the mantelpiece.

'Right, Claire. Tell me about Theo. I want to know everything — I feel like I've missed so much already.'

'Well . . . we live in Hampshire, in a small village. We've been married for eight years and our daughter, Isla, is seven.'

'*Isla*. That's a pretty name. And married! I could never picture Theo being married. Is he happy, Claire?'

'I thought so, yes. No, I *do* think he's happy — the thing is, I don't think he's left me of his own accord, Harriet. Things have happened that point to him not coming home because he can't, not because he doesn't want to, and he wouldn't leave Isla like that, not without talking to me. The police don't want to get involved — they think he's left me. That's why Adam's here. He's a police officer, but he's also a friend. We go back a long way and he's offered to help track To— I mean Theo down, in a non-official capacity. But we're kind of at a dead end. Every lead just ends up going nowhere, until now . . . until we found the photograph. I need your help, Harriet, to try and figure what's going on. Does the name Lydia French mean anything to you?' Harriet shakes her head. No one seems to have heard of her. I stifle my disappointment but before I continue, I have to ask. 'Harriet, you never told me — how *do* you know . . . *Theo*? Did you grow up together?'

Harriet gives me a sad smile, just as Adam knocks over a photo frame on the shelf, the noise a startling clap in the otherwise quiet room. I turn to Adam, who smiles sheepishly, the photo frame now clasped tightly in his hand. Harriet's eyes search my face closely before she speaks again.

'Oh, Claire — maybe you don't know him as well as you thought you did. Theo is my big brother.'

CHAPTER 29

My mouth drops open as Harriet's words fill the air, my stomach rolling in a feeling not dissimilar to a sharp descent in a lift, that feeling of leaving your stomach behind, weightless. It seems I don't know Tom, Theo, whatever his name is at all. Lies, upon lies, upon lies. I don't know whether to believe anything he's ever told me anymore. He always said he was an only child, that he'd wished for a brother or sister but it never happened. How could he do this to me? I blink, trying to somehow make sense of Harriet's revelation, to find a rational explanation for why Tom wouldn't have told me about her, but I can't . . . all I know is that there's another silken strand in Tom's web of deceit. Adam drags out the empty chair next to mine and lays the photo frame in his hand on the table.

'This is you two, isn't it?' he asks Harriet. 'This is you and Theo together when you were tiny.' Harriet picks up the frame, her eyes shining, before she hands it to me.

'He was five and I was three. It's the only photo I have of us as children.' Taking the photo, I run my eyes over it, searching for clues that will show me it's a young Tom. I see it immediately in his chubby, five-year-old smile — the dimple that sits firmly in his left cheek when he really smiles. Not the fake, polite smile he gives to strangers or acquaintances, the true smile he gives to those he loves most. The smile he gives to me, and to our daughter. Harriet has the same dimple, and so does Isla. I hand the photo back to her, an emotion I can't name coursing through my body.

'I think I need to tell you everything.'

* * *

I proceed to tell Harriet what I've discovered so far — that Tom has been living under a different name, that I didn't even know that he was called Theo until today, the betrayal twisting in my guts as painful as if Tom had taken a knife to me himself. I tell her about the wild goose chase I've been on searching for the real Tom Bennett, in my desperation to find out where he is and why he hasn't come home. Tears run down her cheeks as I'm forced to tell Harriet that I never knew she existed. That her own brother had written her out of his life as if she were never there. Adam keeps a respectful silence, making pot after pot of tea and handing Harriet tissues one by one to mop up her tears. I wonder what he's thinking about Tom, about how foolishly blind I've been. It takes some time for the story to come out, and by the time I'm finished we're all exhausted, but the night is far from over.

'Please, Harriet, tell me what happened here, in Lockwood Bay. Why did he leave and cut himself off from everyone? Was it something to do with Lydia French? Is that why Lydia French is looking for him?'

'I don't know anyone by that name.' Harriet frowns, her lips pursed. 'Theo left a note,' she says, the memory of that day clearly painful as she screws her eyes up to take away the sting of tears. 'I got up in the morning and he was gone. He wasn't happy, I knew that. He made sure we all knew it.'

'Take your time, Harriet. We know this must be painful for you.' Adam casts a quick glance in my direction and I look away, desperate for answers but knowing I need to wait for

Harriet to compose herself. Tissues all gone, Harriet sniffs, as Adam stands and walks into the kitchen area, returning a few seconds later with a roll of kitchen towel. He hands Harriet a sheet of kitchen towel and Harriet blows her nose noisily, before she continues.

'Our dad died, the summer before Theo left. Dad had lung cancer, even though he was only forty-five and he'd never smoked a fag in his life.' Harriet gives a rueful smile before her face darkens. 'But then Mum got remarried, God, not even six months later. She was walking down the aisle with Peter, some incomer that she'd met just before Dad died. He made her feel alive again, she said, after looking after Dad. Theo was sick with it. He didn't think Mum was showing Dad any respect, getting married so soon after his death. It was horrible. *Theo* was horrible — he clashed terribly with Peter, refused to speak to him, and argued with Mum all the time. Then, one morning, when I woke up, he was gone. I thought he'd just gone down to the beach or something, you know? Gone to blow off a bit of steam. But when he didn't come back at teatime, Dan—' she stops and looks at me — 'he was my boyfriend at the time, but now . . . well, now he's my husband . . . I guess that makes him your brother-in-law. We went down to Jack's Place looking for Theo, and even though he wasn't there, he'd left a note under a rock outside. It's what we did when we needed to meet up; all of us kids did it. It said he was sorry but he wasn't coming back. He couldn't live in our house, not with Mum being married to Peter. He was going to London to start again and he'd call me. I thought something must have happened to him — that he must be dead. That's the only reason I could think of for him not contacting me. That was in the summer of 2008. I haven't seen him since.'

'And . . . that's it?' Adam asks, his brow furrowed with a frown. 'You never saw or spoke to Theo again? Did no one look for him? Didn't your mum try and find him? I know he was an adult by then, but even so . . .'

Harriet twists her hands together and looks down at the table, suddenly finding her lukewarm mug of tea more enticing than meeting our eyes.

'It wasn't just . . . I mean, things weren't as simple as all that, there was something else . . .' Harriet breaks off, as fresh tears spring to her eyes.

'Please, Harriet,' I say gently, smoothly removing the mug from her hands and holding her cold, trembling fingers tightly. 'You can tell us. After everything I've discovered over the past few days, I don't think anything could shock me about Tom anymore. Anything you can tell me, anything at all, could help me find him.' Harriet finally raises her eyes to mine, the edges rimmed a deep pink from crying.

'OK. OK, I'll tell you. Theo was seeing someone, before he left. A girl called Ruby Baker. They were together, God . . . since they were fourteen or so? Two weeks before Theo left, he was seen standing at the top of the cliff between the bays, arguing with Ruby. The following morning, Ruby's mum rang us to ask if we had seen her — she hadn't come home that night. Theo admitted he'd seen her the night before, and once someone told him they'd been seen arguing, he confessed that they'd had a row. Ruby had told him she was going to London — she had a job there, apparently — he didn't want her to go without him, and they fought.'

'OK . . . but what does that have to do with Theo running away? He sounds like he was confident, sure of himself. Surely he wouldn't have run off over a teenage lover's tiff?' Adam asks, his eyes never leaving Harriet's face.

'Theo was . . . he didn't like things to not go his way,' Harriet says haltingly. 'If Ruby had told him she was going to London, there was no way he'd just let her go without telling her what he thought.' This doesn't sound like the Tom I know, but then who is that anyway? I gesture for Harriet to go on.

'Ruby's mum got it into her head that something happened that night. Ruby hadn't contacted her at all, not once since she didn't come home, and she said there was no way she'd leave and not keep in contact. Ruby's mum said the two of them were close, but Tom always said that wasn't the case. That Ruby hated her mum, hated that she was so strict.'

A shiver starts to snake along my spine at Harriet's words, as I start to grasp what she's getting at. She takes a gulp of her drink and blows her nose again before continuing.

'The police got involved. They questioned Theo, asking him what was said on the clifftop. I think they had to look into it, as Ruby's mum caused such a stink.'

'You mean . . . she thought Theo was responsible?' I wrap my arms across my body, the chill spreading through me. Poor Tom. I don't believe for a second that he could be responsible for Ruby's disappearance.

'Ruby's mum wouldn't let things lie, she kept on saying that Theo must have hurt Ruby. She was obsessed, she started waiting for Theo outside the ice cream shop where he worked, telling customers he was a murderer, until eventually the owner sacked him, saying he was bad for business. Ruby's mum would call our house, hissing vile things down the phone at Theo, my mum, even me. It got to the point where people in the village were starting to turn on Theo too. Don, at the local chippy, was friends with Ruby's mum and he started refusing to serve Theo when he went to pick up our dinner, and everywhere Theo went, people would stare and whisper behind their hands, all because of Ruby's mum and her insistence that he was responsible for Ruby's disappearance. And then he was questioned again by the police, because she wouldn't stop with her accusations. But there was no body or anything — nothing to say that anything sinister had gone on, or that Theo had done anything to her, so nothing ever happened. Theo was furious about being questioned, he swore blind that he left Ruby on the clifftop that night. After everyone began to turn on him . . . his whole attitude seemed to change. Theo was hurt that Ruby's mum could say these awful things about him when all he'd ever done was love

Ruby. Then, the night before he left, our mum asked Theo if he'd had anything to do with Ruby disappearing like that. She told him if he had, he should just be honest and give Ruby's mum some peace. They'd argued about Peter again, and once Mum said that to him that was it, the final straw. He was gone the next morning.' Harriet starts to cry properly, tears rolling down her cheeks in a tidal wave of grief.

'Did Ruby ever come back?' I ask. 'And what about her mother? Where is she now?' Despite what Harriet has said, I feel a pang of sympathy for Ruby's mother, not knowing what happened to her child.

Harriet shakes her head, tears dripping onto the tabletop. 'No, Ruby didn't come back. Her mother died last year without ever knowing what happened to her.'

'Harriet—' Adam leans over and gently takes her hand — 'you say you haven't seen Theo since . . . but have you spoken to him even once since he left?'

Harriet looks up and swipes at the wet tracks under her eyes. 'Once. A few months after he left. I never told Dan. Things were quieter, easier once he was gone. He called from a payphone and said he was in London; he was going to make a fresh start. He'd found a job working behind the bar in a club. The Lion Club? The White Tiger? Something like that. He said if anyone asked for him, tell them he was gone for good. That they were all dead to him.' At this, Harriet breaks down completely, and although I feel awful for bringing all this back to her door, I can't help but latch onto the one word that seems to stand out in Harriet's speech. London. Tom went to London. I catch Adam's eye and he gives me a barely perceptible nod. I know he's thinking the same thing I am. Harriet has just given us our next lead, a good, solid place for us to continue the search.

'I'm sorry, Harriet, really sorry. I had no idea that Tom . . . *Theo* behaved that way. He never told me any of this. He told me he was at Bristol University between 2008 and 2011.' I give a rueful laugh, embarrassed by my gullibility. 'This is why it took me so long to find you. He barely mentioned Cornwall. But Bristol . . . he talked about Bristol all the time. He told me stories, even down to losing his shoe in the river when he was drunk and having to walk home barefoot in the freezing rain. But it turns out he never even went there. I feel so stupid.' So many secrets that Tom has kept tucked away. I can see Tom as Theo now, from Harriet's words, a feisty, awkward teenager, unhappy with his home life and determined to do something about it.

Adam reaches over and takes my hand. 'Don't feel like that, Claire. You weren't to know — he must have had his reasons.'

'Bristol Uni? God, Theo wished he'd got in there but he didn't get the grades. He was obsessed with some poet who lectured there.' Harriet gives a huff of brittle laughter. 'The shoes! That wasn't in Bristol, Claire. That was here. We sneaked out to the pub on the other side of the river because they didn't know our ages and we could get away with a fake ID. Theo got hammered on Aftershock and lost his shoes in the river on the ferry home. Sean — the guy who lived next door to us and hung around with us since we were all small — he had to help him back to the house in the rain with no shoes on. He'd kill Bailey, his son, if he did anything like that now.' Harriet smiles sadly at me, tears glittering on her cheeks. So, Tom was telling the truth when he told me that story, he just changed things to suit the background he'd already created for himself.

'What was he like though, Harriet? What sort of things did he enjoy? How did he feel about . . . I don't know . . . music, books, anything?' I lean forward, desperate to discover what Tom was like before, desperate to see if there is anything of my Tom at all in the Theo Harriet knows.

'Singing,' Harriet says with a smile. 'He loved to sing, even though his voice was terrible. He always used to say a good sing-along . . .'

'. . . clears the lungs,' I finish for her, unable to help the sad smile that creeps across my face, as I think of Tom wailing along in the car to old country songs, telling me that exact thing every time I winced at his singing voice, Isla laughing in the back seat behind us.

'And the ocean,' Harriet says, sobering suddenly, a faraway look on her face. 'Dan loves the water too — he's a trawlerman, always at sea — I think that's part of why I love him. He reminds me of Theo sometimes. He loved the ocean. He would spend hours sitting down on the beach, just watching the waves. He said it made him feel calm on the outside, when he felt stormy on the inside.' Another tear slides down her cheek, and I find my cheeks are wet too. He's still my Tom, even though he's Theo. My Tom loves the sea, the scent of it, the rolling dash of the waves on the shore. Maybe there is a true, real part of him still there, deep inside, part of Theo that he just couldn't give up.

Suddenly, I realise there's one person we haven't spoken properly about yet, someone who might also be looking for Tom.

'What about your mother — where is she now?'

'She died five years ago.' Harriet wipes her cheeks dry and sits up straighter in her chair. 'Cancer again, ironically. When she got sick, Peter left her. He told her he wasn't strong enough to look after her, the bastard. It looks like Theo was right about him all long; he was just there for an easy ride. I cared for her until the end. I tried to find Theo, to tell him that Mum was dying and he should come home, even if it was just to say goodbye. I wanted to ask him to let everything go — to tell him that Mum never meant it when she asked if Theo was involved. She regretted it until the day she died. I tried again after the house was sold, so I could tell him about Mum and give him the money for his half of the house. Dan even hired a private investigator but he couldn't find him either. And now, just when I think I've found him again, he's still missing.' Harriet chokes on a sob, pressing her hand to her mouth.

'What about the investigator? He couldn't find him, but did he turn up any extra information? Anything we could maybe use now to try and track him down?' I leap onto her words, hopeful that maybe the private investigator can give us a lead.

'Nothing.' Harriet shakes her head sadly. 'We pointed him in the direction of the club in London, but when he went there they said they didn't know Theo . . . to be honest I think he just wanted money for very little work. I chased him, trying to get him to dig further but he wouldn't, he said it was pointless. I didn't know where else to turn.'

Adam gets to his feet, beginning to pace across the flagstone kitchen floor. 'What about Roman? Was there someone called Roman that he was friends with?'

'Roman left a long time ago,' Harriet says, a puzzled look on her face. 'He was one of Theo's best friends since primary school. After Theo left, Roman stuck it out here for another couple of years, but then he met a woman from Australia, and ended up moving over there to be with her in . . . gosh, probably 2012? He hasn't heard from Theo either,' Harriet says, pre-empting my next question. 'I hear from Roman once a year maybe, and he always asks about Theo. Oh, Claire, I just want to see him — just once!' She bursts into fresh tears and I lean over and grasp her hand, trying to process the idea that Tom has lied once again — Roman does exist, just not in Bristol, and Tom hasn't had contact with him since he left.

'I'm going to find him, Harriet. I swear I'll find him and bring him home. You two can be reunited; you can meet your niece.'

We talk long into the night, Harriet telling us everything she can remember about her childhood with Theo — how she, Tom and Dan grew up together before Tom left, how she tried hard to move on once she realised Tom was never coming back — and very generously offering up her tiny back bedroom for one of us to stay in, the squashy couch at the back of the kitchen for the other. Adam volunteers to take the couch, pressing me to take the bedroom. It seems as though there aren't enough words to say all that we want to say about our lives with

Tom/Theo, and I wonder at how easily Tom managed to just walk away from it all — from his mother, but especially from Harriet, who still seems to worship the ground he walks on all these years later. Adam listens carefully, offering suggestions as to why Tom might have disappeared, why he might have behaved the way he did, but it doesn't go very far towards soothing the pain he's caused the people who love him. Later that night, when Harriet has gone to bed and Adam is nestled on the battered kitchen sofa, I lie awake in Harriet's spare single bed, springs digging into my back, and wonder if he's done it again now. Just walked away from me and everything we had together. Left me and Isla with no explanation at all.

***

The next morning I'm the first one awake and I stretch out, pushing my hands up over my head in an attempt to straighten out the kinks from a night spent in the less-than-comfortable single bed. I creep downstairs, the scent of the sea on the early-morning air as fingers of lilac and peach sunlight stretch in through the kitchen windows, the faint crash of the waves the only sound in the silent cottage. Putting the kettle on to boil, I move silently from cupboard to cupboard, searching out coffee and mugs, careful not to wake the others until Adam stirs on the couch with a loud yawn and an exaggerated stretch, just as I'm pouring myself a coffee, the aromatic scent filling the kitchen.

'Sleep well?' he asks as he pushes off the blankets, looking far more refreshed than I feel, despite the rough dark stubble that sprinkles his chin.

'Like a log,' I lie, pouring out another mug and passing it to Adam. We sit together at the table, waiting for Harriet to surface, drinking our coffee in companionable silence. Adam watches me as I drink, appearing several times as though he wants to say something. In the end, fed up with watching him wrangle with whatever it is he has to say, I speak.

'What is it, Adam?'

'What? Nothing.' He blows on the top of his already-cool coffee.

'I know you, remember? I know you've got something to say. I wish you'd just spit it out.'

Adam takes a breath, rubbing a hand over his chin with a scratching sound. 'Look, Claire . . .' Before he can finish Harriet appears in her dressing gown, her puffy eyes evidence of her tears last night, tears that I suspect she carried on crying long after we had all gone to bed.

'Did you sleep OK?' she asks, her hair mussed on one side much the same way that Isla's does, another little link in the chain that connects the two of them through Tom. At the thought of Isla, undoubtedly fine with Gwen but still not by my side, my heart skips a beat and I have to work extra hard to force the smile onto my face. Tom has now been missing for six days, and I wonder how on earth Harriet can deal with Dan being away at sea for weeks at a time . . . or maybe it's different when you know they're coming home to you.

'Yes, thanks. I was just envying you and Dan. I feel like I never really knew Tom at all.' I sip at my now lukewarm coffee while Adam stares into the depths of his mug.

'You can get over this, Claire, when you find him. He's . . . he's not a bad person.' Harriet gives a little tearful huff of laughter, as if trying to convince herself her words are true. 'I've spent the last few years telling myself he's not a bad person, and that there's a valid reason why he hasn't contacted me in all this time. He's my brother, I can't think any other way. I'd hate to lose him all over again. It's hard enough after all these years, but I want my family back together. Dan doesn't speak to Jack, you know.' I had realised Dan was Jack's son, but we didn't get a chance to talk about the relationship the previous evening. 'Silly, really, but he blames Jack for Esther walking out. He blames Jack's drinking for the bar burning down. He blames Jack for all of it really, he doesn't stop to think that maybe Esther was going to leave anyway.'

I reach out to comfort her, placing a hand over hers. Harriet has already carved herself a space in my heart, and even if Tom doesn't come home, I don't want to let her go. Adam lifts his gaze abruptly from his mug, necking the last of the coffee before placing his mug strongly back down on the table, the little thud as it hits the wood causing both Harriet and me to look up.

'I'm sorry. I should have told you this before, it's just . . . I wanted to see what Harriet had to say.' Adam's face is sombre, and my heart turns over in my chest. 'It's about Tom.'

Harriet and I wait expectantly for Adam to carry on. I knew there was something he wanted to say, but I know Adam — he doesn't like to be pushed.

'Claire—' Adam turns to me — 'last night, I started searching the internet, trying to find a club in London with a similar name to the ones Harriet mentioned yesterday. There are quite a few, but I think I may have found it. I found a website, for a club in Soho called the Tiger Club. The website didn't tell me much, it's just a few vague sentences and a couple of pictures. There's a members area that you need to sign up to where presumably there's more information available, but there's a fee involved and I didn't want my credit card details to be held on there, so I just kept to the public areas.'

'Go on.' My heart is almost bursting out of my ribcage, suddenly terrified about what Adam is about to tell me.

'It hasn't been updated in a long time — the pictures are all pretty old. The thing is, Claire, I think they do know Tom there. There's a picture of him on the website.'

'There's a picture of Tom? Are you sure?' My heads spins and I grip the edge of the table, trying to quell the dizziness.

'Like I said, I don't think the public parts of the website have been updated for years. I don't know about the private sections. I wasn't sure at first. The picture isn't great — it's a group shot and Tom isn't the centre of the photo, so I didn't want to say anything until I knew for definite.'

'So why say something now? What's made you so sure?' Harriet sounds puzzled, and I know exactly how she feels — another tangle in Tom's web of lies.

'I did a reverse image search and it brought up another photo. A clearer picture where you can see his face.' Adam holds out his phone, and I feel almost dizzy with anticipation. Harriet and I lean in. Harriet gasps, her hand flying to her mouth, and I swallow, my throat swollen with tears.

'That's him. That's Theo.'

CHAPTER 30

My mind drifts as the cold seeps into my bones and the fire of a fever starts to warm my brow. I think about my family, how I want so badly to see their faces again, to tell them I love them, and that I'm sorry for all the times I let them down. This is all down to the photograph — maybe if the photograph had never been taken, none of this would ever have happened. I would be at home, or at work, the same as any other day. A single tear tracks its way down my cheek, itching my skin as it rolls towards my chin. I keep my eyes closed behind the scratchy blindfold that keeps me in the dark, and behind my eyelids I see my sister's face, as clear as if she were standing in front of me. I see her chubby cheeks as a toddler, when she would follow me around everywhere I went, desperate to keep up with me. Memories flash through my mind, a carousel of images. Me, running, chasing her, her laughter bubbling like a fountain as she tried to get away before I could scoop her up in my arms. Her, snuggling up to me, a blanket over us both as rain hammered at the window, the weather outside squally and wild. If she were here now, I would tell her how much I regret pushing her away when we were growing up, that she wasn't that embarrassing, not really. That secretly I loved the way she looked up to me, the way she wanted to emulate me so badly. I would tell her I regret the way I behaved, and the time I spent away from her. I would tell her that I love her, and I wish I had cherished every moment we had together. That if I could have that time again, I never would have left her alone.

CHAPTER 31

The car journey back from Cornwall passes mostly in silence, tension filling the air until it threatens to strangle me. Adam stares out of the window, watching the landscape racing by, after trying and failing to engage me in conversation. He tries to talk about Tom, attempting to understand his behaviour before he left Cornwall, and I snap back at him, unable to help myself. I'm full of conflicted emotion — part of me feels excited, almost to the point of agitation, butterflies rippling through my stomach, so keen am I to head for London to see if the Tiger Club yields any answers about where Tom might be. The other part of me is trying to deal with yet another betrayal, another lie from the man I thought I knew inside and out, his deceit chipping away at the foundations of our relationship. I make it clear early on that I don't want to talk. Despite his tact in not mentioning it out loud, there is the overwhelming sensation that the more we uncover about Tom, the more convinced Adam is that he's left me of his own accord. I'm still certain he hasn't — the Tom (*Theo, Claire, his name is Theo*) of twenty years ago is totally different to the Tom I know now. People change, they grow up, and Tom is kind, reliable, an amazing father, with no sign of this dark side hidden inside the boy I'm supposed to believe he once was. There's no way he would do this to Isla — is there? I have to admit that in light of everything I've discovered, a tiny voice at the back of my mind does keep trying to ask the question, *But are you really sure? Are you really one hundred per cent, hand on heart convinced he wouldn't just walk away from both of you?*

Now, as we get closer to Easthampton, I feel guilty at behaving so badly — the person I'm really angry with is Tom, for not being honest about where he came from, but Adam is here with me now, so he's the one that bears the brunt of my frustration. As we pull up to the traffic lights on the outskirts of town, Adam still gazes blandly out of the windscreen, watching a mother battling with a toddler in a pushchair with shopping bags hanging from both handles.

'I won't come in when I drop you off,' I say. He doesn't respond, the silence growing thicker, and I sigh. 'Adam, I'm sorry. I know I've been a wanker today.' I try to catch his eye, but he carries on watching the mum with her pushchair, now halfway across the road. Finally, he turns to look at me, a frown creasing his brow.

'Yeah, you have been a wanker.' He lets a small smile lift the corners of his mouth. 'It's not that though, Claire. I'm tired — it's been a tough, emotional couple of days. I just want to get home and shower, put some clean clothes on and feed Peggy. I'm looking forward to a night in my own bed.'

'Peggy? Who's Peggy?' The lights change and I pull away smoothly, turning right to head towards Adam's house, rather than left towards Gwen's.

'My cat. Someone's been looking after her. So, I need to get back.'

I remember how devastated Adam was when his old cat died — he'd had her for years, and brought her with him when we moved in together. She died not long afterwards, and Adam never replaced her because I'm allergic to cats. I'm glad he's got another one, although I can't help wondering who the *someone* is who's looking after her — maybe Peggy isn't the only company Adam has in his life. Adam doesn't offer any information, instead keeping his eyes on the road, and minutes later, I pull up outside his small, terraced house.

'What will you do now?' Adam asks as he gets out of the car, leaning down to grab his overnight bag from the rear footwell.

'I want to spend some time with Isla, and I suppose I'd better update Gwen on what we found in Cornwall.' I'd given her a brief update over the phone before we left, but I know Gwen will want all the details. 'Then head into London, I guess. Check out the Tiger Club and see if anyone there remembers Tom.'

'Are you sure you want to go there?' Adam asks, frowning. 'I mean . . . do you know what you're walking into? Maybe it would be better to do some digging around here first, before you go charging in there.'

'I need to go there, Adam. I told you before, I'm no good at sitting around online, making phone calls. I need to feel like I'm actually *doing* something.' Tom might have lied to me, things might not be as I thought they were, but I still love him. I still want him home safe, and right now the Tiger Club is all I have to go on.

'Just . . . keep your head. Don't go in there all guns blazing. And don't get your hopes up too high.' Adam sighs. 'There's every chance that no one will remember him.' He pauses. 'Do you want me to come with you? I'm not sure you should go alone.'

'Thanks, Adam, but no thanks.' I shake my head. 'I think I need to do this alone.' I'm not sure anyone at the Tiger Club will speak to me even if they do remember Tom, and I don't think rocking up with a police officer on my arm will do me any favours. 'I do appreciate you, you know. Now, go home and get some rest. I'll call you once I know anything more.'

Adam finally smiles and reaches out to squeeze my hand through the open window before his face is serious once more.

'Claire. While you're in London . . . just be careful.'

* * *

Isla hurtles down the stairs and into my arms as Gwen pulls the front door open, a hint of a smile on her face as she tries to disguise the concern in her eyes. I pull Isla close, breathing in the scent of Gwen's unfamiliar washing powder and shampoo, my heart filled with the shape of her in my arms.

'I missed you, Mummy,' she murmurs into my shoulder, snuggling her face as close to me as she can.

'I missed you too, baby.' I kiss her hair, before holding her slightly away from me so I can drink in her face, searching out all the familiar features she shares with Tom — her eyes, and her dimples.

'Is Daddy here?' she asks, just as I expected, peering over my shoulder to check the front path.

'Not yet, darling, but I think I know where to look.' I meet Gwen's eyes over the top of Isla's head.

'Isla, why don't you run upstairs and get that drawing you did for Mummy? I'm sure she'd love to see it.' Isla nods, and runs back up to the room Gwen swears is just a spare room but is decorated exactly the way Isla loves it. Gwen watches her go before she turns back to me. 'Is that true? Do you really know where to look?'

'I think so . . . Gwen, I can't believe Tom has a sister and he never told me.' Gwen's face changes as my own crumples, the tears that I've tried to hold in for too long spilling down my cheeks. 'He isn't who I thought he was, and I don't even know what's going to happen if I do find him.'

Gwen tugs me gently by the arm, leading me into the kitchen and pouring me a large glass of red wine. 'I think you'd better tell me everything.'

I push the wine away, sinking wearily into a chair at the table. 'It's a long story, but his sister told me when he left Cornwall, he went to London. That's where I'm going tonight . . . to see if this could be the thing that leads me to him.'

CHAPTER 32

Soho. It's been years since I visited the place and I'd forgotten quite how vibrant and alive it is. I blink as I exit the tube station, the warm evening air feeling fresh and cool after the stuffiness of the train. I spent a lot of time in Soho back in the day, after I finished university and moved up to London for work. We used to head into Soho on a Friday night and spend the nights drinking, chatting and dancing, Adam able to slam the tequila with the best of the city boys. He used to meet me in town on the nights when he wasn't on shift. It's strange now to think Tom and I might have crossed paths here without even knowing, that it's entirely possible he might have been mere feet away from me while I was dancing and doing shots with my mates. In those days I only had eyes for Adam, and wouldn't have even considered looking at another man, even one as handsome as Tom. I can't think of him as Theo, not yet. To me, he's still my Tom, the quiet, patient man I married, and I find it hard to tally the man I know with the feisty Theo, the boy who felt so passionately about things that he could walk out on his family, never to be seen again. Sure, the Tom I know gets annoyed about things, but he rarely loses his temper, not in the way Harriet described, and I wonder whether he really has changed . . . or whether he was just hiding that part of himself from me all this time.

A little after ten o'clock in the evening, I check in to a cheap hotel round the corner from the Tiger Club. I've decided the only way to get any information is go to the club, find someone who's worked there for a while and see if they remember Tom. Maybe they'll know Lydia French and I can finally start to put the puzzle pieces together. Changing into the kind of outfit I haven't worn for years, and thanking God that I kept up my gym membership, I run my eyes over my reflection in the mirror. Tom wouldn't recognise me — I barely recognise myself — and I tug down the lacy crop top that barely covers my midriff. The tiny skirt is hardly any better. Pulling up the internet browser on my phone, I pace the thin, grubby carpet in my room, searching for the Tiger Club to check opening times, then pull out Tom's mobile to see if there have been any further texts. The screen is blank, the only alerts several voicemails from Jonah that I haven't listened to and promotional codes from Deliveroo. There have been no more messages from the unknown number, and I'm certain that's because Lydia French has found him — there's a creeping, cold sensation that tickles the base of my neck, telling me she no longer needs to send texts to threaten Tom because she's already keeping him from coming home. My heart skips a beat at what could be happening to him right now. As the cold hand of fear grips me tightly, I wonder where he is, if he's being fed, if he's warm enough. Is he even still alive? From what Harriet has told me, Theo was the kind of boy who was fearless, the kind of boy who could get himself into all sorts of trouble. Is that what has happened to Tom? Does he still have that reckless side that could have got him into something bigger than he ever expected? I try and fail to stop the thoughts that lead me down the darkest routes — thoughts of kidnap, of blackmail and beatings or worse. I'm so engrossed in my own terrifying reflections that I nearly miss the buzz of my phone. Snatching it up, I answer quickly, heart knocking in my chest.

'Claire?'

'Hi, Adam.'

'Look, I did some more digging on the Tiger Club. Claire, you need to be careful.' Adam's voice is urgent, and I wonder what on earth he could have dug up to make him so jittery. 'So, there's this guy who I think might own the club. His name isn't on any paperwork, but I've asked about and he's definitely involved in it. The Met have had their eye on him for quite some time. His name is Carlos Bremen — Claire, he is seriously bad news.'

'What do you mean, *bad news*? Is he some sort of gangster or something?' I swallow hard, an icy trickle of fear starting to drip down my back. *Does this guy know Tom?*

'Claire, I'm serious. He calls himself a "businessman" . . . If Tom had anything to do with him . . . Well, just be careful, that's all I'm saying.'

'Ok, I promise I'll be careful. I'll stay away from this Carlos guy.' Restlessness snaps at my heels again and I spritz myself briskly with perfume and smooth down my hair. 'Adam, I have to go.' The thought that Tom might somehow be involved with this 'businessman' makes my pulse thud in my ears and I snatch up my jacket, hurrying from the hotel, my heels clacking on the pavement as I rush towards the Tiger Club.

I see the neon sign as I approach, hear the dull thud of music wafting out as patrons come and go. Thick-necked bouncers stand on the door, huge and intimidating, black t-shirts tight against their rippled muscles, and I shake off the tingle that zips along my nerve endings at the sight of them. Reaching the main door, trying to appear more confident than I really feel, I give a quick smile to the pair of them, my heart banging in my chest like an old tin drum, and both of them stare back at me impassively. I push it open, the beat of the music from inside reaching my ears, the bass thudding in my chest. The door opens into a small reception area, dimly lit by a cascade of fairy lights lining the walls and a large gothic-style mirror hanging behind the desk. A red deep-pile carpet gives an illusion of luxury, but I can't help noticing that it's worn in places — a tiny glimpse of what lies beneath the glamorous facade. A woman stands behind a desk, large breasts spilling out of a tight, low-cut top, with a small gold badge that reads, 'Colleen'. A large man in a suit lounges against the wall by her side. The earpiece in his ear and the bulge of his muscles through his tight suit jacket show him to be a bouncer, and although he doesn't seem as intimidating as the others outside, I move quickly to the desk to pay the entrance fee, wanting to keep a low profile until I've managed to ask my questions.

'Sixty quid, please.' Barely looking at me, the woman holds her hand out for the money, large silver hoops in her ears swinging as she reaches for the stamp to mark the back of my hand. I fumble for the notes in my pocket and hand it over to her, the stamp she punches down hard on my skin leaving a smudged black tiger face. I thank her and she ignores me, so I push through the thick velvet curtains leading into the main bar. The music here is deafening, a constant thudding bassline that jolts through my whole body. The lighting is dim, and a stage is set up at one side of the room, opposite the bar. Framed by heavy red curtains, a spotlight shines down on the stage, illuminating a woman who stands in high heels and a tiny set of matching underwear, clearly in the middle of her routine. The men seated at the tables in front of the stage are all transfixed by her as she bends and twirls, her long blonde hair snaking down her back and almost reaching the floor as she slides her hands down her legs towards her ankles. Bottles of champagne litter the tables and wads of notes are clutched in their sweaty fists, ready to press onto the girl when she's finished her dance. My heart sinks a little, even though I had my suspicions. Calling itself a 'gentleman's club', the Tiger Club is nothing more than a very expensive, upmarket strip club. It makes me feel slightly nauseous to think of Tom working in a place like this, and I wonder if this is why he's so supportive of women's rights. Turning away and smothering the distaste that rises like sap, I walk slap bang into a woman, dressed almost identically to the girl on the stage. She gives a lascivious smile, verging on vulgar, and licks her lips at me.

'Dance?' she breathes, leaning in close enough for me to smell the alcohol on her breath.

'Um . . . no, thanks,' I manage awkwardly, half twisting away from her.

'Come for a job?' she asks, one hand reaching up to stroke my collarbone as she laughs. Sweat prickles along my hairline and I take a step back, trying to get some distance between us.

'No, thanks, really.' I hold up a hand and she gives me a filthy look, the smile dropping from her face, before turning away, her eyes already seeking out her next client. Letting out a shaky breath, uncomfortable in the thickly charged atmosphere of the dance area, I head towards the bar. It's not terribly busy, most clientele availing themselves of the tables with the best view of the stage, so I sit at a bar stool and wait to catch the barmaid's attention. Finally, she notices me waiting patiently, her eyes flicking over me quickly.

'What can I get you?'

'Gin and tonic, please.' I have to lean over and shout for her to be able to hear me. She thumps a gin glass in front of me, gin sloshing over the side and onto the slightly sticky bar. There's no fancy sprig of foliage like you'd find in most Soho bars, no straw, not even an ice cube. As she turns to leave, I reach out and grab her sleeve. She stares down where my hand rests on her forearm, her eyebrows raising in a little 'V' of disapproval.

'Do you mind?' She glares at me, tugging her arm away.

'Wait a minute — please. I just want to ask you something.'

'I don't do what they're doing up there. Not for men *or* women. So don't even ask. I just pour the drinks.'

'No, that's not what I want. Please, would you look at this, it'll only take a second of your time.' I grope in my jacket pocket for the photograph of Tom and Harriet and pull it out, smoothing out the wrinkles in it, something that seems to have become part of the ritual in showing the photograph to people. The barmaid takes a sneaky look around the bar, making sure she's unobserved before holding her hand out.

'Give it here, then. Quickly, I'm busy.' Not strictly true, the bar having emptied out slightly, the men all drifting over to the tables by the stage as a new girl starts her routine under the harsh glare of the stage lights. I watch her carefully as she drinks in the picture, her dark eyes casting quickly over Tom's features. She purses her lips slightly, a small frown creasing her brow before she shakes her head at me.

'Never seen him before in my life. Why do you care anyway?'

'He's my husband, and he's missing. I think he used to work here, it would have been around three or four years after this photo was taken. I wondered if you recognised him. His name is . . . Theo.' I remember at the last minute that anyone who worked here would have known Tom by that name. The girl looks around the bar, seeming almost afraid, before shoving the photo into my hand.

'Look, I told you I don't know him, all right? If you're not going to have another drink or buy a dance off one of the girls then just piss off out of here. Please, just go.'

'What about Carlos?' I ask, throwing his name out in desperation. I know Tom was here at some point . . . he told Harriet that himself. If this girl can't help me, then despite my promise to Adam and the icy finger stroking the back of my neck at Carlos's name, maybe I'll have no choice but to deal with him. 'Is he here? Can I speak to him?'

'Have you got a death wish or something? Just *get out*.' There is the unmistakable scent of fear pouring off her in waves, and I can't understand why she would be afraid of me, until a hand clamps down tightly on my shoulder and I realise I'm not the source of her fear. As I half turn in my seat, the hand tightens its grip, making me wince. Looking into the mirror behind the bar, I see a man I recognise as one of the bouncers from the door, standing behind me, holding me tightly.

'This woman bothering you, Pippa?' He peers down at me, so close I can see the shaving rash that marks his chin. I squirm away from him, resisting the urge to rub at my sore shoulder as he lets me go.

'I was just—'

'Like the lady said, if you're not going to buy another drink or a dance, just piss off. Before I have to force you to leave.' He looms over me, a full head taller than me. I can barely hear him over the crashing of my pulse in my ears, and my knees feel like cooked spaghetti. His rancid breath hits my face and I recoil slightly.

'OK, I'm sorry. I'm leaving.' Raising my hands in a gesture of defeat, I give the barmaid one last look, but she averts her eyes and refuses to meet my gaze.

***

Outside, I breathe in one gulp after another of hot, humid air, the scent of beer and takeaway food lying heavy on my tongue. Even the polluted flavour of London is better than the wicked breath that thug breathed all over me. I lean over, resting my hands on my bare knees, the sour taste of fear making my mouth slick. Despite the terror that blasts through my veins, leaving me shaken and cotton-mouthed and with damp palms that I swipe over my too-short skirt, I don't leave. Instead, I wait, just far enough away from the club to avoid suspicion, before seeing the barmaid step out of the side door of the club into the alleyway that runs along the side of the building. Sidling silently along the wall, I edge closer, eager to avoid detection by the bouncers. As I turn into the narrow, cobbled alley, the girl has turned her back to me, leaning against the wall by the huge industrial bins. I get closer, inching my way along the wall towards her, and realise she's talking on a mobile phone as she smokes a cigarette.

'No . . . I dunno, she was just asking questions. Poking about.' She sucks in hard on the cigarette, before expelling a long breath of smoke that sits in the muggy, airless evening like a dark cloud over her head. I duck into the doorway opposite — from the smell that lingers, it belongs to the takeaway on the other side of the alleyway entrance. 'She said he was missing, that's all. Apparently, he's her husband. No, I never told her anything. *Jesus Christ, I said I don't know, Carlos.*' She kicks at an empty burger wrapper that lies discarded on the cobbles, her shoe scuffing noisily along the pavement. 'She's gone now, Kev threw her out, but yeah, OK, I'll keep an eye out, see if she does come back.' Finishing her cigarette, she throws the butt to the floor, grinding it out under the heel of her shoe. The door of the club bursts open before I realise what's happening.

'Oi! You! I thought I told you to piss off!' Looking up in alarm, I see Kev the bouncer bulldozing his way towards me, the barmaid turning back with a startled look on her face. As I race off around the corner trying to shake Kev, my last thought is: she lied to me. The barmaid does know Tom. And so does Carlos Bremen.

CHAPTER 33

Slowing my pace once out of sight, I walk until the adrenaline coursing through my body has ebbed away, leaving me sweaty and trembling. I find a small bar, and realising I haven't eaten properly again today, stop for a bite to eat and a drink.

My head is spinning with everything I've learned over the past few days. I've discovered a whole new Tom I never could have imagined before — and it's looking more and more likely that something or someone from his past is the reason behind all the secrets and lies. Tom must have been hiding from Carlos or Lydia French, why else would he have changed his name? Or was it because of Ruby's disappearance? Was he afraid her mother would track him down and try to ruin his life all over again? I slug back the last of my Diet Coke, the cold bubbles soothing my parched throat. I need to speak to the girl behind the bar again, get her somewhere away from the club and find out exactly what she remembers about Tom, what she knows about Carlos Bremen and whether she knows Lydia French. I don't think she'll be too forthcoming given that she's already lied to me, but it's the only lead I have right now, and there's no way I'm going to let it slip through my fingers. Feeling better now I have some sort of strategy,

I pay for the meal and start to walk back slowly towards the Tiger Club. I call Adam as I walk, knowing he'll be worried and want an update. His phone rings for a long time before he answers, a little out of breath as though he ran to pick up.

'Adam? It's me, Claire.'

'Claire, where are you? Are you still in Soho?' His voice is low, brisk with anxiety, and for a moment I wish I'd let him come with me.

'I'm fine. I've visited the Tiger Club and I've found someone there who remembers Tom. Although, she didn't exactly tell me that.' I don't tell Adam about getting thrown out of the club.

'What do you mean? Claire, be careful, these aren't nice people you're dealing with.'

'I know that — I've already become acquainted with the bouncers. But I'm OK, I promise. Listen, the girl said she doesn't know Tom, but she *does* — I heard her on the phone to a guy named Carlos in the alleyway. That has to be Carlos Bremen, right? I'm pretty sure if I can get her away from the club and the bouncers she'll speak to me. I'm going to talk to her, find out what she knows. I just need to get her away from the club first so she can talk without being worried about being overheard.'

'Claire, are you out of your fucking mind? This Carlos guy . . . from what I've heard he's ruthless. He does whatever it takes to get what he wants.' A strong note of anxiety still runs through Adam's voice, despite me trying to reassure him everything is just peachy, and I shudder internally at his words. *He does whatever it takes.*

'It has to be done, Adam. *My husband is missing*. I think there might be a chance Carlos Bremen has something to do with it — why else would this girl call him? If Carlos has Tom, or he's put Lydia French up to luring him out, this girl knows something.' I take a deep breath and lower my voice. '*I* need to do whatever it takes to get Tom back — especially seeing as the police won't help me. I'll follow this girl home if I need to. I'll promise her that I won't tell anyone she's spoken to me, and I'll see what she knows. She might be my only chance to find out whether Carlos has Tom. She might know who Lydia French is and why she posted that advert. It might be my only chance to find out where she's keeping him.' My voice breaks slightly, the lump in my throat making it hard to speak.

'Claire, before you go off all hare-brained, please just listen to me for a moment. I've done some digging and I found something that . . . well, it's not good.'

'What? Tell me, Adam.'

'There was a guy, before, from one of these clubs. Nothing was ever proven, not according to my source, but he worked for one of the clubs connected to Carlos Bremen. Something happened — a row, an argument, I don't know — and he disappeared. I don't know any names, all I know is he pissed off Carlos Bremen and no one has seen him since. This is why I'm telling you to be careful. There's talk that Carlos had him dealt with, if you get my meaning.'

'Fuck.' I wipe my forehead with a shaking hand. This is more than I can handle. A week ago, I was a conveyancing solicitor with a strong marriage, a beautiful kid, life was as perfect as I could have ever imagined it. Now, I don't recognise my own life. I'm struggling to understand who it is I'm looking for anymore — is it Tom, my calm, placid husband, the man I thought I knew, or is it the fearless and hot-headed Theo? 'OK, Adam, I hear you. If Tom is involved with Carlos, then I need to tread carefully. I'll speak to the bartender and see what she can tell me — it would be a start.'

'Claire, I don't think you—'

'*No*, Adam. Please. I need to do this.' I lower my voice, huddling over the phone as someone knocks into me from behind. 'If it was me who was missing, ten years ago, would you have given up just because you were afraid?'

There's a heavy pause, swollen with some emotion that I can't name, then Adam speaks. 'No,' he says quietly. 'I wouldn't. I wouldn't give up on you, not even if you were the one missing now.'

I blink, my breath sticking in my throat. 'Then you should understand,' I say softly, and hang up.

CHAPTER 34

Conversation over, I find myself back at the club. Moving silently down the alleyway to the right of the building, I slip into the alcove of a doorway to the takeaway shop next door — the perfect vantage point to watch the back entrance to the club without being spotted — my heart rate is swift and sounding loudly in my ears. It's late, the sun long gone below the horizon, but the night air is still hot and thick, spiced with cigarette smoke. Sitting sideways on the concrete step in the doorway, I lean back against the bricks and close my eyes for a brief second, the miles and emotions of the past few days finally catching up with me. My bones feel weary and my eyelids are heavy, imagining Tom and Isla playing on the beach at Lockwood Bay, the waves breaking gently on the shoreline as seagulls shriek overhead.

Realising the shriek of the seagulls is actually a hen party crossing the entrance to the alley as they make their way raucously back to their hotel, my eyes snap open and I shift on the step, the bricks digging into my thighs through the thin fabric of my skirt. Movement catches my eye, the staff at the Tiger Club beginning to leave through the heavy black door that marks the side entrance. Drawing back into the relative safety of the doorway, I watch the girls leave, their bodies now covered in jogging pants and t-shirts despite the warm night air. All appear years younger than they did up on the stage, now the night's make-up has been washed away and hair has been tied up into ponytails. They kiss each other's cheeks and light cigarettes and puff on vapes as they call goodbye to each other before disappearing down the alleyway towards the tube station. Several of the bouncers leave, and I shrink back further into the shadowy crevice of the doorway, pressing myself against the wall. The heavy door slams shut and no one else leaves the building. There's been no sign of the barmaid, or of my friend, Kev the bouncer. She must have left earlier, or through the front entrance. I'm never going to find Tom, or bloody Lydia French. No one is going to tell me whether Carlos Bremen has something to do with all of this.

Failure tastes bitter on my tongue as I move towards the open air of the cobbled street, ready to head back to my hotel, when the sound of the heavy, black door creaking open causes me to stumble backwards into the darkness of the alcove. Holding my breath, sweat beading at my temples, I watch as the barmaid exits the building, her hair pulled back into a ponytail. The bouncer who threw me out earlier closely follows her, his muscles rippling under the tight-fitting suit he wears despite the heavy summer heat. He leans in close to speak to her and her face changes, a pout appearing on her lips as she shakes her head. He speaks to her again, trying to grab her arm, but she pulls away, a look of annoyance on her face, before turning and walking towards the entrance to the alley. The bouncer watches for a moment, a slight sneer on his face, before turning and re-entering the club.

My breath coming in short pants as the nerves kick in, I peer out from my hiding place just in time to see the flash of her red shoulder bag as she turns right out of the alley, presumably headed towards the tube station like the other girls. Stepping out of the darkness, I quickly walk after her, anxious not to lose her on the still-busy streets of Soho. I follow her at a distance as she strides towards the tube, making sure I'm several paces back and behind other people so if she does happen to glance back, she doesn't notice me. Lifting my chin and pulling my shoulders back, I walk with a confidence I don't feel, aware all the time that the barmaid might not be the only one who's being followed. Tom would have walked this way, I think, my chest tightening. Only, he wouldn't have worried about being followed or taking a shortcut down a dark alley.

The barmaid steps up her pace a little and, glancing at my phone, I realise how late it is. The last tube runs soon, and I match my pace to hers, keeping my eyes on her red bag. She enters the tube station at Piccadilly Circus and I jump on the eastbound train to Cockfosters one carriage down from her. At each stop I peer out of the doors nervously, ready to hop out the minute I see her depart the train. I don't have long to wait. Five stops along and I see her get off at Caledonian Road, swinging her distinctive red bag up onto her shoulder as she leaves the train. No one else leaves the station, so I hang back for a moment on the platform, stooping to fiddle with my shoe with my heart beating ten to the dozen, sure that this time she'll turn round and spot me. She strides on ahead without looking back and after a few seconds I stand, the blood rushing to my head as I follow her out onto the street. For a moment I lose sight of her slim figure as a bus rounds the corner, and then I see her on the opposite side of the road, still walking briskly, her ponytail swinging. Keeping my head low, I cast quick side glances in her direction, remembering the smell of fear that rolled off her as the bouncer loomed over my shoulder. I'm convinced she knows something. She stops outside a townhouse on Rufford Street, fumbling in her bag for her keys, and I jog lightly across the road towards her.

'Hey!' I whisper-shout to her, raising one hand in her direction to show I mean her no harm. She whips around to face me, her ponytail flying. Dismay crosses her features as she realises it's me. She fumbles her keys out of her bag and starts jabbing frantically at the lock.

'Please wait, I just need to talk to you,' I gasp, as I draw level with her, pushing my fringe out of my eyes. She stabs urgently at the lock, the key slipping, before managing to jam it in. 'Please . . .'

'*No.*' Finally turning the key and creaking the front door part way open, she turns to face me, one foot inside the hallway already. 'I can't talk to you. You have no idea what you're getting yourself into. I told you earlier, *I don't know anything.*'

'*Stop.*' I grasp her by the shoulder, my fingers snagging the silky fabric of her top. 'It's *you* that doesn't have any idea. He is *missing*, do you understand? I know you know something — I heard you on the phone — and I'm not leaving until you tell me everything. Does Carlos have Theo? Is that why you're too frightened to talk to me?' The girl stumbles slightly as I tighten my grip, desperation clawing at my insides. 'He left our house on Tuesday and he hasn't *come home since.*' My voice cracks on the last words, my throat closing over as I try and swallow. 'We have a child together, do you have any idea what we're going through?'

She tugs herself free, rubbing at her shoulder, her eyes wide with fright, before giving a spiteful little laugh. 'Missing. What a fucking surprise.'

'What? What's that supposed to mean?' Confused, I take a step back, my hands slide from her shoulders and drop to my sides. 'Does the name Lydia French mean anything to you?'

'Her? What do you want with her? She's just another one who got sucked in by Theo and his bullshit. The last I heard she was in prison. And what I *mean* is *good fucking riddance*. Yeah, I knew Theo, OK?' Her dark eyes glitter with icy rage in the harsh glare of the streetlamps lighting the pavement close to the house. 'And do you know what? He was a bastard. Whatever's happened to him, he deserved it. I was glad to see the back of him — and you should be too.' With that she shoves me backwards, harder than I would have expected, and slams the door closed in my face. Sighing, I lean against the front door, the cool panel of glass refreshing on my hot forehead, and close my eyes in defeat.

CHAPTER 35

As I walk back down the path from the girl's house, the sound of her mocking voice ringing in my ears, I fail to spot the two men who loom out of the bushes until it's far too late to do anything about it. Their shadows fall across the pavement, under the bright shaft of moonlight that crosses the path, and they're on me before I even realise they're there.

'Told you to mind your own business, didn't I?' My heart sinks as I recognise the voice of Kev the bouncer, and he's not alone. I try to shuffle away from them, fear rising in my throat, my hands shaking as they step closer.

'Look, I'm sorry, OK? I'm leaving.' I try to keep the panic from my voice as I hold my hands up in a gesture of defeat, moving sideways as if to step around the pair of them, but Kev matches my sidestep and blocks the pavement.

'Do you really want to mess with Carlos?'

'I'm sorry,' I repeat, almost dizzy with fear. 'I'm looking for someone, that's all. I'm looking for my husband — I'm sorry if you thought . . .' Panic makes my brain foggy and I can't get the words out quickly enough.

'Maybe we should let you make it up to us.'

I can't move. Can't run, can't scream. I'm frozen from the eyes down as the bouncer steps towards me, running his tongue over his lips. I always thought if something like this happened I would be prepared. Ready with a scream in my mouth and my keys jammed between my fingers. It turns out, I'm not ready. He reaches out a meaty hand, running it over my hair, along my jawline and down to my exposed collarbone.

'Please.' The word is a whisper and I pray that the barmaid is watching, calling 999 as we speak, but no light comes from the house behind me.

'Poking your nose in. Asking questions about things that don't concern you.' He chuckles low and deep, a sound that turns my bowels to water.

'Please don't hurt me. Don't . . . rape me.' The words are strangled as the second bouncer moves closer. I can smell my own fear, sour and ripe in the still night air. 'I have a child . . . a daughter. I'll leave, I swear, I won't—'

The first punch lands square in my guts and knocks the wind from me, nausea rising up in my stomach and filling my mouth with saliva as I struggle to heave in a breath.

'I'm not a *fucking rapist*,' Kev spits. Bile fills my mouth and I spit, bent double by the force of the blow.

'Please . . .' I manage to wheeze out as another blow comes from behind, to the ribs this time, and I fall to my knees. A slap to the ear now, just to jazz things up a bit, knocking me sideways on the cold, hard tarmac, my ear ringing and stinging with heat. I try to pull my arm up to cover my ear from another blow, but a hand grabs mine, squeezing it tight before bending the fingers back painfully. I groan, spit and bile dripping from my mouth as I roll over to get to my feet, trying desperately to get away.

'Hey!'

I don't know if I imagine the shout that hangs in the still night air, but Kev's face is thrust perilously close to mine, his thick sausage fingers hauling me up by the straps of my top. 'That was just a warning. Come back again if you want more.' A laugh in the background tells me, woman or not, they're more than happy to teach me a lesson. The two hands let go of my lacy crop top roughly and I fall to the ground, my legs weak and wobbly. As my head hits the tarmac everything goes black, and my last thought is of Tom, wondering if I'll ever see him again.

* * *

Ugghhh. Everything hurts. Trying to open my sticky, aching eyes, the bright, white lights overhead make my eyeballs hurt and I give up, surrendering to blissful darkness. A jackhammer thumps through my skull, the pain making me nauseous, and there's a low groaning sound coming from somewhere in the room. My throat is dry, and as I struggle to swallow I realise the groaning is coming from me. I don't know where I am, and I'm too tired to try and figure it out. Managing to raise my eyelids just enough to peep out and get a sense of my surroundings, I see a dark-haired young woman at the end of the bed, watching me closely, a clipboard in her hand. She leans forward as she sees me trying to open my eyes as if she wants to say something, but the effort exhausts me and I close them again, sinking gratefully back into the darkness.

I don't know how much time passes before I wake again. This time, I manage to open my eyes fully, despite the harsh white light still permeating the room. Struggling to push myself into a sitting position, I wince as every muscle and bone in my body screams out in pain, a sharp stabbing in my ribs that makes my head swim. My skull still thumps with an insistent hammering and wearily I slump backwards onto the pillows behind me. I'm in a hospital. In a private room, not a ward, and there are no other patients nearby. A drip snakes out from the back of my hand, and my fingers have been strapped together. As I breathe in, I'm aware again of the sharp pain piercing my ribs, and when I press them gently the discomfort is great enough to convince me they might be broken. I'm wondering what to do — whether to press the buzzer and call the nurses to tell me how I got here, to ask for some painkillers to drown out the thumping in my head — when the door to my room silently swings open and Adam and Gwen walk in.

'Oh, Claire.' Gwen leans over, her voice thick, the scent of her floral perfume overriding the harsh disinfectant smell that hangs in the air.

'Claire — how are you feeling?' Peering at me with concerned eyes, Adam perches on the chair next to the bed, while Gwen fusses with my bed covers, loosening them slightly so I have some freedom to move around.

'Like I got hit by a bus.' I give a little smile, but wince again as the tiny muscle movement causes my head to throb.

'Do you remember what happened?'

Raising my hand to my hairline, I find a little shaved patch with a neat line of stitches marching through it and battle the urge to cry.

'Claire?' Adam presses again, as Gwen gives him a sharp look.

'Isla is at home with Hannah,' Gwen says, reaching out to brush my hair back, avoiding the line of stitches at my temple. 'I don't want you to worry about her, don't worry about anything except feeling better. It's Brody's birthday party today, so she's gone for a sleepover. I couldn't bring her . . . I didn't know what I was going to find when Adam called.'

'Adam called you?' A frown tugs at my forehead and I wince.

'I found you, Claire. Outside the house in Rufford Street.' Adam's eyes search my face as I try to remember. Rufford Street. The barmaid. I followed her. 'Those . . . men.' Adam's face twists. 'I saw them hurting you. I shouted and they ran off. Claire, they took your bag.'

My bag is gone. The photo I had of Tom and Harriet is gone. My heart sinks, and I realise Adam is talking to me.

'I brought you straight here, you were in a hell of a state. You hit your head on the pavement, and I was terrified we were going to lose you. What the hell were you doing there?'

I cast my mind back, attempting to remember what led to me ending up here, but everything has a fuzzy veil over it, nothing is clear.

'I was going to call you after I spoke to the barmaid from the club, I remember that,' I say as I unpick the tangled memories. 'What day is it now?' Swallowing is painful and I gesture at Gwen to pass me the water glass sitting on the movable tray next to the bed. Gratefully, I sip at the cool liquid, soothing the fire burning in my throat.

'It's Tuesday evening. It's late.' Gwen checks her watch. 'We shouldn't even really be here now, but the nurses said as it's a private room and you hadn't woken up yet it should be OK. She thought it might help if you woke up to familiar faces.' So, I've been unconscious for nearly twenty-four hours — and Tom has been gone for a whole week. The last thing I remember is . . . I struggle to piece together the images swirling frantically in my mind . . . the girl's flat. Trying to talk to her before she slammed the door in my face. It comes back to me in a rush, the fists slamming into my ribs, the scent of blood and violence hanging in the air.

'What about the girl? She told me she was glad Tom was gone. "Good riddance," she said.' I struggle against the pillows, trying to push myself up into a position where I can swing my legs free from the bed and get out of here.

'What girl, Claire?' Adam rests his hand on my arm to calm me, sensing my agitation. Black spots dance at the corner of my vision and I lie back against the pillows again, waiting for it to stop. 'What were you doing outside that house?'

'The girl from behind the bar — you know, Adam, the one I was going to see from the Tiger Club. The one who said she didn't know Tom, but I knew she did.' I run my tongue over dry lips, things coming back to me in patchy fragments. 'I was jumped. Attacked. I *did* go to the girl's flat . . . I . . . followed her back there after her shift.'

I hear Gwen suck in her breath in a disapproving hiss but ignore it.

'She was there on the doorstep... I grabbed her arm and asked her what she knew.' I risk a glance at Adam, his face pinched with displeasure. I knew he wouldn't like my plan, but it was the only one I had. 'I'm sorry, Adam. I didn't know how else to get the information. She told me she was glad Tom was gone. That Tom was a bastard. I got the impression that something happened — something bad — and Tom ran out again. Just like he did to Harriet.'

I stop to draw breath, my ribs hurting like a bitch, tears close to the surface.

'When I left two guys stopped me in the street, just outside her house — bouncers from the club. The last thing I remember is them hitting me. They attacked me... they said something about not messing with Carlos. I tried to tell them I wasn't, that I was looking for Tom, but they just kept hitting me. Adam, I think Carlos is definitely involved — he has to be.'

'Claire, we need to call the police. You've been attacked — and you know who did it.' Gwen's dark eyes are serious as she sits on the edge of the bed, taking my hand in hers. Adam stands behind her, one hand on her shoulder.

'Adam, please.' I stare up at him beseechingly. 'I'm not reporting this to the police. If Carlos is involved, there's no way I can bring the police into it — he would kill me, given what you've found out about him. I'm the only one who can find Tom now. Adam, the girl — the one from the club — she knows Lydia French.' *Oh.* I remember one other detail about the previous evening — the girl telling me Lydia French is in prison, right before she told me I should be glad to be rid of Tom. I tell Adam everything I can remember, as long as he swears not to involve anybody from the force.

'It's my job, Claire,' he sighs. 'I'm supposed to protect people from scum like Carlos.'

'But it's my decision at the end of the day — please, Adam. This is the only way I'm going to be able to find him. If the police get involved things could get really messy, especially when it comes to Carlos. Can you check and see if what the girl said is true? Can you see if Lydia French is still in prison?' I don't know what I'm going to do if it transpires that she's still behind bars. *Maybe*, a sneaky voice whispers in my head, *maybe if she is, it means Tom really has left you. That he doesn't want to be with you anymore.* Shaking the thought away, I'm exhausted. I lean back into the pillows, my skin feeling clammy. Gwen takes notice, and nudging Adam's arm, they stand to leave, Adam promising that *for now* he won't say anything to the police.

'But I swear, Claire—' he stops in the doorway, one hand on the frame — 'any more violence, even the hint of the threat of violence, and I'm calling them in. Understood?'

I nod, weakly. 'Adam, wait.'

He turns, as Gwen's footsteps disappear down the corridor. 'What?'

'How did you know I was there? At the house on Rufford Street.'

Adam pauses for a moment, scrubbing his hand over the stubble on his chin that he still hasn't shaved. 'You aren't the only one who knows how to follow people, Claire.'

CHAPTER 36

Painkillers ensure I sleep like the dead that night, and when I wake late the next morning the sun has moved across the room, illuminating a long stripe across the bed covers, leaving me hot and sticky. My head hurts to move, and as I raise my hands to my face to gingerly trace the injuries marking the skin, I realise that, once again, I'm not alone. A large, broad-shouldered man in his early forties sits in the hospital chair next to my bed, his huge frame dwarfing it. He has dark hair slicked back from his forehead, revealing a scar that crosses his eyebrow, reaching up towards his temple. At first, I think Gwen called the police after all. But there's something about this man that triggers the hairs on the back of my neck. Combined with the sharp blue suit that looks as if it has been tailored especially for him, all my instincts shout danger. He leans over and pours a fresh glass of water from the jug on the nightstand and hands it to me, gesturing for me to drink. I take a small swallow to refresh my sore throat and wait for him to speak.

'Well, Claire Bennett. You have been in the wars, haven't you?' His voice is a rich, deep baritone, strong and resonant, and it crosses my mind that he probably has a fantastic singing voice. *Get a grip, Claire.* Feeling at a disadvantage from my viewpoint, I raise the hospital bed and push myself a little further up the pillows to meet his dark, brooding eyes. There is a hint of something sinister in there, a flatness, like a snake's eyes, that makes me more than a little uncomfortable. I wait for him to speak again, before the silence becomes unbearable.

'I'm sorry, I don't . . . do I know you?' My voice is raspy, my throat sore and gravelly, my head still aching and full of cotton wool. I want more water, but feel reluctant to ask this man for anything.

'No. See, that's the thing, Claire. You don't know me, and yet you seem to think it's OK to be asking questions about me and my business.' He reaches into his jacket pocket and pulls out a cigar case. Shaking one out of the tin, he clips it and then holds it under his nose, breathing in the scent of tobacco.

'I'm sorry — I didn't mean to cause any offence. I'm just looking for my husband.' Adrenaline starts thumping its way around my body and I lay my hands flat on the blanket in front of me in an attempt to disguise their shaking, as I realise who this must be, sitting in my hospital room.

'Ahhhh, yes. Your husband. The elusive Theo.' Another sniff of the cigar, before he rolls it gently between finger and thumb. 'Guess what, Claire? I'm also looking for Theo. I've been looking for him for quite a while now, in fact.' My heart beats double time in my chest — I'm pretty sure the guy sitting in front of me is Carlos Bremen, but I'm wary of letting him know that I know who he is.

'Why are you looking for my husband?' My voice sounds tiny, squeaking like a child's as it rasps its way out of my bruised throat. I clear my throat to try again, but the man lets out a booming laugh, and I shrink back against the pillows as the sudden noise makes my head ring.

'Again with the questions!' He shakes his head, still rolling the cigar between his fingers, tiny pieces of tobacco starting to flake from the clipped end, dotting the white of the hospital blanket on the bed. 'Let me tell you, Claire, in different circumstances you would have been quite an asset to my team. Tenacious, strong-willed, persistent. All admirable qualities. Unfortunately, in this case, you're only getting in my way. Do you really want to know who I am?'

I nod slowly, the movement causing the nausea to return, my eyes skittering away from his.

He leans close, his mouth next to my ear, the faint scent of tobacco on his breath. 'My name is Carlos Bremen. I have other names, but you can call me Carlos.'

Leaning back in the tiny hospital chair, he bares his teeth at me in some semblance of a grin and I try to smile back, the bitter taste of fear on my tongue. In a show of bravado, I push myself upright and force myself to meet his eyes.

'So, Claire, what I want to know is, what do you think you're doing? Why are you hanging around my club, asking about my team, even though you've been warned to stay away? You followed one of them home . . . that's bang out of order, Claire. Unacceptable.'

'Look, Carlos . . . Mr. Bremen. I'm just looking for my husband, that's all. He's gone missing. I'm retracing his steps, and I think there's a possibility he used to work for you. Do you know where he is?' I'm careful not to use Tom's name, hoping I can protect him for a little longer, until I know exactly what I'm dealing with.

'Me? Why would I have anything to do with it, Claire? I'm just a businessman, trying to make an honest living.' He gives me a slow wink and I swallow hard. Just the sight of him, sitting next to my hospital bed, is intimidating.

'And where does Lydia French come into it? I heard you were asking about her too.'

'I saw a photograph on my social media — some kind of sponsored advert. It was a plea from Lydia French, asking for help in finding her husband and child; only, it was a photo of Theo and our daughter. He left for work as usual that day, but he never came home. I thought she'd taken Theo . . . only now, I'm not sure. I was told she was in prison.' I blink back the hot tears that spring to my eyes, powerless to stop them sliding down my cheeks.

'Oh, Claire. No need to cry. You see, the thing is, Theo and I have a history together. And he has a history of running off — did you know that?' I don't speak, unsure what the correct answer would be. 'But I'm prepared to look past all of that, in order to help you find your husband.'

'O . . . K. You want to help me find Theo? You really don't know where he is? I thought maybe . . .' I tail off, unwilling to finish my sentence.

'You thought what, Claire? Come on, spit it out. After all, we're friends now, aren't we?' He grins, and I'm reminded of a shark, circling its prey.

'I thought maybe he was with you. Maybe Lydia French was searching him out for you.'

'Claire, I haven't seen Theo for years, why would I know where he is now?' He gives a short bark of laughter, humourless and harsh. 'He owes me something, Claire, and I'll help you find him if you make him repay what he owes me. I've waited a long time to see Theo again.' He leans in towards me, lowering his voice to a conspiratorial whisper. 'And now I know where to find you . . . well, let's just say I'm not going to rest until I get what I'm due.'

My blood turns to ice, my mind whirling — what could it possibly be that Tom owes this man? Did he take something with him when he left? Something precious to Carlos? Does it have anything to do with the money I found under the floorboards? I don't want to accept his help, but the thinly veiled threat of what he will do to me, to us, if he doesn't get what he wants is terrifying. Carlos won't let this lie, not now he knows Tom has a family, and I need any information he can give me. The air crackles with tension as he waits for me to answer.

'OK . . .' I swallow down the fear bubbling like lava in my chest, willing to agree to anything if it means my family is safe. 'OK, I'll accept your help.' The words almost choke me as I realise what I'm getting myself into. 'What is it you want from my husband? What is it he owes you?'

'He owes me an apology for starters, Claire. He made me look a mug in front of everyone — he fucking ruined me. People thought I was some sort of idiot, some sort of pushover. You've no idea, Claire, of the lengths I had to go to, *the things I had to do*, to prove to people I was still the same Carlos.' He cracks his knuckles and I wince. 'He's lucky this much time has passed, because in all honesty, if I'd found him before, I would have killed him for what he did. I loved her, Claire. I loved Lydia, and her and Theo, the two of them did me over.' He stares hard at me, flat, dark eyes betraying none of the emotion of his words. The eyes of a psychopath. Registering his words, my heart leaps into my mouth. Carlos loved Lydia. Lydia and Tom betrayed Carlos and what? Ran off together?

'I'm sorry, Carlos. For whatever they did to you. It's entirely possible Theo has done it to me now, but I need to know where he is.' My best course of action is to try and show Carlos I understand where he's coming from. 'I need to know he's safe, even if he has . . . run off. We have a child together, and I don't think Theo would leave her intentionally.'

'There's just one other thing, Claire, before I leave.' Brushing my words away, he reaches behind him and picks up a hand mirror from the windowsill and hands it to me. I peer into it, shocked at the state of the injuries to my face. There is a split across my nose, and while it doesn't feel broken, the bruising has spread out across my face, giving me two shining black eyes. My bottom lip is split, held together by three neat, black stitches, which explains why my throat is so dry — it hurts to close my lips together. Angling the mirror to the right, I see the shaved patch in the side of my thick, blond hair, the whiteness of my scalp bleeding through, and the spikes of several more stitches sticking up from the bald patch above my hairline. I look a mess. 'If you come round the club, or near any of my girls again, this is just the beginning. This—' he waves his unlit cigar in the direction of my face — 'will look like a vacation compared to what I'll have done to you next time. And stay away from Pippa. She's a bartender, not a fucking grass.' He places the cigar in his mouth. 'I'll be in touch.'

With that he stands, tucks a business card between my arm and the hospital blanket, and marches out of the hospital room, leaving me dazed. I peer at myself again in the mirror, before laying it down on the blanket and closing my eyes. I don't need to see my battered, ruined face to know I've found myself tangled in something deeper than I ever thought possible, and Tom is the one who led me here.

CHAPTER 37

I should fight. I should be tugging and pulling, trying to free myself, but any energy I had is gone, and my wrists are on fire where the handcuffs pull tight with every movement I make. The old me would never give up, would never surrender, but I'm older. More tired. Lessons have been learned. My head aches with fever and with every passing hour it feels as though my bones are freezing from the inside out, the hard concrete floor making it impossible to find a comfortable position. My stomach shrieks with hunger, made worse by the tiny scraps of fruit and bread that are brought to me with seemingly no pattern, the food always appearing just as I've given up hope of anything to eat. I try to stay alert, ears pricked to hear my captor return, but I find myself jerking from sleep time and again without even realising I've dozed off. I'd give anything for my own bed — any bed — for a blanket to fend off the excruciating cold. Something clangs overhead, a sharp repetitive sound that seems to echo around my skull, and I wish I could raise my hands to cover my ears before the noise drives me insane.

As my urge to physically fight back is almost extinguished, I rack my scrambled brains to think of a way out of this. I need to beg my captor, to see if I can make them feel anything for me. I need to appeal to their better nature — beg them to let me go. If I promise never to tell, if I agree to pretend that none of this ever happened, maybe they'll let me go. The thought of leaving, of walking through my own front door into the arms of my family is overwhelming and my throat thickens. I can't afford to cry.

This time, I'm awake when I hear the squeal of the door opening and as soon as the gag is pulled from my lips, I open my mouth to make my case.

'Please . . . I swear I'll never tell anyone what happened here. I'll keep my mouth shut about everything, I promise. Just let me go. No one will ever know, it can be our secret.' I try to swallow but my mouth is too dry and it feels as though the two sides of my throat are sticking together, fibres from the gag leaving a nasty, bitter taste in my mouth.

'Our secret?' Finally my captor speaks for the first time and horror spreads through my veins like ice over a lake. It's a voice I know so well. 'Don't you think we've got enough secrets between us?'

CHAPTER 38

After a visit from the doctor the next morning, I discharge myself against his wishes. My bumps and bruises are not life-threatening and, although painful, no one ever died from a couple of broken ribs. I fix myself up the best I can in the tiny hospital bathroom and pull on clean clothes — luckily Gwen left me a small holdall with a change of clothes and a toothbrush, before she left to hurry back in time to collect Isla from school. I'm guessing she's disposed of my battered, blood-stained clothes from Monday night.

I rang Adam earlier this morning to tell him I would be leaving the hospital this afternoon, and after trying to persuade me to stay, at least until the doctors pronounced me fit to leave, he finally caved in and agreed to come and pick me up. I sit on the bench outside the hospital, among the smokers, some sporting hospital gowns and cannulas in the back of their veiny hands, waiting for him to arrive. The sun, which felt so welcoming at first after two days holed up in a hospital bed, soon starts to make me feel dizzy, and I'm relieved when Adam pulls up in his battered Fiesta.

'Come on, get in.' He jumps out of the car and helps me into the passenger seat, ignoring my winces as my stitches tug and my ribs groan. 'You look like shit, by the way. You should have waited until they said it was OK to leave.' Grim-faced, Adam glares at the old man with a cigarette who tries to attract my attention by pulling his hospital gown open as we pull away.

'I don't have time to sit around in a hospital bed.' I pull down the sun visor, peering into the small mirror. My face really does look worse, if that's at all possible. The skin around my eyes is a deep blue-purple, verging on black, and I look as though I've gone ten rounds with Mike Tyson. Sighing, I flip the visor back up and gently press my fingers to the bridge of my nose, flinching at the pain. As we drive, Adam stares hard at the road, concentrating on getting me home, but there's a set edge to his jaw and I know there's something he needs to tell me.

'Adam. What is it?' I ask, but he ignores me, pulling expertly into the right-hand lane, narrowly missing a taxi that hurtles up behind him, the taxi driver letting him know exactly what he thinks of Adam's driving through some pretty obscene hand gestures. Adam doesn't react, just raises his eyes to the rear-view mirror and tuts to himself.

'Adam, please, just tell me. I know you — I know when you've got something to say.' Adam pulls back over to the left-hand lane, ready to turn at the next set of lights, letting Mr. Angry in his taxi rush past him.

'First, you need to take some painkillers.' He points to the glove box, where I stashed the small pharmacy bag handed to me by the doctors on my departure from the hospital. 'Then, yes, I do have something to tell you.' He busies himself with the rear-view mirror again, as he glides to a stop at the red traffic light ahead. Dry swallowing two co-codamol, I sit quietly, having learned a long time ago that when Adam is in this mood, it's best to just let him go with it. Finally, he turns to me, his face serious.

'I went to the Tiger Club.' Adam drops his eyes, and I stare at him incredulously.

'Adam? What the fuck! After you told *me* it was dangerous, and then you saw the state of me yesterday? Jesus.'

'I know, but I needed to speak to that girl — the one you followed.' There's an edge to his voice that tells me I can be disapproving of him all I want, but I was the one who started this.

'You do know Carlos visited me in hospital yesterday?' I can't help my voice from rising. 'He sat next to my hospital bed and told me he was also looking for Tom. He threatened me, said that this—' I jab a finger towards my face — 'will be nothing compared to what he'll do to me next time. And then you go and start poking around at the club! Bloody hell, Adam, you're going to get us killed.'

'What? No, I didn't know that — because you didn't think to tell me! Don't you think if I'd known then I wouldn't have gone?' Adam's face is flushed, a muscle working overtime in his jaw.

'Look, I'm sorry, OK? I didn't get a chance to tell you — once he was gone I took more painkillers and passed out. If I'd known what you were planning, then of course I would have told you. But bloody hell, Adam, you were the one who warned me off Carlos and the club in the first place.'

'It's my job to question people, Claire. I know how to handle this stuff. Maybe you should have left it to me in the first place, at least then you might not have been hurt.'

I say nothing for a moment, unwilling to admit that Adam is right. 'And did you speak to the girl?' I say finally, butterfly wings flapping in my stomach at what Pippa might have revealed to Adam, especially after the way she spoke about Tom.

'I think you're right, Claire. I'm sorry I doubted you. I just put it all down to Tom being a bit flighty and leaving when things get too much for him. But I'm starting to think Lydia French is involved too. The girl, Pippa, told me Tom does know Lydia. She worked at the Tiger Club. Tom worked with her the whole time he was there — according to this girl, she was a bit infatuated with him.'

'Infatuated?' This almost — but not quite — ties up with the story Carlos Bremen told me.

'That's what she said.'

'God.' This is disturbing news, but it gives credit to everything I've been thinking all along. 'Carlos told me something similar . . . but he said Tom and Lydia did the dirty on him. Do you think they had a relationship behind Carlos's back? Did she tell you why Tom left the club?'

'No, nothing else. She was antsy enough as it was, and once she'd told me that, she couldn't get rid of me quick enough. Obviously she was worried Carlos would come back and catch her talking to me. I got the impression there might have been something between Tom and Lydia, even if it was little more than wishful thinking on Lydia's side. Maybe Tom liked the attention and led her on? Pippa did confirm Lydia was in prison, but that was all I got out of her before she made me leave.'

I sit back, leaning my head against the headrest. The painkillers are giving me a spacey feeling, making it hard for me to take in what Adam had just told me. Adam believes me that Tom didn't leave. And Tom definitely knows Lydia French.

'So, what's the plan now?' Adam doesn't take his eyes off my face as he speaks. The lights change to green and someone behind us toots impatiently. 'The Tiger Club is a definite no-go. The girl doesn't have any more information about where Tom could have gone, and even if she did there's no way you could go back there, not now Carlos knows your face.'

'What about Lydia French? Did you get anywhere with the prison thing?' I ask.

'There's no way I can get into the police computer system to check without a red flag being raised, and I'm sorry, Claire, but I risked my job enough last night by using my badge to get Pippa to talk to me.'

Despite my disappointment at his words, a wave of gratitude floods over me — Adam doesn't realise how much his help means to me, and although I can't help thinking I was wrong to get him involved, there's no way I could have made this much progress without his support.

'Thanks, Adam. Maybe Carlos will turn something up.' Hopefully he wasn't lying when he said he had nothing to do with Tom's disappearance. I'm already regretting agreeing to accept Carlos's help, not just because he's crazy, with no regard for the law, but also for fear of what he might do to Tom once he does catch up with him. The threat he made about not resting until he got what he was due rolls around in my mind, my heart stuttering in my chest every time I picture his face. I lean my head back again, rolling my shoulders and fighting the urge to close my eyes and sleep. A tug of longing for Isla sweeps over me; it feels like weeks since I've been with her. I lay a hand on Adam's forearm. 'Can you take me to Gwen's? I really need to see my daughter.'

CHAPTER 39

I gingerly slide my way out of the car when we pull up at Gwen's and Adam waves me off. Gwen stands in the doorway, nervously clutching at fistfuls of her skirt as I walk up the driveway to meet her. She hugs me as I reach the front door, apologising as she feels me wince, before guiding me through to the kitchen.

'Here.' Gwen eyes my battered face carefully, guiding me towards the table before she rummages in her handbag and pulls out her make-up bag. 'Sit down. I need to fix you up a bit before Isla sees you.'

'How's she been? I'm sorry to have just left her with you like this . . .' I have to take a deep breath, and Gwen tuts as she gently dabs foundation over my bruises.

'It's fine, Claire. We're family. I love Isla and I love you . . . you would do it for me if it were the other way round. I'm guessing there's still no word from Tom?'

I close my eyes as Gwen's cool fingers dab lightly at my skin. 'Nothing. I think I might be close to finding Lydia French though.'

'So, you definitely think she has something to do with it? Tom hasn't just . . . left?' Gwen asks, her face crumpling slightly as she blinks back tears.

I pick up a lip gloss and swipe it quickly over my lips, peeking at my reflection in my phone camera. I look monstrous, but less monstrous than before. 'I don't know, Gwen, to be honest. After what happened to me in Soho, I'm concerned Tom is tangled up in something serious. I need to find out exactly what's gone on before I involve the police, so it's best if I just keep trying on my own. Can I see Isla?' I'm longing to hold my daughter, and I don't want to go over everything again. I'm just too tired, and there's nothing Gwen can do to help.

Gwen jumps to her feet and goes to the bottom of the stairs to call Isla again. She appears a few minutes later, eyeing me cautiously.

'Isla! Oh, I've missed you.' I hold my arms out to her, my heart breaking when at first she hangs back, unsure of the bruised and battered face in front of her. 'It's me, Mummy. I'm sorry, darling, Mummy looks a bit of a state.' Isla slowly peels herself away from the doorframe, shuffling slowly across the laminate floor towards me. I bend down on one knee and hold my arms out to her. She gets within feet of me, still anxious, before she throws herself across the last patch of floor between us, tumbling into my arms and making my ribs shriek with pain.

'Mummy, what happened to you? Where have you been? Where's Daddy — is he back?' Her small face gazes earnestly up at mine, her tiny fingers tracing gently over the spiky, black stitches at my temple.

'I fell over . . . nothing serious. I slipped on a wet banana skin.' Isla gives a tiny laugh, the sound of it pouring over my skin like rain on a parched pavement. We saw it in a cartoon once and she laughed until she peed a little bit. 'Daddy is . . . he's not back yet, but it won't be much longer and I'll bring him home.' I meet Gwen's worried gaze over the top of Isla's head. 'Can you stay with Aunt Gwen for a little bit longer?' Gwen gives a slight nod and Isla turns her face into my shoulder, shaking her head.

'I just want to come home, Mummy.' Her voice is thick with tears.

'Please, baby . . . I need you to be brave, remember? I'm going to get you home as soon as I can . . . as soon as I find Daddy, I promise.' We hug for a long time, Isla's arms tight around my neck. Kissing her forehead, I nudge her. 'Go on, go and play.' She squeezes me one last time and runs from the room, her tiny feet slapping on the steps as she runs back upstairs. I get awkwardly to my feet, every bone in my body aching.

'God, Gwen, I hate leaving her.' It was hard enough leaving her just to go to work every day. This is unbearable.

'I know,' Gwen soothes, her voice thick with emotion. 'But you need to, Claire, if you're still determined to do this on your own. You don't need to worry about anything here. I'll look after Isla, don't worry about her, you just go and find Tom.' I nod slowly, apologising again, heading towards the staircase to say goodbye to Isla, when the buzzing of a mobile phone stops me. Pulling my phone out, I'm puzzled when the screen of my phone is blank. The tone buzzes again and realisation dawns on me. It's Tom's phone and when I pull it from my pocket, it shows one unread text message, again from an unknown number. A different one this time. Is it from Lydia French? Does she have a burner phone? Or is there someone else involved? Ruby, the girl who disappeared from the clifftop in Lockwood Bay? Another faceless person intent on harming Tom? Shaking, I swipe sideways and open the message.

YOU DIDN'T THINK YOU COULD GET AWAY WITH IT, DID YOU?

My mouth fills with bile, and I have to swallow hard in order to stop myself from being sick.

'*Shit.* Shit . . . Oh God.' I'm trying to unlock my phone with shaking fingers, entering the passcode wrong twice as I try to get to Adam's number so I can call him.

'Claire? Claire, what is it?' Gwen's face is pinched and white, concern etched sharply into her features. I pass her Tom's phone, the text glaring out from the backlit screen, and her hand flies to her mouth as she reads it.

'What are you going to do? I mean, who sent this text? Is it Lydia French?' Her eyes are wide as she hands me back the phone.

'I don't know, Gwen. I don't know what's going on, or who has Tom. If Lydia has him, then who sent this text message? I tried replying to the last message like this one and got no response. I need to speak to Adam.' I ring Adam's phone again, and finally, after the third missed call, he picks up.

'I've had a text,' I blurt out, before he even has a chance to say hello. 'It's on Tom's phone.' I tell him what it says and wait for him to speak. Adam pauses for a moment, as if carefully choosing his words.

'Claire, I was just going to call you. I've been looking further into Lydia French. Now we know she worked there, I tried searching for her name alongside the Tiger Club — I thought maybe whatever she went to prison for might have had something to do with the club. She was charged and convicted of manslaughter in early 2009.'

Manslaughter. I thought maybe fraud, or something to do with drugs, but I never thought that the woman looking for my husband would have been arrested for manslaughter. A buzz on my phone alerts me to a text.

'Hang on, Adam, I've got a text.' Pulling the phone away from my ear, I check the screen. There's one message, from an unknown number. I open it, my stomach flipping when I see it signed off 'Carlos' — how the hell did he get my number? I re-read the message, the words making my blood run cold. The sick feeling in my stomach intensifies and I feel the heavy weight of Gwen's eyes on me, as she and Adam anxiously wait to hear my response.

'Adam, Lydia French was released from prison three months ago.'

CHAPTER 40

The news that Lydia French has been released from prison is not entirely unexpected, and it almost comes as a relief, laying to rest the thought that has niggled at the back of my mind this entire time. The one that says, *What if Lydia French has nothing to do with this? What if it is simply a case of Tom intentionally leaving without a second thought for you or Isla?* Keeping the flurry of emotions running through my mind in check, I say goodbye to Isla properly, squeezing her tight and promising her I'll be back to fetch her soon. She cries a little as I leave, and I feel desperately guilty at leaving her so soon after I got back. Thanking Gwen again for all her help, I begin the short walk back to my house. I've arranged to meet Adam there, in order to decide where we go next. As I turn into our road, I see him sitting in his car outside the house, his face set as he taps away on his phone. Looking up to see me beside the window, he gets out of the car and pulls me in for a hug. I breathe in the familiar scent of him. The smell of his aftershave has an underlying twist of nutmeg, taking me back ten years to another time, a time when everything was so much simpler. I pull away, confused by what I'm feeling.

'Oh God, Claire, your face.' I take it Gwen's make-up skills haven't done the job, as Adam runs his eyes over me.

'Pretty sure it's not as painful as it looks,' I lie, as I walk up the garden path to the house, vividly aware of the space where Tom's car should be. 'Are you coming in? We need to talk about where to go next.'

'Claire, I think we need to call the police.' Adam's voice is calm and firm as we step inside the house. He switches into police officer mode, taking control of the situation.

'No. No police. We can't.'

'We have to! Tom is still missing — it's highly likely Lydia French is involved and not because she wants to play Happy Families, Claire. You've been badly beaten up, and you know who's behind it all. We need to call the police, and pass this on to them. This is too big for us to deal with on our own.' Adam stares me down, but I don't look away.

'Adam, I can't call the police, OK? It's not just Lydia French to consider. There are other people involved, nasty people; you know that, you're the one who warned me about them in the first place. *We don't know what has happened to Tom. If he's . . .*' I take a deep breath, readying myself to say it out loud. 'If Tom is still alive, then involving the police might be the catalyst that gets him killed. I need to find Tom before that happens.'

'Is this about Carlos Bremen?'

'Partly. And partly because I don't know how deep this thing goes for Tom. Look at the text message.' I hold Tom's phone out to him, and watch closely as he scans over the text. 'See what I mean? What is it that he's supposedly got away with? Come on, Adam, I've told you what Tom is like. He's . . . perfect. He's a good dad, a good husband. He goes out of his way to do the right thing for other people. He's a *nice person*. And if he's made a mistake in the past, I want to deal with it without getting the police involved. If . . . *when* we find him, then we call the police, and get Lydia French back in prison, away from Tom, away from all of us. Then we can sit down and talk about whatever Tom is supposed to have done.'

I can see it takes every ounce of Adam's restraint to keep his mouth shut, and it doesn't take long before his resolve cracks and he shakes his head. 'Claire, I don't think you understand how serious this is . . . how *risky*. It's common sense to involve the police — they're more likely to be able to deal with this than you are. Carlos Bremen is *dangerous*. I've told you, people who've crossed him have gone missing before. Doesn't that tell you the kind of people you're dealing with here? Sorry, Claire, but I'm finding it really hard to condone your actions.'

'And if I do call the police and they find Tom, and we end up getting him killed, how will you feel then?' My voice is dangerously quiet as I struggle to dampen down the emotions bubbling away under my skin. I need Adam's help, but I need to do this my way.

'*Jesus Christ*, Claire.' Adam spins away from me, running his hands through his hair in frustration. 'Fine, if you think you know best, we'll do it your way, but you can't say I didn't warn you. There's every chance that this could all go wrong, you know that?' He steps past me, shoving his hands into his pockets as he stares moodily out the back window, when my phone rings. I glance at him nervously, *number withheld* flashing on the screen. Scowling, Adam nods at me as if to say, *Go on*, and I press the green button to connect the call, and switch it to loudspeaker.

'Hello?'

'Mrs. Bennett? Easthampton Police.' I raise my eyes to meet Adam's, and he shrugs, turning back to the window. I know he wants me to tell them everything, but I can't. Not yet. 'We're just checking in on a report you filed last . . . Tuesday? Regarding your husband, Tom Bennett.'

'Umm . . .' I clear my throat, the words sticking like thorns. 'Err . . . yes. Yes, I made the report.'

'We're just checking to see how things are going . . . whether you've had any further developments? Obviously, if things are resolved between you and your husband then we do need to close the file.' Adam goes to speak and I put my finger to my lips.

'Thank you so much. I should have contacted you before . . . I mean, I spoke to my husband.' Adam stares at me in outrage, and I turn my back to avoid his hard gaze. 'We're . . . having a trial separation at the moment. For now. We're both very sorry to have wasted your time.' I clear my throat again and make the right noises until, satisfied, the policeman rings off.

'You're really going to do this? On your own? You bloody fool.'

'What else can I do, Adam? I can't go back to the club — and certainly not with the police in tow. If I do, Carlos will most probably kill me. He's looking for Tom too, you know. What if he finds him before us? He's not going to hand him over to me if I'm dragging the police along behind me.'

Finally, Adam nods in recognition that what I've said makes sense. 'OK, I get your point. No police, for now anyway. So, what are we going to do?'

'To be honest, Adam, I have no idea. Every avenue I try to follow is a dead end. I don't know where to go next.' I lick my lips, stinging the stitches holding the skin together. 'We know Lydia French worked at the Tiger Club with Tom, she was infatuated with him, and then she went to prison. We also know she's now out of prison, but God only knows where she is, and I haven't got a clue where to start looking. Carlos obviously doesn't know either — he told me Lydia was out of prison, but not where I could find her.'

'Right, well, I've got a plan. It might not work; the whole thing might backfire completely. And don't forget, Claire, we don't know for definite Tom is with Lydia French.' Adam lays his hand gently on top of mine, resignation in his voice. 'I believe what you're saying, but we still don't know the truth. He might have gone of his own accord, remember? He's done it to Harriet, and he's done it to Carlos.'

'Tom hasn't done it to me, Adam. He wouldn't do that. Not to Isla.' Angrily, I swipe my hand back. 'I'm sure he hasn't. Lydia French was in prison for manslaughter — you can't tell me she's not dangerous, and you can't tell me this is all a coincidence.' I'm not going to let myself believe Tom's left us, not until he tells me that himself.

'OK, OK. He hasn't chosen to leave. Now listen, do you want to hear my idea or not?'

CHAPTER 41

I spend the long, uncomfortable hours alone, listing my regrets, all the things I wish I'd done, all the things I wish I'd never done. So many things I've said, so many nights I wish I could take back. I'm not perfect — I know that — but I've tried to be a better person the last few years. To be the person I wish I'd been all along. Now, I'll never get the opportunity to put things right. I think of my sister, wishing I had spent more time with her, regretting the way I left her behind. I try to sleep, but my shoulders burn and ache when I try to move, so I have to stay in one position, relishing the moments when everything feels numb. Waiting for the fire to tear through my limbs every time I shift position in my light sleep.

Sleep. I'm craving the oblivion of a deep sleep like nothing else, my limbs heavy and my eyes dry from lack of it. My captor brings me more water, bread and fruit, and although I try to engage in conversation to ask why, there's never any response, not after that one single sentence spoken in the dark. I'm weak, broken, the fuzziness of a fever clawing at my brain. My lips are cracked and my eyes hurt, but despite the state I'm in, the answer comes to me in a small moment of clarity. I know why I'm here. I remember the events that led to this moment like it was yesterday. I wait anxiously for my captor to reappear, my heart racing as I hear the familiar sound of the heavy door creaking open.

'Please . . .' I say, before food and water appear. 'I promise, I won't say anything, please just let me go.'

My captor's voice is cold, with none of the warm emotion I'm used to from those dulcet tones. 'You didn't think you could get away with it, did you?' A laugh, brittle and icy. 'There can only be one winner in this — you know that, don't you?'

I nod. A single tear slides down my cheek. I should have known. The past will always come back to haunt you, no matter what you do to try to make amends.

CHAPTER 42

'We need to find Lydia French.'

That's Adam's big idea? Resisting the urge to scream in frustration, I gesture for Adam to go on.

'Every trail we've followed to find Tom has been a dead end, correct? So, we need to find Lydia French. I know you've been saying this all along, but now . . . I think you're right. We need to follow the trail that leads to her — if we can find her, then there's a chance we can find Tom. I believe you. I believe there's something more sinister going on than just Tom getting a bee in his bonnet and running off.'

Realising what Adam is getting at, a little spark of hope leaps in my chest. He's right — I've been so focused on places that *Tom* might go, it hasn't even crossed my mind to follow the trails leading to Lydia French.

'Adam — you're brilliant. The only thing is, where do we start? The club is the only lead we have for Lydia, and Carlos hasn't seen her. Plus, Carlos made it pretty clear it's not a good idea for me to show my face round there. I don't want to piss him off, especially now he seems to be helping us. I'm still wary of him.'

'That's not the only lead, Claire. We have the prison as well, don't we?' Adam smiles and pulls his warrant card from his back pocket, throwing it down on the table with a slap. 'If I do this for you, there's every chance I could lose my job, my home, everything, if my gut instinct is wrong. If it goes right . . . well, maybe there's something in it for me. It sounds harsh, Claire, but if Tom has been taken by this woman, and I help you find her, then maybe my boss won't pass me over for promotion.' Adam doesn't meet my eyes, instead staring down at his hands intently. 'By rights, I should be calling this in and handing it over for my colleagues to deal with, *but* I also get what you're saying about Tom being involved in something . . . unsavoury.'

'What do you mean?'

'There's one person who absolutely *must* know where Lydia French is — it'll be a condition of her being released — and that's her probation officer. She'll have to report to them every week, and they'll know where she's supposed to be living. If I can get hold of them, maybe I can find out where she's staying and we can go from there.'

* * *

The next morning, my nerves are jangling as I sit at the kitchen table waiting for Adam to get ready. He stayed over on the couch the previous night, as we sat up late into the evening talking about his plan, deciding it was too late for him to trek all the way home only to have to come back in the morning. I try not to think about what Tom would think if he knew about it. We never really discussed my relationship with Adam after Tom and I got together. It took me a long time to get over the guilt, but at the same time I knew I'd made the right decision. I couldn't live without Tom.

After phoning around his police contacts yesterday afternoon, it didn't take long for Adam to track down Lydia French's probation officer. Adam is going to head to her office in Camden this morning, to try and see if she can find a way of getting hold of Lydia, hopefully giving Adam a current address. I watch as he stands in front of the living room mirror hanging over the fireplace, smoothing his hair down and checking his parting is straight. I've lost count of the number of times I've watched Tom get ready in front of the same mirror before leaving for work in the morning, and there's something comforting about it, at a time when I feel upside down and more than a little in turmoil.

Adam catches me watching in the mirror and turns with a frown. 'Claire? You OK?' He adjusts the collar of his shirt and tucks the hem into his jeans.

'Are you sure you won't get in trouble for this?' I'm nervous, not just because today we might potentially find Lydia French, but also for Adam. He's risking his job by doing this. The idea also crosses my mind that when I do find Tom I might be too late, making ice swim through my veins, a cold shudder slowly rolling from the back of my neck down to the bottom of my spine. How could I ever forgive myself if I didn't find him in time?

'Yes, as long as they don't know about it. If I'm right, and we end up finding Tom, then I'll come clean.' Adam's voice is firm. 'We have to do this, Claire — this is the only way we're going to find Lydia. I'm not going to mention any names; I'm just going to see if I can get an address for her.'

'I want to come,' I announce, the thought of waiting here all day unbearable, pacing back and forth as I wonder what's going on.

'Absolutely not.' Adam's tone is firm, leaving no room for argument, but I insist anyway.

'I promise I won't get in the way. I'll stay in the car. Please, Adam,' I beg, allowing my eyes to fill with tears. 'I can't wait here alone all day, I'll go mad. Please?'

Adam eyes me closely, and I see his mouth soften. 'This is a bad idea,' he sighs. 'OK. But you stay in the car. You let *me* handle everything.'

* * *

We pull up outside a boxy, seventies-style building on the outskirts of Camden that's seen better days. Adam quickly looks over at me, his gaze confident, while my palms start to prickle with sweat. He gives me a brisk smile before sliding out of the driver's seat, phone in one hand, police-issued notepad in the other.

'Wait here,' he says, as I unclip my seatbelt, ready to walk up to the building with him, my promise to stay in the car forgotten. 'Claire, I can't take you in with me, even if you weren't in that state. You look like you've been cage fighting or something.' The bruising has fully bloomed now despite my best efforts at covering it with make-up, dark flowers of purple and indigo decorating my face, making me look puffy and, even if I do say so myself, slightly dangerous. 'I don't think I'll be long, so wait here for me. Do *not* — and I mean it — do not even think about getting out of this car.'

I nod my agreement, feeling increasingly on edge as Adam makes his way up the path to a heavy-framed door, pressing a buzzer on the metal plate next to it. A moment later, the door swings open and Adam disappears inside. I wait patiently at first, but as the minutes tick by I get more and more frustrated. I drum my fingers on the dashboard, waiting for Adam to appear at the door, various scenarios playing out in my head as I curse my superb talent for overthinking. A man in a green Barbour similar to one Tom has walks past, led by a tiny yellow Chihuahua, and glances in curiously at the window. I do a double take as I catch sight of the jacket, thinking for a moment it *is* Tom, before disappointment takes over when I realise he's too short and his hair is all wrong. The man catches sight of my bruised and battered face and turns away, scurrying quickly along the pavement towards the traffic lights. I continue waiting, reluctant to turn on the radio or get out and stretch my legs, until thirty-five minutes after Adam disappeared inside the building, I see his frame silhouetted in the glass of the door, and he steps out with a squat, older lady with an elfin haircut just behind him. Adam turns and speaks to the woman, shaking her hand and nodding in agreement with something she says, before he says goodbye and begins walking back to the car. The woman watches as Adam approaches the car, tugging open the door and climbing into the driver's seat. He turns and, catching the woman still watching, raises a hand, before firing up the engine and pulling away from the kerb.

* * *

Adam drives us to a café about half a mile away, with a tiny car park at the rear. We head in and Adam steers me to a booth at the back, tucked away in a corner where we're not noticeable at first glance to anybody who enters. He orders two full English breakfasts and two pots of tea. Finally, once the food has arrived and he's satisfied we can't be overheard, he's ready to talk.

'So, that was Lydia French's probation officer.'

'The short woman who watched us drive away?'

'Yep. That's her. Virginia Carter. Hopefully, she doesn't suspect I'm nothing to do with Lydia's case and she's not going to report me.' Adam takes a big bite of his sausage after dousing it in brown sauce.

'So, what did she say? What did you tell her?' I'm on tenterhooks, waiting for Adam to fill me in.

'Well, first of all, I told her I was working on a missing person's case and Lydia French's name had come up in connection with the person that we're looking for. She wanted to ask questions, obviously, but I managed to get away without revealing anything. I told her at the moment it was all strictly confidential. She bought it, but I'm a bit worried that after seeing you in the car, she might make some calls and try to find out what it's all about, but we'll deal with that if it comes to it.' Adam appears to be pretty cool and calm, but under the table I can feel his foot tapping against the lino, a sure sign he's not feeling that cool at all.

'Do you think she will? I don't want you to get in any trouble, Adam.' I'll feel terrible if Adam loses his job for helping me, but I'd do anything to find Tom. 'Did you get the address for Lydia? Did Virginia Carter tell you anything about where she might be?' Too anxious to eat, I push my plate to one side, my breakfast left untouched, my stomach tangled in worried knots.

Adam holds up the notepad triumphantly. 'Got it. She told me Lydia works as a caretaker for several blocks of flats not far from here. It's on the same estate as the block she lives in. She lived there before she got sent down and apparently her mum kept up the payments on it while she was in prison, so there's no other address for her. This is our best place to start — there's just one problem.'

The initial rush of excitement that Adam has managed to obtain an address for Lydia French fades as I register his words — of course there's a problem. There's been nothing but problems ever since I called Tom's mobile on that first morning, which seems like months ago now, to see if he knew who Lydia French was.

'What's the problem?'

'Lydia is supposed to sign in with Virginia Carter every Thursday morning. It's a condition of her parole. Claire, Lydia French didn't sign in last week.'

CHAPTER 43

The implications of Adam's words are clear. Lydia hasn't checked in with her probation officer. Tom hasn't come home. The two are quite obviously connected and I'm certain now, one hundred per cent sure, Lydia French is with my husband. The question is, is Tom there through his own volition? There is a tiny seed of doubt, given Tom's history, but it's dwarfed by the certainty I feel whenever I think about Isla and the way Tom is with her. He wouldn't leave. Whichever it is, there's only one way to find out.

'So, we're going to her flat, yes?' I pluck the notepad from Adam's hands, my eyes running over his spidery black writing, committing the address to memory. I know roughly where it is after working on the sale of a house just around the corner from there last year. It's a block of flats at the end of York Road in Camden, slightly run-down, but with more and more of them being snapped up from the council and becoming privately owned.

'Are you sure you want to do this, Claire?' Adam's voice is quiet, worry lacing his words. 'What if Tom's with her off his own bat? What if he's been waiting for her to come out of prison?'

'Then surely she would have checked in, wouldn't she?' Adam's suggestion that Tom wants to be with Lydia French instead of me makes my stomach roll and I push my chair away from the table, ready to leave. 'If Tom's been waiting for her and now they're finally together, why would she do anything to jeopardise that? Are you coming or not?'

'I'm coming.' Adam stands, an expression I can't read on his face, but he sucks it up and doesn't say another word, instead tapping Lydia's address into the satnav when we get in the car. The roads are quiet, especially for a mid-morning on a weekday, and I'm lucky enough to spot a parking space almost directly opposite Lydia's building. It feels like things finally might be going my way. Adam turns to me, his face sober.

'Wait here. I'll go up and see if she's home.' He catches sight of the alarm on my face. 'No, Claire. I'll go alone. I won't tell her who I am; I'll just check things out, see if she's actually there.' He pauses for a moment. 'I'll see if she's there alone.'

Before I can protest, Adam slides out of the passenger seat and jogs lightly up to the front door of the flats. I know Adam's right — it *is* best if he goes up there alone, we don't want to spook her — but it's beyond frustrating to be so near and yet so far. I resist the urge to get out and follow him, conscious that if Lydia sees me from the window of her flat she may bolt, instead pulling out my phone and checking for messages. There's one from Gwen, asking me to check in, so I quickly tap out a reply, updating her on what we've found out over the past few hours. Moments later, Adam slips back into the passenger seat.

'Well?' I demand, anxious to hear what he has to say.

'Nothing. Lydia wasn't there. I knocked, but there was no sign of life whatsoever. I even peered through the letter box, but there was nothing out of the ordinary.'

'Shit.' I think for a minute. 'She'll have to come back at some point though, right?'

Adam nods thoughtfully. 'See that window?' He points to one on the top floor, right at the end of the building. 'That's the window outside her front door. I could see you waiting in the car from there. We could wait? See if she turns up?' There's no other option. Neither of us have any idea where Lydia might be, and if she does have Tom and is keeping him somewhere else, I assume she'll have to come back at some point to change clothes and shower.

'OK,' I agree. 'We wait. However long it takes.'

We wait for hours. Several people go in and out of the flats, but as we look up to the window outside Lydia's door each time someone enters, no one goes near her flat. It's mid-afternoon, and I'm hot, hungry and close to calling the whole thing off, when a slight young woman lets herself into the block of flats. I don't pay much attention, but Adam sits up straight and nudges me.

'Claire, look.' He points to the top-floor window, where we can just make out the figure of the girl letting herself into Lydia's flat. 'I'm going up. Alone.'

'No, not this time.' I reach for the door handle as Adam sighs beside me. 'I don't care, Adam. I waited in the car earlier, I did what you wanted, but I'm not waiting anymore. I want answers.'

'Jesus, Claire,' Adam mutters, but he doesn't try and stop me when I open the car door. We scramble out and I take a deep breath to calm the adrenaline coursing through me, my legs feeling oddly light as we walk towards the entry door. The buzzer to the building is broken and the door swings open as I lean on it. Making our way up the concrete staircase to the top floor, the smell of must and urine filling our noses, we step over small piles of litter that have been swept to one side. Graffiti is scrawled across several of the walls, but as we arrive on the top landing, it is clean and quiet. Adam tugs on my arm, pulling me to a stop.

'Wait here a moment,' he says, pushing me into the alcove of a doorway to the flat next door. 'I don't want her to see you — if she answers the door she might know who you are, especially if Tom is in there.' Adam holds a hand up as I go to speak, to tell him I have every right to go in there and demand to know what is going on. 'No, Claire, trust me. I'm a police officer, I've done this hundreds of times before and I know what I'm doing.'

Defeated, I hang back, shadowed by the alcove so the girl is unable to see me, but I'll be able to hear everything that is said. Before he knocks on Lydia's door, Adam taps on the door of the flat next door, crouching down and peering through the letterbox. I catch a glimpse of some empty food wrappers and a dirty blue blanket scrunched up in the corner of the living room, but no furniture, and Adam gently levers the flap back into place. No one answers.

'It's empty,' Adam confirms. 'I don't want to leave you there and then the tenant opens the door on you and gives us away.' He turns to the door of Lydia's flat and knocks, a sharp, urgent rap. I hear footsteps and resist the urge to peer round the corner of the alcove. Instead, I press myself further into the doorframe, sweat beginning to prickle under my arms as I strain to hear what's being said.

'I'm looking for Lydia French.' I catch a glimpse of Adam's hand as it ducks into his back pocket and pulls out his warrant card.

'She's not here.' A girl's voice, high-pitched and young, drifts out of the open door.

'When will she be back?' Adam's voice carries more than a hint of steel, and I know if he was on my doorstep I'd spill the beans within minutes.

'I . . . I'm not sure. She'll only be a few hours, I'm sure. I think she's gone to work; she's normally home about five o'clock. I'll get her to call you when she gets home.' I realise the girl thinks Adam is something to do with Lydia's probation. No wonder she doesn't want to elaborate.

'And you are?' Adam ignores her assurances that Lydia will call later.

'Summer. I'm her sister.'

'Right, Summer. I'll be back. Oh, and I would appreciate it if you didn't tell Lydia I was here. I'll catch up with her soon, I'm sure.' As Adam steps back I see him give the young woman, Summer, a wink and the door slams shut. Sucking in gulps of air, I find I've been holding my breath through the entire conversation.

'That didn't go too well.' Disappointed Lydia's sister didn't offer up any answers, I fall into step beside Adam as we head back towards the door leading to the grotty, smelly staircase.

'It's fine. There's no rush now, sometimes you just need to take things slowly.' Adam pushes the door open and starts to run lightly down the stairs, seemingly not bothered by the grime and the whiff of decay filling the corridor. 'We just go back there tonight. She said Lydia will be home at around five o'clock, so wherever she's keeping Tom, it's not in there. We go back after five and we wait for her. We'll get her, Claire, don't worry.'

* * *

We spend the afternoon sitting outside the flats, and by the time Adam gives me the nod to step out of the car I'm wound tighter than a watch spring, the thought that I'm almost there — possibly within touching distance of Tom — making me antsy, jumpy with anticipation. I don't know what Lydia French is going to reveal when we finally catch up with her, and my nerves are stretched to breaking point. I shiver slightly as I step out onto the pavement, unsure as to whether it's caused by the drop in temperature or if someone has walked over my grave.

'Are you sure we won't be too late?' I ask, as Adam leans on the door, pushing it wide open, the rubbish in the bottom of the stairwell whipping into a mini cyclone in the breeze. Neither of us have seen Lydia enter the building, but Adam spotted a rear entrance on the way in earlier.

'It's perfect timing — she won't be expecting us, trust me.' We climb the four flights of stairs to Lydia's flat, my broken ribs screaming with the effort, and Adam bangs on the door knocker so hard that tiny chips of red paint flake off. Within seconds the door creaks open and I catch my first proper glimpse of Lydia's sister. She's a tiny, fragile thing, with no colour to her at all — insubstantial, that's the only word to describe her. With her pale face and icy blonde hair that snakes down to her waist, she's like a dandelion clock — one puff and she would be gone.

'She's not here.' Her voice is barely above a whisper and her eyes are puffy and rimmed with red. 'I told you I'd get her to call you when she got in.' The girl looks as though she's been crying since we left, and even Adam takes pity on her.

'Look — Summer, is it?' The girl nods, tugging the sleeves of her cardigan down over her hands. 'I'm not from the probation office. I'm a police officer — but I'm not here about that. I need to speak to Lydia about something completely unrelated.'

'But I thought . . .' Summer looks confused, looking from Adam's face to the warrant card he holds in his hand and back again. 'I think you'd better come in.'

We step into the claustrophobic hallway of the flat, and Summer shows us through to the living area. It's tiny, with a sagging green couch at one end, the other end a cramped kitchen area made up of a few cupboards and a stainless-steel sink. Despite the small proportions, it's clean and tidy and Lydia is obviously very proud of it. I cast my eyes quickly about the room for any signs that Tom has been here, but there's nothing.

'Please, sit down. Would you like a cup of tea?' Summer is trying hard to play hostess but I have neither the time nor the patience for it.

'Summer, please. Where is Lydia? Don't tell me she's at work, because I don't believe you.' Adam's voice is firm and he looms over Summer, standing head and shoulders above her. 'We'll wait here for her to come back. We can wait all night if we have to.' At his words, tears start to stream down Summer's pale cheeks as she tugs again and again at her sleeves, pulling them down over her hands until they're completely hidden.

'I'm sorry,' she gasps through her sobs. 'I thought you were from the probation team. Why are you here if not for that?'

'We're here for Tom Bennett, Summer. He's gone missing. You might know him better as Theo. This is his wife, Claire.' Summer's mouth gapes open in shock, and it's clear to both Adam and me the name means something to her.

'I don't know where Lydia is. She left the house last Tuesday morning to go to her office and she hasn't been home since.' Jesus. The same day Tom left. Everything I suspected from the beginning has been right.

'Summer?' Struggling to keep my voice calm, I speak to her for the first time. 'I think you better tell us everything.'

'I don't have to tell you anything — you're not from the probation team. I don't have to speak to you if I don't want to.' Summer's voice is shrill and her hands flutter around her waist like nervous butterflies as she speaks.

'No, you're quite right,' Adam says calmly, not raising his voice above Summer's strident tones. 'You don't *have* to speak to us at all . . . there's nothing that makes you legally bound to tell us anything about where Lydia could be.'

I stare at Adam aghast. I thought he was supposed to be getting information from Summer, not telling her she didn't need to co-operate.

'See, the thing is, Summer, you say you don't know where Lydia is anyway,' Adam goes on, his tone flat and uninterested. 'Don't you think it would be wise to help us? And then that way, we could help you find her. You're worried about her, aren't you?' Marvelling at the way Adam has effortlessly turned this around, I wait for Summer to respond, worried that if I speak she'll shut down.

'But how do I know you are who you say you are?' Summer asks, some of the fight already going out of her. 'How do I know you don't want to hurt Lydia, or throw her back in prison?'

'Honestly, Summer, take another look at my ID. I'm a police officer — it's my job to help people, not hurt them. And I don't want to put Lydia back in prison, especially if she's done nothing wrong.' Adam passes Summer his warrant card. 'I just want to ask Lydia some questions, that's all. She's not in any trouble. And let's be honest, three heads are better than one, aren't they?'

Summer makes a show of bringing the card up to her face, glancing between the photograph and Adam. Finally, she passes the card back to Adam, satisfied with what she sees, her desperate worry about her sister's failure to return home overshadowing any concerns she might have that we're not on the level.

'OK,' she says, after a moment. 'I'll tell you everything I know.'

CHAPTER 44

Summer takes a deep breath and sinks down onto the couch. I raise an eyebrow and glance across at Adam, who says nothing as he perches on the armchair across from Summer. 'I'm not telling you this because I want to help you, you know. I'm telling you so you'll help me find Lydia. She's my older sister and I've been without her for long enough. She's been in prison for the last eight years, since I was fifteen, after she killed a man.' She sips at a glass of water on a nest of tables next to the couch, taking a moment to gather her thoughts. 'It was an accident — I don't want you to think she did it on purpose. Lydia isn't like that. There was a fight . . . The man was struck on the head and died. But I need to tell you, I don't think Lydia did it. I think she was set up. She's not a bad person.'

'Sorry, Summer, I know she's your sister—'

Adam signals at me to stop talking, and I grit my teeth in frustration.

Summer lifts her chin defiantly. 'She's *not a bad person*,' she repeats. 'It was an *accident*. The charge was manslaughter, not murder. She was let out of prison three months ago after the parole board decided she had served her time. She was a model prisoner, never got into any trouble, so they took that into account. She came home at the end of April and since then all she's talked about is finding Theo. She asked around but Theo was gone. Lydia couldn't go to the club where they used to work, so she just kind of kept walking the streets, asking around in the places where they used to hang out together. It turns out Theo disappeared from London pretty much as soon as Lydia was arrested, and no one's seen him since. Until Lydia saw his face on a travel brochure in town. It was just a freaky coincidence, she was walking through town and there he was — older, but still undeniably Theo. He was sitting in the sun, with a kid on his lap.'

'That's my daughter. *Our* daughter.' The cruise line did use our photograph after all. I feel a hot ball of anger fizz in my stomach, aimed partly at the cruise line, and partly at myself — if only I'd never submitted it. I think back to the day I first saw Lydia's post and I have to cough to clear the lump that fills the back of my throat. Summer doesn't pay me any attention, just carries on talking as though I haven't spoken.

'So, she came back all excited that she'd found him — or she thought she had. She had this bright idea of using social media to see if she could flush him out — well, it was more my idea, really. I thought if we could get it on Facebook there would be more chance of *someone* knowing where Theo was. And I didn't like the idea of Lydia walking the streets all day every day looking for him. She scanned in the picture from the brochure and then put out a plea to help find him. She used a sponsored post so she could target people who liked to travel, people who liked cruises. She thought there might be a chance of someone remembering him from their holiday.'

I sit back in my chair, feeling light-headed. So that was how it had ended up on my timeline — a fateful coincidence put Lydia's advert on my screen. I thank my lucky stars it did. I wouldn't have had anywhere to start looking for Tom if it hadn't.

'I saw it.' My tone is sharp and Summer avoids my eyes. 'How do you think I knew Lydia was involved? She referred to them as *her* husband and child. What kind of person does that?' I feel the pressure of Adam's hand on my arm and realise I've raised my voice.

'She didn't mean anything by it. She just thought if people thought they were her family, then they would be more inclined to help, to let her know if they'd seen Theo. I called the travel company and told them I worked for a modelling agency, and I wanted Theo's details. They said they would have to contact him themselves, that they couldn't pass on any details.' Vaguely, a dim memory swims into view — Tom waving a letter from the travel company at me, before tearing it up and throwing it in the bin. I was irritated with him at the time for interrupting me when I was working on a tricky contract. Was that where all of this began?

'Go on.' Adam leans forward, listening intently, and suddenly I can visualise him at work, giving his suspects his undivided attention until they confess all.

'So, I found a guy who worked for the cruise company. I struck up a conversation, chatted him up a bit and eventually he asked me out. We went out a few times and I managed to persuade him to get me Theo's details. That's how I found out where he lived, his phone number and what his name is now. I gave Lydia his number so she could contact him.' She covers her face with her hands for a moment. 'Look, I'm not proud of it, OK? If I'd known what was going to happen then I never would have done it but Lydia loves him . . . *loved* him. She just wants to see him again, that's all.'

'If that's all — if she only wanted to see him, to speak to him — then why hasn't Tom come home? What about the threatening messages on his phone?' Adam may have looked the picture of sympathy when Summer was talking, but now his voice is hard.

'I don't know! All I know is Lydia wanted to see Theo — she said there were things they needed to talk about, stuff from before.' Summer wipes her nose on her sleeve, leaving a silvery trail that makes my stomach flip. I feel a flicker of sympathy for her — she's little more than a child — but anger still simmers under my skin, rage that my life has been turned upside down because of this girl's sister.

'You said you gave Lydia our address. Why not just come and knock on the door? Why not just tell us Lydia wanted to see Theo when she got out? You keep telling us she isn't a bad person, but if all she wanted to do was talk to him she didn't need to threaten him.' I'm confused, unsure how all of this has turned into such a tangled web.

'Lydia thought if she just turned up on the doorstep Theo wouldn't see her. That he'd call the police. She was worried if he called the police they might say she'd broken the terms of her parole and send her back to prison.' Summer is openly sobbing now, and although I feel bad for her, I need to harden my heart against her and remember she's partly to blame for what's happened.

'The texts are threatening, Summer. They say, "I KNOW EVERYTHING" and "DID YOU THINK YOU COULD GET AWAY WITH IT?" Why would Lydia send things like that to Tom?'

Summer shakes her head and slides a tissue out from the sleeve of her cardigan, dabbing ineffectually at the tears rolling down her cheeks. 'She just wanted him to talk to her. All I know is she loves Theo and felt she needed to see him. She said there were things that needed to be said, that needed to be dealt with before she could move on. I thought she meant so she could move on and be with someone else. Eight years is a long time to be hung up on someone. I thought she only wanted to talk to him, I didn't know she'd do something like this.' Summer sniffles into the tissue and I have to resist the urge to shake her until her teeth rattle and she finally starts to make some sense.

'What do you mean, you didn't know she'd *do something like this*? Summer, please.' I grasp both of her hands in mine. 'Where is Lydia? You need to tell us if there's anything else you know.'

Summer shakes her head forlornly and heaves in a deep breath. 'That's why I'm talking to you, Claire. That's why I let you into our home. On Tuesday morning, Lydia rang me to tell me she was going to see Theo. She said she was going to get "closure".'

'Right. Closure, OK.' I shove my hands into my hair and wait for what's coming next.

'I'm worried because that was the last time I spoke to Lydia. She's not answering her phone and she hasn't been home since.'

CHAPTER 45

Standing abruptly, I start to pace, my heart pounding and my hands beginning to shake. I knew it. I knew all along that she had him, and now I know for sure she does. I never realised quite how far Lydia was prepared to take things.

'Show me the rest of the flat,' I say, my voice clipped.

'What? Why?' Summer throws Adam a panicked look as I head towards the kitchen area and start pulling out drawers and opening cupboards.

'Claire—'

'Maybe Tom came here? Maybe Lydia left something that will show us where they are.' I push past Summer into Lydia's bedroom, sure there must be some sign proving she has Tom. Instead, I find a room that doesn't look too dissimilar to my room when I lived alone. Clothes scatter the bed, as though she couldn't make up her mind what to wear before she left the house. Skincare products litter the bedside table, the lid left off one bottle, a small perfume bottle next to it. It's a scent I bought once but never wore after Tom complained, wrinkling his nose saying he hated the smell of it. As I turn to leave, I catch sight of the corner of a photograph peeking out from underneath the pillow on the bed. Pulling it out, I gasp as though winded, the picture delivering a punch to my lower abdomen. The proof I needed that Lydia French is obsessed with my husband is right there in front of me — a photograph of Tom, his hair shorter and the ghost of dark stubble across his cheeks, the lights of the Tiger Club shining behind him, as he smiles into the camera with a woman who can only be Lydia French. Hastily, I shove it into my pocket, feeling it burning a hole as I steady my shaking hands and try to ignore the sweat breaking out all over my body.

'Where is she, Summer?' I stride back through to the living area, rage and panic coursing through me as Summer stands before me, her tiny body quaking at my raised voice. 'What has she done with my husband?' I step towards her, blind with rage, desperate to find Tom before it's too late.

'Claire, calm down. Please, we need to think about things rationally — we need to call the police.' Adam steps between us, his voice soothing, as he grips me by the wrists, his fingers wrapping tightly around my skin.

'*No!*' Both Summer and I cry in unison. I shoot Summer a look, almost daring her to speak again, before turning to Adam. 'No, Adam, please. No police.' I think of Carlos, sitting in the chair beside my hospital bed, menace oozing from every pore. 'Summer, think very carefully. Where could Lydia have taken Tom? You must know places, old haunts where she used to hang out — come on, think!' I grasp her by her upper arms and she gasps, before Adam tugs me away from her tiny frame.

'Please, Claire, you need to calm down. Summer — can you think of anywhere that Lydia might go? Anywhere they might have gone together that might hold some significance for her? Any places she might go when she's feeling threatened?'

Summer gulps and rubs at her upper arms, and through the fear cloaking my shoulders, I feel a wave of guilt for grabbing her so roughly, that secret, nasty Claire — the one I didn't know lived inside me — rising to the surface again, just like when I grabbed Pippa in my desperation for answers. *Just like the Claire who upped and left Adam without a backwards glance, running off into the sunset with another man, breaking Adam's heart.*

'We've got a lock-up, about three miles from here. She had it before, it was our dad's, and when he died Lydia got it. When she... went away, our mum carried on paying the rent on it for her, for when she got out. My mum doesn't believe she did it either. Lydia would have done anything for Theo, you know.' Summer plucks at the threads on her skirt with shaking hands, avoiding eye contact.

Pulling out my phone, I open the Maps function and shove it roughly towards her. 'Tell us where it is. We need to get to Tom before Lydia takes things too far.'

Summer gives me an uncertain look but takes the phone, still convinced her sister is harmless. I know she doesn't believe Lydia has it in her to hurt Tom, but despite her reassurances that she loves him, I believe otherwise. Who abducts a person because they love them? Who snatches someone away from their family because they want 'closure'? And what's to stop Lydia handing Tom over to Carlos when he rejects her advances?

'Here. It's on this road.' She splays her fingers to enlarge the map. 'Lydia has one of the biggest ones, right at the end of the row.'

'Have you been to the lock-up, Summer? Surely that's the first place we should be looking,' Adam points out. 'If she's got Tom then there's every chance she's holed up in there with him. It's familiar to her, and she knows no one else has access, especially if it's in an area where there are just garages.'

I'm inclined to agree, but Summer shakes her head slowly, as if trying to dislodge her thoughts. 'I've called her mobile a hundred times but it was just ringing and ringing, and now it goes to voicemail. She would call me back if everything was OK, she always does.' Her voice sounds small and her eyes are ringed with black circles. 'I went to the lock-up and banged on the door but she didn't answer, so she can't be there. There was no one around and I don't even know if there's a spare key. I don't know where she would be — I was too young to know all the places she hung out before she . . . left.'

'Let's try the lock-up first. Just because she didn't answer the door doesn't mean she's not in there. It might mean she doesn't want you to know she's in there. I'll break in, if I have to.' Adam's voice is brisk, and I feel a sense of relief that he's taking charge. Fear and adrenaline have left me drained, my ribs aching and a thudding in the stitches at my temples that won't go away no matter how many painkillers I swallow. Adam pauses, running his eyes over me intently. 'Are you ready?'

I nod swiftly, desperate to find Tom, to find out what's happened to him over these last few days, despite the fact it's me who put him in this position.

CHAPTER 46

Adam drives over to the lock-up Lydia French has held in her name for the past ten years, since she lost her father.

'We need to be careful when we get there, Claire.' Adam briefly takes his eyes from the road. 'We don't know if Lydia's in there with Tom alone, or if she's got help from someone else. Also, we don't know how rational she is by now; she's been gone for over a week already with no contact.' *Ten days, to be exact.* Adam turns back to concentrate on the road ahead and doesn't see the worried look that Summer gives him. 'And you're going to have to tell Carlos you've found Tom. If he is there, Carlos is going to want to see him — you know that, right? Now he knows who you are he's not just going to leave things, especially if he knows you have Tom back.' Adam licks his lips and I realise he's just as nervous as I am at the thought of dealing with Carlos. 'Better to get it over and done with, than have him turn up on your doorstep in a few months' time. Isla could be there. We don't know how he's going to react . . .'

'You're not going to hurt her, are you?' Summer's voice from the back seat is laced with a tremor.

'Summer, the last thing we want is for anyone to get hurt. And we don't know, Lydia might not even be in there, we just need to be on our guard. We don't know what state of mind she could be in, if she's even in there.' Adam tries to be understanding, but I can hear the underlying steel that runs through his words.

'But she loves Theo . . . she's always loved him. She always said she would have moved heaven and earth for him. She just wanted closure from everything that happened.'

I feel sick, Summer's words hitting me like tiny barbs. Obviously, I knew Tom had relationships with women before me, but to hear the way Lydia has been talking about him leaves a greasy layer on my skin that I'm desperate to wash away. It takes me a moment to realise that it's fear I want to wash away. Fear that Tom feels the same way about Lydia.

'Closure can mean anything,' Adam says with a grim look on his face, before expertly following the bend in the road that leads to the paved area outside the garages.

The garages sit in a row, the tarmac in front of them cracked and split with age. A large oil stain sits in the middle of the row and Adam skirts round it, gesturing to Summer to watch where she walks.

'Which is it?' Adam whispers, his words still loud in the thick twilight. Although set back from the road, this is a residential area and the last thing we need is someone to look out of their flat window and report us to the police. Lydia's lock-up is at the far end of the row, the red paint peeling off the wood around the locked garage door, a sharp contrast to the two units that come before hers, both of them freshly painted and in pristine condition. Lydia and Summer's mother may have paid the rent on this garage while Lydia was in prison, but she certainly didn't want anything to do with the maintenance of it. As we approach the door, Summer whimpers slightly and makes as if to turn back, before I steady her with one hand on her shoulder.

'Summer, please. We need to do this. It's not just about Lydia anymore.' Adam stares her down until at last, she nods.

Checking the flats across from the row of garages, there's no sign of movement — no people smoking on their balconies, and only a few lights lit in the windows. Nervously, I look to Adam to give the OK to try the door. There's little risk of anyone seeing us if something does happen; nevertheless, I find myself peering anxiously both ways down the road, sure we are about to be found out and arrested for breaking and entering. Adam taps lightly on the door to the lock-up and tugs at the door, but there's no response, the door tightly locked.

'Lydia,' Summer calls. 'It's me, Summer. Let me in.' Still no response.

'What do you want to do, Claire?' Adam pauses with one hand still on the door handle, watching me carefully.

'There's only one thing we can do, Adam. We break the door down.'

Summer gives a little cry at this and positions herself between me and the door. Adam gently grasps her by the upper arms and moves her to one side.

'Summer, please.' Adam says quietly. 'Tom could be in there on his own — he could be hurt. Lydia isn't there. She would have answered the door to you, wouldn't she?'

'Unless something happened to her as well — you keep mentioning this Carlos, how do we know he hasn't got Theo? How do we know he hasn't done something to Lydia?' Summer asks quietly, tears filling her eyes again.

'Carlos hasn't touched him. For one thing, Carlos wouldn't want to get his own hands dirty, and for another, I think he would have told us if he had found Lydia already. He wants to find Tom just as much as we do.' I give her a sharp glance as Adam readies himself to charge at the door. It's flimsier than I imagined, and after just one hefty shove the door comes away from the frame, leaving me wondering how Lydia had managed to go so long without being burgled, or having squatters move in while she was in prison. Forcing the door from the frame completely, Adam gestures for me to wait, in case Lydia is there and is hiding. He steps inside, and when he turns to me with a brisk nod, I follow. The air is stale and stiflingly hot. It's clear no windows have been opened recently, the air thick and muggy from the warm sunshine that has been streaming in through the grimy window.

'Hello? Lydia? Tom?' I call quietly, my voice booming in my ears in the deathly hush of the lock-up. There's no one here. There's no sign anyone's been in here, not even since Lydia went to prison. A bicycle leans against one wall, both tyres flat and the chain rusty. Shelves lean crookedly across the walls, holding cans of paint, their lids glued shut through years of festering in this dark, dusty space. A large shape, covered by a thick blue tarpaulin, takes up most of the space. Summer steps in, her feet leaving neat footprints in the dust covering the thick, concrete floor.

'She hasn't been here, has she?' she gasps, fresh tears pooling in her eyes.

'It doesn't look as though she has. Although . . . wait a moment.' Adam turns slowly on the spot, taking in the thick, unspoiled dust coating everything. Everything except the tarpaulin. He runs a finger through the dirt on one of the shelves, rubbing his forefinger and thumb together with a frown.

'Claire.' Adam draws my attention to the narrow pathway in the space between the tarpaulin and the wall. Looking down, I see the dust has been disturbed, a mash of footprints marching backwards and forwards, almost too difficult to see in the dingy gloom of the garage.

'The tarpaulin isn't dusty,' I say, pointing to the clear, smooth sheet. Adam steps in front of the covered object and tugs it away, revealing what lies underneath. My knees give way slightly and I stagger, holding one hand against the grimy wall to keep me upright, bile scorching the back of my throat when I see what's underneath the plastic.

'Oh shit, Adam. That's Tom's car.' My breath comes in ragged pants as panic threatens to overwhelm me. 'Summer — where the fuck is your sister? If you know anything you need to tell me right now . . . she has my husband!' My voice is tinged with hysteria and Adam holds my arm, sensing that all I want to do is shake Summer until the truth falls out of her mouth.

'Claire, *calm down.*' Adam holds onto me tightly and I draw in a deep breath in an attempt to stop the panic from choking me. 'Summer, you can see what this looks like, right? This is Tom's car — the car he was driving last Tuesday when he went missing. To me, it's looking like Lydia and Tom are together — and this car is going to be evidence, if the police get involved. So, you need to think very carefully.'

Summer gives a little wail as the full implications of what Adam has said sinks in. It's looking more and more likely that Lydia isn't the sweet, innocent sister Summer thinks she is. Unable to stop myself from pacing the concrete floor, I rub my hands together, anxious to get going again now we know neither Tom nor Lydia are here.

'Where do we go next, Adam? Summer, where else would Lydia go? Think, Summer, please.'

Adam pauses at the back of the garage, where he is rolling the tarpaulin into a ball, waiting to hear Summer's response.

'I don't know . . .' Summer stutters, her eyes ringed with pink. 'I just don't know . . . I'm sorry, Claire. I never thought . . . She loves him so much; she just wanted to make things right with him, that's all. She didn't do it, Claire, what she was meant to have done to go to prison. She just wanted to talk to Tom about it, to make it all right, that's what she said.' Summer plucks at the loose threads on her skirt again. 'It was me who sent that second message. The one that said, "DID YOU THINK YOU'D GET AWAY WITH IT?" I found Tom's number scrawled on an old receipt — I don't know where Lydia got it. I was just so . . . panicked. She said she was going to see Tom and then she never came back. I wanted to scare him into calling me so I could find out whether he'd seen her.' Summer starts to cry again, but I have no sympathy for her. Angrily, I shove my way outside, stepping into the cool evening air. Even with its faint tang of petrol and pollution, it's a damn sight fresher than the air inside the lock-up. Adam follows after me, hurrying round to stand in front and block my exit.

'Claire, where are you going? You can't just run off all half-cocked about this; we need to have a plan. We need to think, where did they spend time together?' Adam aims this at Summer, but she's a weeping puddle of tears and I ruthlessly step past her, headed back towards the car.

'I don't care . . . I just need to . . . do something. Look at it, Adam — Tom's car is in *her* garage, hidden away. She must have him somewhere near here. If she didn't want to hurt him, why would she hide the car like that?' But Adam isn't listening; instead he's frowning hard, as though trying to recall something just out of reach.

'Her office,' Adam says a moment later, a satisfied look on his face. 'Summer, you said she left to go to her office on Tuesday morning. Let's go and see if she's been there, we might find something that will tell us what she's thinking. Summer, where is Lydia's office?'

Summer looks up, surprised she hasn't thought of it herself. 'Back towards the flat. She walks to work normally. It's not that far. She finishes at five and is home by ten past usually.'

'How are you about breaking and entering twice in one night?' Adam asks me, a mischievous smile on his face.

'Oh, you won't need to break in,' Summer pipes up as she gets to her feet, brushing the dust and dirt from her skirt. Digging in one pocket she pulls out a set of keys. 'I've got the spare key.'

* * *

Adam screeches the car to a halt on double yellow lines behind a long line of parked cars, and I have the car door open before the engine is even switched off. I hit the ground running, scanning the building numbers as I go, searching for the one that houses Lydia's office.

'This one!' Summer tugs at my arm as I almost miss it, my breath catching in my throat, stitches throbbing at the short run from the car. The building is in darkness, and there's no sign of a security guard. Summer jiggles the key, struggling to get it in the lock, and I push her aside to do it myself, impatience making my fingers thick and clumsy, until at last, I force it in. The door slides open and with a quick glance to make sure we're unobserved, we enter the hallway, searching out the room that belongs to Lydia.

'The company looks after lots of flats,' Summer tells us as we creep along the eerily quiet corridor, my heartbeat crashing in my ears. 'Lydia was lucky there was a vacancy close to our block. She looks after our flat, and all the others. Light bulbs, getting rid of graffiti, all that stuff.' Remembering the graffiti littering the walls of the stairwell, I'd say she wasn't doing a very good job, but obviously her mind has been elsewhere. At the end of the darkened corridor, Summer stops us.

'It's this one,' she says, digging out another key. 'This is Lydia's office.' We step into the small room and Adam flicks on the light. It's untidy — an old computer around ten years out of date sits on the worktop that serves as a desk, paperwork litters the rest of the empty workspace, and bunches of papers hang from bulldog clips on nails in the walls. An overstuffed filing cabinet leaks more paperwork, and when Summer sees what else sits on the desk, she lets out a cry.

'Summer? What is it?' Adam tears himself away from the filing cabinet, where he is leafing through documents.

'That's Lydia's lunch.' Summer points with a trembling finger to the carrier bag sitting on the desk next to a filthy teacup. 'I make her a packed lunch every day — that's the one I made her on Tuesday.' She covers her mouth with a shaking hand.

'So, she didn't eat it on Tuesday, and she hasn't been back since. Tom left for work as usual on Tuesday but never got there, and he hasn't been heard from since either.' My heart is beating double time as I realise this, along with Tom's car tucked neatly away in Lydia's garage, is the proof I needed. Why would Lydia not come home, unless she was keeping

Tom somewhere? Maybe wherever he is, she can't leave him in case he escapes or draws attention to himself? Once again bile burns the back of my throat.

'We need to think logically.' Adam is firm, taking charge again. 'Summer, think. There must be somewhere Lydia would have taken Tom.'

Summer starts moaning, wittering on that she doesn't know, Lydia never tells her anything, when something catches my eye. It takes me a moment to process it, but then I give a shout.

'Adam!' I point to the space above the filing cabinet. A wooden board hangs there, with nails embedded at different heights. Every nail has a set of keys hanging from it, all apart from one. Adam grabs Summer by the arm, pulling her roughly towards the board.

'Which are missing? *Which keys are missing, Summer?*'

Summer stutters as Adam points at the gap on the board.

'Summer, please!'

'Err . . . it's . . . it's the plant room. The keys for the plant room in our block are missing.' Summer's teeth are chattering, her face paler than ever, but I pay her no mind as we run towards the exit.

CHAPTER 47

Heart pounding, I follow Summer, racing towards the block of flats where she lives with Lydia, Adam hurrying along behind me. Summer shoves the broken front door open and we follow her towards the other set of stairs — the ones that lead down, away from the ground floor, our feet pounding on the concrete steps. We reach the last few steps down to the basement corridor when Adam stops, raising a hand in my direction.

'Wait a minute. Just stop there, just for a second.' He pushes past us, jumping down the last few steps and walking to the far end of the corridor, where a dark green door without a number is shrouded in shadow from the concrete staircase overhead.

'Claire? Why are we stopping?' Summer grabs at my arm impatiently, and I brush her off, peering into the gloomy darkness to see what has caught Adam's attention.

'Adam? What is it?' Whispering, I creep down the last few stairs, as Adam raises a finger to his lips to shush me.

'That's the plant room,' he whispers back, his voice low and calm as he gestures towards the huge padlock holding the door securely shut.

My eyes widen as I take in what he's saying. 'Oh God, Adam — do you think she has Tom in there?'

'I don't know. It might be nothing, but it's worth a shot, don't you think? No one else apart from the caretaker would have access to this room. The keys are missing — that has to tell us something.' Adam roots in his bag, clearly looking for something.

'Shouldn't we call someone? There might be a spare key — the other ones might be lost. It might not be Lydia.' Oblivious to our frantically whispered conversation, Summer's voice floats over my shoulder. She has stopped crying, for now at least, and looks young and fragile, the dark circles under her pink-rimmed eyes only serving to make her look even more delicate. She wrings her hands together as she tries to convince us Lydia has nothing to do with the missing keys.

'No time,' Adam whispers with a quick glance towards me, before pulling a huge pair of bolt cutters from within the depths of the bag. With one practiced movement, he slices clean through the padlock. Peeling it off, he hands it to me and then slowly pushes the weighty door open. The air is heavy with the scent of machinery oil, and thick with dust. It's clear no one uses this room, and the caretaker only comes in when they really need to. Adam raises his finger to his lips once again and like church mice, Summer and I tiptoe in after him. Sweat beads at my temples and my stitches itch as I follow Adam. My pulse crashes in my ears so loud I'm surprised the others can't hear it. My palms are slick with sweat and I suddenly have a terrible sense of foreboding — the feeling that once I leave this room, nothing in my life will ever be the same again. The deeper into the plant room we go the darker it gets, and Summer fumbles for my hand as she trips over something, causing a metallic clang to ring out.

'Shhhh.' Adam turns to look at Summer, a frown on his face, before he stops dead. 'Listen,' he whispers, 'can you hear that?'

I stop behind him, feeling a chill at my back, creeping up my spine and making my skin tighten with goosebumps.

'What?' I say, my voice low. 'I can't hear anything.'

'Wait . . .' Adam pauses and we fall silent, ears straining in the thick darkness blanketing the hot, musty room, the only light the thin torch light from Adam's phone. 'There it is again.' This time I hear what Adam hears — a shuffling sound as though someone is shifting their weight.

'It could be mice,' Summer whispers, fear etched onto her face, but the noise comes again, this time with a metallic scraping alongside it. Adam and I lock eyes and we both take a cautious step forward. My heart is hammering so hard in my chest I feel as though it may burst through my ribcage, and my feet suddenly feel leaden, unwilling to move any further.

'Hello?' Adam calls out in a low voice. 'Is someone there?' The shuffling noise comes again and a clanging of metal on metal. Adam pulls the bolt cutters out the bag, handing them to me. 'Wait here, I'm going to take a look.'

'No, Adam.' I grab his arm, stopping him. 'Let me look . . . If it's him . . . It could be Tom . . .'

'I'm trained for this, Claire, you're not. If it's him, I'll shout . . . Just stay two steps behind me, OK?' he whispers, and I nod reluctantly, hot wings of panic flapping in my chest. We creep forward, Summer behind us, and Adam puts a finger to his lips again, as we reach the corner of the huge boiler system. He peers around it, and my breath catches in my throat as a muffled moan reaches my ears.

'Shit.' Adam stops abruptly, whatever he's seen causing him to almost lose his footing. 'Oh shit. Oh God.' His hand rises to his mouth, and unable to wait any longer, I push past him to see what it is that has him so shocked. Preparing myself for the worst, sure I'm about to see my husband in some terrible condition, I have to blink, shake the sweat out of my eyes, and blink again before I can fully comprehend what I'm seeing, as there, handcuffed to the pipes feeding the heating system and wearing nothing but underwear, is the woman I now know to be Lydia French.

CHAPTER 48

'Jesus Christ,' Adam breathes, as Lydia raises her head slowly towards where we are standing, stock-still, shock reverberating through both of us. Filthy rags are tied tightly around her head, covering her eyes and filling her mouth, and at the sound of Adam's voice she flinches.

'What? What is it?' Summer roughly shoves me aside before I can stop her, gasping as she takes in the sight of her sister, dirty and helpless, tied to the metal pipes that feed the huge boiler system. A wail rises in her throat and I pull her towards me, anxious that her shrieks will alarm Lydia and alert whoever is keeping her here. Adam walks slowly towards Lydia, making a quiet shushing sound as she shrinks away from him.

'Lydia, shhh, it's OK.' Adam lays a hand on her thin arm and she makes a small yelping sound in the back of her throat, the material shoved in her mouth making it impossible for her to speak. 'I'm not going to hurt you, I'm here to help you. We'll get you free, and then you need to tell us what happened to you, OK? I'm a police officer.'

Lydia nods as I watch in silence, still in shock at this unexpected turn of events. I feel disembodied, as though I'm watching everything on a life-size cinema screen. This was the last scenario I was expecting to find when Adam broke the padlock on the heavy outer door. Taking charge of the situation, Adam takes the bolt cutters from me, and tells Lydia to hold still while he slides them around the handcuff chain. One sharp squeeze and the chain falls into two pieces and Lydia is free, albeit with a handcuff bracelet on each wrist. She rubs at her sore wrists and rotates her shoulders to get the blood flowing, shifting on the concrete floor into a more comfortable position, although the thinness of her frame must make any seated position uncomfortable.

Adam gently unties the rag from behind Lydia's head and her dark eyes squint in the dim light. He pulls the fabric from her mouth and roots in his bag for a bottle of water, which he presses gently to Lydia's cracked and swollen lips. She sips hungrily, taking the bottle herself before moving her head away and staring at me. I don't know what to think — I was so convinced I'd walk in here to find Tom in the position Lydia is in, I don't know how to process the scene in front of me. With a stifled cry, Summer tugs herself free from my embrace and kneels on the cold concrete floor in front of Lydia, taking no notice of the dust and filth that clings to her skirt.

'Lydia? Oh, *Lydia*. Who did this to you? What happened?' Summer looks wildly up at Adam, as if expecting him to hold all the answers. Adam gives a tiny shake of his head, laying a comforting hand on Lydia's shoulder. Summer gives a little sob as Lydia shrinks away from Adam's touch, exposing the livid purple bruises that dot her arms and shoulders.

Lydia still hasn't spoken a word. Adam flicks his fingers at me and I shake my head, confused.

'Your sweater,' he hisses and I tug it off and pass it to him. Adam wraps it over Lydia's shoulders, her eyes meeting mine as he does so. The haunted look filling those dark eyes spurs me into action.

'Lydia, I'm Claire Bennett.' I crouch low on the floor to meet her at eye level.

'Claire? You're Theo's wife, aren't you? He told me about you.' Her voice is raspy from disuse and she winces as she swallows, before taking another sip from the water bottle.

'Did he?' I look up at Adam, confused, but he says nothing. 'Who did this to you, Lydia? Was it Carlos — did Carlos keep you here? What about Tom — what did he do with Tom?' I have to stop myself from firing twenty questions at her, so I sit back on my heels and wait for her to finish drinking, when the clanging of the outer door opening startles us all. Lydia visibly flinches and a look of terror crosses her features, as she seems to shrivel before my eyes, curling herself into a tight ball in the shadows of the heating system. I reach for her, wanting to tell her we'll protect her from whoever has done this, even as it crosses my mind that if it's Carlos none of us is a match for him, when a voice reaches my ears — one I've been waiting to hear for what feels like the longest time.

'Claire?' Straightening up, I turn to see Tom's outline framed by the light of the open doorway behind him, the familiar cut of his shoulders, the swoop of his hair brushed back from his forehead. He walks towards me, a look of horror on his face. My heart jumps in my chest at the sight of him, the thought *he's OK* leaping into my mind as I realise I've found him . . . he's alive . . . he's not hurt. My feet move towards him as though he's a magnet and I raise my hands, wanting to pull him close and not let go, but his expression stops me and slowly, slowly, I begin to comprehend what I'm seeing. I lower my hands to my sides, shock buzzing through my body, my knees wobbly, and take a shaky step back.

'Tom? What are you . . . why?' My stomach churns as the full force of what has happened hits me. Behind me, I hear a rustle as Adam gets to his feet and stands by my side.

'Tom,' Adam begins, 'what the hell . . . ? What you've done . . . it's against the law.' Quicker to grasp the situation, Adam dives straight in, switching to police officer mode.

Tom gives Adam a withering glance before turning his gaze on me. 'Claire — this isn't what it looks like, I promise.' He reaches out to me, his wedding ring catching the light.

'Really, Tom?' Adam says, a strange look on his face. 'Because from where I'm standing there's really only one way this looks.' I step forward, squinting as the light streams in through the doorway behind Tom.

'Adam, stop. Tom . . . you need to explain what's going on. Do you know how worried I've been? I've been searching everywhere for you. You left Isla, for Christ's sake!' I can't stop the anger bubbling up in my chest. 'You lied to me, Tom, about everything. Everything we've built together is all just . . . lies. You never even told me your real name! What . . . I don't understand what's going on.' Swallowing hard, I push down the tears clogging my throat.

'What have you done to my sister, you bastard?' Summer's on her feet, cheeks flushed with fury as Adam restrains her from flying at Tom.

'Shut up! All of you — just stop!' Tom booms, his face contorting as spittle flies from his mouth, his cheeks flushed a deep, angry red. As he waves his hand I spy the large carving knife he grips in an iron fist, and for the first time I'm no longer afraid *for* him, I'm afraid *of* him. 'You don't understand . . . none of you understand!'

'OK, Tom.' I hold up a shaking hand. 'We'll be quiet. Just . . . please explain it to us. To me.' My heart hammering in my chest, I take a step towards him in an attempt to calm him, but he turns, the knife now pointing in my direction.

'Claire, listen to me.' Tom's voice is steady now, the voice I hear every day when I wake up. 'You don't understand . . . she was going to destroy everything.' His voice thickens and my tears spill over, sliding down my cheeks. My instinct is to go to him, to wrap my arms around him and tell him everything is going to be OK, but I don't move. I don't know him anymore. I don't know this man standing in front of me with Tom's face and Tom's voice — he's nothing like the man I married.

'Who was, Tom? Who was going to destroy what?'

'*Lydia*.' He waves the knife in her direction, as she cowers away from him in a way that makes my heart hurt. 'She was going to ruin everything we have, Claire. I couldn't let that happen.'

'Why don't you explain what happened from the beginning? Tell us the truth, Tom,' Adam says quietly, his eyes never leaving the knife. Tom's eyes briefly flicker over Adam, his mouth twisting with distaste before he turns his gaze back to me.

'Claire — I couldn't let her do it. You wouldn't understand.'

'Try me, Tom.' My nerve endings feel exposed, frayed at the edges, every word landing like a tiny electric shock. I don't know who he is any more — I don't recognise the man standing in front of me as my husband.

'Lydia and I were . . . friends. More than friends.' He casts a nervous glance in my direction. 'But she was dating Carlos, the owner of the Tiger Club.'

'I know Carlos.'

Tom swallows, adjusting his grip on the knife, and I feel the bittersweet taste of satisfaction as this information lands. 'I worked for Carlos but I didn't want to anymore. It started off as bar work, then working the door, and then . . . other stuff. Carlos was into things I didn't want to be a part of. I wasn't always the Tom you know, Claire.' He pauses, one hand rising as if to reach for me before he thinks better of it. 'At first I liked being part of Carlos's group — I liked the notoriety it gave me, I liked people giving me free drinks, free drugs, whatever I wanted because I was part of his team.' Tom looks at me, desperation radiating from every pore as his words tumble over each other, frantic, as though they leave a nasty taste in his mouth. 'But it all got too much — Carlos was dabbling with stuff I didn't agree with, but no one just walks away from that man.' Tom looks away now, as though emotion has got the better of him, but I'm unsure. I don't know which of his reactions is real anymore.

'Go on. I need to know all of it, Tom. I need to know the truth.' My lips feel numb, my brain slow to comprehend. This version of himself Tom is describing . . . this is Harriet's Theo. Not the Tom I know. *Knew.*

'I met Lydia at the Tiger Club. She seemed like a nice girl, and we were friends. I knew she wanted more, but I also knew Carlos would kill both of us if he found out. I thought . . . I thought I'd figured a way out. I needed Lydia's help, so I made sure I got close to her — gave her what she wanted — and she agreed.' From the corner, Lydia moans and Summer mops at her forehead with her sleeve. Lydia looks feverish, sick, her face pale save for two spots of colour blazing hot on her cheeks. Tom doesn't even appear to notice Lydia, he's so caught up in his own memories, and it strikes me that I never knew him, not at all.

'What did Lydia agree to?'

Tom sighs. 'I knew Carlos was out doing a deal, that particular evening. I told Lydia I knew the code to the safe. I would break into the safe and take the money sitting there from the previous day's club takings and meet her outside in the alley. My fingerprints were already all over the office, so they would expect to find them on the safe — it wouldn't be a problem if the police picked them up.'

'You *robbed* him?' I think of the money under the floorboards and swipe my hands over my jeans, sick at the memory of the notes in my hand. 'Jesus, Tom. Carlos is a fucking *gangster*.'

'You think I didn't know that? We were going to take the money and go, get away from London and start a new life somewhere else. Together, away from Carlos, away from the vile, immoral people I was involved with. I found a new name, a new identity, all ready to start again where no one could find me.'

'What went wrong? How did you end up like . . . this?' I wave my hand in his direction. 'That's not you, Tom. You're organised, methodical. Something terrible must have happened for you to fuck it up this badly.'

An expression I can't read crosses Tom's face, and there's a flicker of fear in my gut as I remember this isn't the Tom I know. This is *Theo*. 'As I was taking the money out of the safe, one of Carlos's guys came into the office and caught me. It was Lester, his main man. The guy who cleared up all of his messes.' His voice is bland, cold enough to send a shiver down my spine. 'I had no choice.'

'You killed him, Theo.' Lydia's voice is weak, and at first I think I misheard her, until I hear Summer's gasp of shock. I meet Tom's eyes in horror, waiting for him to deny it all, to tell Lydia that she's got it all wrong.

'Tom?'

'I couldn't let him stop me, Claire. I had to get away.' Tom's voice breaks now and he raises the knife again, taking a step back, inching towards the still-open door, fear making his forehead shine with perspiration. 'He threatened to tell Carlos, and there was a struggle. He was a big man, stronger than me, and he had his hands round my throat. He was choking me, I thought I was going to die. So, I hit him. I hit him with the metal paperweight that sat on Carlos's desk. And that's when Lydia came in.'

'Tom . . . *you* killed someone.' I feel winded, gut punched, my mouth gaping as I try to draw in oxygen. I've been living with a murderer. I've borne the child of a *murderer*.

'The guy went down like a stone, his . . . his head was split open, blood pouring out everywhere. He was dead before he even hit the floor, and I did it. I was the one who killed him. Lydia told me to go, that she would deal with it all, but as I left, I wiped my fingerprints from the paperweight and handed it to Lydia. I knew what I was doing. I knew they'd find my DNA in that office anyway, but I was there all the time, of course they would find it. I knew by wiping my prints off the paperweight and handing it to Lydia I was setting her up. But I couldn't go to prison, Claire, I just couldn't, not after everything I'd done to try and make something of my life. Not after leaving everything behind.' Tom looks at me now, a defiant spark in his eyes, and my heart twists in my chest. There's a crackling cough from behind me and then a raspy voice speaks up.

'You set me up.' Lydia's eyes are fiery with fever, but she knows exactly what she wants to say. 'You set me up; I went to prison for eight years for you, Theo. You handed me that paperweight and then the minute you set foot outside that room you called the police. That's why I contacted you. That's why I needed to see you.' Tom looks from Lydia to me, a sick look on his face.

Adam steps forward. 'Tom . . .'

Tom whirls around, his face changing. 'What the fuck are you even doing here, Adam? I bet you couldn't wait, could you? Couldn't wait to swoop in on Claire the minute my back was turned.'

'Tom!' Fury spurts through my veins, a white-hot lava trail leaving ash in its wake. 'I asked Adam for help. I *wanted* him here.'

Adam's face is impassive, unmoved by Tom's anger. 'What about Ruby, Tom? What happened to Ruby that night on the cliff in Cornwall?'

Tom's face is stunned, the colour leaching from it, leaving his skin waxen like marble, as he looks from Adam to me and back again.

'You know about that?' he whispers, and I nod, sick at the thought of what he's about to say next. When Tom speaks again, his voice is stronger, an undercurrent of rage running through it. 'Ruby was going to leave me. She was going to leave, and not even think about what she would be doing to me, leaving me there on my own. I couldn't let her go — I wasn't about to let her ruin all the plans I had for us.' Tom stops for a moment, drawing in a deep breath and composing himself.

'Did it happen how Harriet said?' I ask quietly.

Tom looks up at Harriet's name. 'We argued, I pushed her and that's when she fell. I couldn't stop myself, I was so angry. I looked over the edge but she was gone. There was nothing I could do.' His tone is icy cold, his eyes dark, no emotion. He looks towards me and I raise my eyes to meet his, even though a shiver runs through me as I do so — every woman he's ever been close to has been hurt. 'Everywhere I go, whatever I do, no matter how many times I try to start over, someone always tries to take that away from me. Claire, you have to understand. *Lydia wanted to take everything we had together.* She got her sister to contact me, to tell me she was out and wanted to speak to me. She called me from the insurance company she works for, trying to get me to agree to see her. She had people following me, and I freaked out. I knew what she wanted — she said she just wanted to talk, but I knew she was out for revenge. She was going to tell you everything, Claire. I tried so hard to disappear, to make myself a different person. A better person. I didn't want to be the man who lashes out when things go wrong — I wanted to be *Tom*.'

A pleading note enters Tom's voice, and he steps towards me, holding out his hand. I stare at his outstretched palm, on the verge of reaching out and taking it, wishing that if I did, all of this would disappear and we would just be us again. 'I wanted to be the Tom you know, Claire. I worked so hard to create our family together, and she was going to destroy us. I couldn't have that.'

'You've destroyed us, Tom. Not Lydia. You could have had all of that still, if you'd just been honest in the first place.'

'We still could.' Desperation seeps into Tom's voice and I take a step back, my hand dropping to my side. *How did we get from where we were, a happy, stable family, to this?* My mind is blown, everything I thought I knew shattered to smithereens. I rake my fingers through my hair, trying to make sense of it all.

'Tell me what happened after Lydia contacted you.'

Tom drops his hand, his eyes narrowing. 'I thought I'd managed to cover my tracks well enough — I needed to change my name once I left the club. I was terrified if they started looking into the murder at the club that night, they would link me back to Ruby in Cornwall, so I had to change my name, get away. I had to kill Theo off for good. I thought I'd done it, until you stupidly sent that photo into the cruise line and Lydia tracked me down.'

Tom points the knife towards me, but I hold firm, holding my hand up and refusing to shrink away from him, even as my pulse ratchets up to the point where I feel dizzy.

'She wanted to meet. I had to agree to it.' Tom's eyes are pleading now. 'I didn't know how she found me at first. I just received a text saying, "I KNOW EVERYTHING," after I'd managed to avoid her sister's calls and blocked her number. I knew then I had to meet her, or everything would have come crashing down around us. Lydia wouldn't leave it, she was obsessive even before and I knew she'd be pushing at me until I gave in. I had to stage it just right though. I left for work as usual, so you didn't suspect anything. Oh God, Isla! Where is she? Please tell me she's safe.' Tom looks at me, eyes wide with panic.

'She's . . .' I trail off, reluctant to reveal her whereabouts. 'She's safe.'

'Claire, I didn't know what to do. I was trying to keep her safe, to keep both of you safe.'

I don't respond, unable to trust my voice not to give away how I'm feeling. Tom carries on, intent on trying to explain himself.

'I arranged to meet Lydia in a pub round the corner. I wanted to sound her out . . . see what she wanted, but straight away she told me she would tell you everything. She said she'd set up a Facebook advert and was hoping you'd see it and if you didn't . . . well, I deleted it, as soon as I possibly could, and the message you sent to her. Just because I don't use social media, doesn't mean I don't know my way around it.' Tom gives a tiny smile, the corners of his mouth just lifting. 'I had to do this, Claire. She said you deserved to know the truth, to know the real man you married. She wanted to make me suffer the way she did.'

'Why didn't you just kill her?' Adam asks bluntly. 'Why keep Lydia here? If you were that worried about it all, why not just get rid of her for good?'

Tom eyes Adam coolly for a long moment, and when he speaks his voice is chilly. 'I'm not a *murderer*, Adam. I didn't hurt

Ruby on purpose — it was an accident. The other guy . . . it was him or me. I didn't want to *kill* Lydia, I just wanted to show her I wasn't prepared to lose everything I worked so hard to keep.'

'Oh, Theo, you stupid fool.' Lydia staggers to her feet, leaning on Adam's shoulder for support. 'I didn't really want to tell Claire anything; it was just a way to get what I really wanted. I've tried to tell you over and over the last few days that I just wanted my share of the money. I don't give a shit what you're up to now. I got over you a long time ago; I just didn't get over losing my share of the cash. You didn't think I wanted you for *you* did you? When I could have taken that cash and been long gone?'

Tom blinks in shock, shaken by the idea Lydia only wanted him for the money, that she was playing him all those years ago, just as he was playing her. Lydia has played the part of a simple, love-struck fool to perfection, fooling all of us.

'Why did you do it?' My voice is louder than expected and it rings around the enclosed space. Any sympathy I might have briefly felt for Lydia is now long gone. 'Why tell Tom to go and that you'd deal with the fallout from Lester's murder?'

Lydia gives a feeble laugh, and grabs at her ribs, where lilac bruises lightly dust her pale skin. 'I was going to meet him as arranged, go along with his little plan. I'd take my share of the money and then I planned on telling the police he did it, but I hadn't banked on the paperweight. I took it, by instinct, and then that was it. In the split second it took me to realise he'd done it deliberately — passing it to me so my fingerprints would be on it — it was too late. Theo called the police as he left and they arrived before I had a chance to get out. They had my fingerprints on the murder weapon, they had me crouched over the body. There was no way I was getting out of it — who would believe me? I already had a record for other stuff. Better to just do the time, and figure out a way to put things right when I got out. I can't believe you thought I was that stupid, Theo. I can't believe you actually thought I wouldn't know you set me up.'

Now it makes perfect sense — Summer saying over and over Lydia just wanted to put things right. I thought she'd kidnapped Tom in some weird revenge plot, to punish him for not loving her back maybe, but all she wanted was the money. Taking advantage of the fact we're somewhat stunned, in one swift movement Tom utters a war cry and lurches forward towards Lydia, brandishing the knife high in the air. The blade gleams as it slices through the air, coming within inches of her face, as Summer screams and tries to pull Lydia away from the razor-sharp edge. I rush towards Tom, trying to seize him around the waist, anything to stop him from making this whole situation worse. Tom is screaming unintelligible words, rage and fury I never knew he was capable of pouring out of him. As I fight to get to him before he can reach Lydia, Adam makes a grab for him and with a clearly practiced movement, brings Tom's arms down and round behind his back, forcing the knife from between his fingers. It clatters to the ground, spinning away from Tom, and Adam shoves him hard against the wall, shouting to me to pull the handcuffs from his back pocket. Numb, I move towards Adam, time seeming to slow down as if I'm underwater. Snatching the cuffs from my fingers, Adam expertly secures Tom's wrists.

Lydia French leans against Summer's shoulder, the venom that poured out of her in Tom's direction leaving her weak and exhausted.

I step forward, reaching out a hand to Tom's shoulder. He opens his eyes and I'm thrown back in time to the morning of his disappearance, when I woke first. The scent of him fills my nose and I breathe in deeply, as something deep inside my chest cracks. I think it might be my heart.

'Why?' I whisper, tears spilling over my cheeks as I press my face close to his. 'Why couldn't you just be honest?'

Adam has kicked the knife out of reach, and he and Summer are occupied taking care of Lydia, tugging my sweater over her head as she lies down, fever exhausting her. I take this moment while no one is watching us to try and understand why Tom has done this.

'You'd leave me, Claire.' Tom looks at me, his eyes ringed by purple shadows, his expression broken. 'You're a good woman. You and Isla are the one thing I haven't fucked up — and that's because I wasn't Theo, I was Tom. You're better than anything I've ever had in my life before, and I knew if you knew the truth about me, if you knew *the real me*, and the things I've done to try and keep everything as it should be, then it would be over between us.'

'But all the lies . . . I can't get my head around why you would lie about other things — like Bristol? And Harriet? You never told me about Harriet . . .'

'I wanted to give you something of me, Claire. The real me. I couldn't tell you the truth, not without giving away Theo, but I wanted you to know some of the things that were important to me. Some of the things that make me who I really am. Bristol was one of them. For years all I wanted was to go to university there and be taught by Greg West, but I failed my exams. And then Ruby fell, and I couldn't stay to retake them, I had to leave.'

'It didn't have to be like this, Tom. You've run from everything your whole life — we should have been the one thing you stayed and fought for. It was supposed to be us against the world.' I rest my head against his shoulder, one last time.

'Oh, Claire, if only you knew. I've been fighting for us every day since I met you. That's why I had to keep all of this a secret. That's why I could never tell you the lengths I would go to, to keep you.' I look up as Tom gives me a sad smile, and at that moment I really do feel my heart break in two. 'It's not too late, Claire. We could still be us. We could run, go away somewhere they'd never find us.'

I look up at him, at the familiar face I thought I'd grow old with. It's tempting. To run, to change our names, to live the life we *should* have together.

Adam looks over at us, tucking his phone back into his pocket. 'I've called the police. Help is coming, Claire. It's OK. It's all over.'

Tom's gaze roams over my face, pleading. 'Claire?'

I step back, my face awash with tears as Adam puts out an arm and pulls me close to him, my weight sagging against his shoulder as he guides me towards the plant room exit, the faint sound of sirens on the air.

Forcing myself to meet my husband's gaze for the last time, I say the only thing left to say. 'Goodbye, Tom.'

EPILOGUE

Four months later

'Isla, you're going to have to say goodbye now.' I peer over her shoulder and wave at Harriet's smiling face on the Zoom screen. 'Sorry, Harriet, it's bath time.'

Harriet smiles and waves goodbye as Isla slides off the chair with a grumble and heads towards the bathroom. It's been a tough few months, but Isla seems to be dealing with things OK, as far as I can tell.

She was devastated when I told her Tom wouldn't be coming home, and it was hard to find the words to explain why without making her think Tom was a monster. Because despite it all, I can't think that way, can't think that I've dedicated the last decade of my life to someone who could do the things Tom has. Now, we seem to have settled into a routine, me and Isla, with support from Gwen. I'm no longer working towards partnership at the firm. After everything that's happened, partnership is something that can wait, Isla needs to come first. I've cut my hours to school time as much as possible, Gwen stepping in now and again if I need her to, and I've realised that by working all those hours before I've missed out on something far more precious than success. I got a far better buzz from watching Isla perform at her harvest festival than I ever did in the office.

Adam has been a rock too. He got offered a promotion last week following his work helping uncover Tom's lies, and I don't think I'm imagining it when I think he's hoping that there might be something between the two of us. It's far too early for me to think about anything like that. Despite Tom's lies and the way he behaved, my heart is still too tangled with his to even contemplate another relationship. I'm not sure I'll ever be ready, if I'm honest.

And Tom . . . Tom is awaiting trial for what he did to Lydia. Charges have also been brought for the death of Carlos's right-hand man, although Tom's lawyer is claiming self-defence on that one, and he's being questioned again about the night Ruby Baker disappeared. I've been to see him a few times, but each time is harder than the last. While he reaches out to take my hands across the table, while he apologises over and over, I can't shake the lies out of my head. I never knew him. I knew Tom Bennett, a kind, gentle man who wouldn't hurt a fly. The man who swept me off my feet, who held my hand and cried as I pushed our child into the world. A man who would never leave me to change the kitchen bin because he knew it was my least favourite job, a man who would catch crane flies and gently scoop them out of the window rather than squash them under his heel. But I was married to Theo Cooper, a hot-headed, volatile man who would rather commit violence than let something he wanted slip through his fingers.

I scrub Isla dry with her Barbie bath towel, comb her hair and read her two stories before she's settled under her duvet, her eyelids drooping before I've even left the room. *Everything will be OK*, I think as I gently pull her door closed.

As I reach the top of the stairs there's a tapping at the front door and I find myself smiling. Adam is due over, complete with a takeaway curry and a bottle of sauvignon to celebrate his promotion. While I may not be in the market for any romance, Adam is good company, and I'm looking forward to catching up over some nice wine and crappy television. I jog lightly down the stairs and pull the door open, my smile fading as I realise it's not Adam on the doorstep.

'Hi.' It's a woman I don't recognise. She's around my age, slim, with long red hair that tumbles around her shoulders like she's just walked out of a shampoo advert. She's exceptionally pretty — I would even say she's beautiful, but for the ugly scar that twists from her left temple to halfway down her cheek, the skin pitted and thick. 'I'm looking for Theo Cooper.'

I swallow, my mouth suddenly dry. I thought the reporters had given up for now, although I'm fully expecting them to land back on my doorstep when the trial date is set. 'He's not here. Obviously.' I stare at her, allowing my gaze to rest on the scar for just a fraction of a second too long. 'Who are you?'

The woman shifts, adjusting her bag over her shoulder before she speaks, lifting her eyes to meet mine. 'My name's Ruby.'

THE END

THE JOFFE BOOKS STORY

We began in 2014 when Jasper agreed to publish his mum's much-rejected romance novel and it became a bestseller.

Since then we've grown into the largest independent publisher in the UK. We're extremely proud to publish some of the very best writers in the world, including Joy Ellis, Faith Martin, Caro Ramsay, Helen Forrester, Simon Brett and Robert Goddard. Everyone at Joffe Books loves reading and we never forget that it all begins with the magic of an author telling a story.

We are proud to publish talented first-time authors, as well as established writers whose books we love introducing to a new generation of readers.

We won Trade Publisher of the Year at the Independent Publishing Awards in 2023 and Best Publisher Award in 2024 at the People's Book Prize. We have been shortlisted for Independent Publisher of the Year at the British Book Awards for the last five years, and were shortlisted for the Diversity and Inclusivity Award at the 2022 Independent Publishing Awards. In 2023 we were shortlisted for Publisher of the Year at the RNA Industry Awards, and in 2024 we were shortlisted at the CWA Daggers for the Best Crime and Mystery Publisher.

We built this company with your help, and we love to hear from you, so please email us about absolutely anything bookish at feedback@joffebooks.com.

If you want to receive free books every Friday and hear about all our new releases, join our mailing list here: www.joffebooks.com/freebooks.

And when you tell your friends about us, just remember: it's pronounced Joffe as in coffee or toffee!

www.ingramcontent.com/pod-product-compliance
Ingram Content Group UK Ltd.
Pitfield, Milton Keynes, MK11 3LW, UK
UKHW020627170225
4621UKWH00051B/608